The Tramping Methodist
Sheila Kaye-Smith

Sheila Kaye-Smith (1887 – 1956) was an English writer, known for her many novels set in the borderlands of Sussex and Kent in the English regional tradition. Her 1923 book The End of the House of Alard became a best-seller, and gave her prominence; it was followed by other successes and her books enjoyed worldwide sales. Her earliest novels partly fit into the 'earthy' rural category, together with that of Mary E Mann, Mary Webb, D. H. Lawrence, and Thomas Hardy.

The Tramping Methodist

CHAPTER I

OF THE METHODIST AT BREDE PARSONAGE

My father was Rector of Brede, and held in plurality the livings of Udimore, Westfield, Piddinghoe, and Southease. He himself took charge of the first three parishes, which lay near each other, and my elder brother, Clonmel, assisted him as his curate. Between Piddinghoe and Southease an underfed, overworked curate-in-charge galloped an underfed, overworked horse every Sunday.

My father's office was almost a sinecure—there were only two services a week at Brede, and only one at Udimore and at Westfield. On Sunday evening my father took off the priest with his surplice, and lived the life of a fox-hunting squire till he put on his surplice again the next Sunday morning. Clonmel was not a priest even in his surplice, but from week-end to week-end, a combination of the jockey, the sot, and the brute.

We were a large family—my father and mother, my brothers Clonmel, Archie, and Christopher, and my sisters Fanny and Matilda. I have it on the authority of several neighbours that the Lytes of Brede Parsonage were renowned for their good looks, my father and Clonmel being specially fine men. As for me, I think I can do no better than describe myself in the words of my mother when a visitor admired my face: "Yes, Humphrey would be handsome if his brows were not so black, and if he were not always frowning."

I can clearly remember that frown, though time and peace have long since worn away all traces of it, except two upright lines between my brows. I first noticed it when, as a child of six, I caught sight of myself in a mirror and saw the sullen, swarthy little face, with its beetling brows and angry grey eyes beneath them. I then realised how I deserved the epithets constantly hurled at me by my parents and Clonmel of "Little beast! Little devil!"

I was an unfavourable specimen of childhood—stiff, moody, sullen, and untractable, my bosom always seething with furious passions. I had no affection for my family, as I knew they did not love me or take any interest in me. Archie and Kit were coarse and rough, Fanny and Tilly were vain and would-be-genteel; my mother neglected me, and my father and Clonmel kicked and beat me. So I shunned them all, and would mope by myself about the house, sitting for hours, my head sunk on my breast, in the recess of some windowseat, or on the attic stairs, where, as they were rickety and unsafe with age, I was sure of comparative peace.

My life was miserable, and my heart was full of bitter passions; but one day a kind of happiness dawned for me. My brothers and sisters and I were gathering blackberries in a field near Starvecrow, when the sun suddenly pierced his noontide wrapping of clouds, and shed his beams on the pastures. Then I noticed for the first time how lovely was the country round my home. I saw the Brede River winding through emerald marshes, like a string of turquoise on a woman's green gown. I saw Spell Land Woods with their foliage gilt right royally, and the glorious scarlet of the roofs of Dew Farm against a background of bice and blue. I felt as if I had been blind up to that hour, and had only just opened my eyes on a world which God saw was very good.

Thenceforth I was an ardent lover of Nature, a mistress who never grows old. I rose early each day that I might see the mists scuttle from the valleys like ghosts at cock-crow, and the sunrise pierce the woods with copper darts. I never went to bed till the fold-star had risen beyond Udimore, and the owls had begun to hoot in the woods of Brede Eye. I used to take long rambles in the lanes and fields, and one night I spent on the lee-side of a haystack by the Rother Marshes. I saw the Zodiac wheel slowly above the horizon, the scales hang over the Five-watering, and the Virgin stand as close as she dare to the flushing moon. I saw the mists creep along the grass and along the breast of the river, writhe between the pollards, and scud like ghosts over the level. I was severely beaten for my escapade when I returned home, but the memory of that night shall go down with me to the grave.

It was well for me that I had this love of field and hedgerow, for my life was empty of all other loves. I hated books, and never opened one of my freewill, though by dint of much whipping I had been taught my letters. My younger brothers and I did not go to school, as we were needed for work on the Parsonage Farm, and our education was confined to three hours' daily reading with our father. I hated this, and, regardless of blows, played truant at every opportunity. It was after one of these revolts that the turning-point of my life was reached.

I had been wandering in Loneham fields, instead of plodding through Ovid in my father's study, and on my return was thrashed by Clonmel, and locked into an attic with the assurance that I should stay there on bread and water till the end of the week. At first I was delirious with rage, and lying on the dirty floor, I sobbed wildly and tearlessly, till I fell asleep through exhaustion. When I awoke I felt calmer, and began to examine my prison. It was bare of all furniture, save for an old chest, and on opening this I found a quantity of musty books. These were no consolation to me, and I shut the lid. But as the hours wore on, loneliness and fear overpowered me. I had always been a superstitious child, and even in the room where I slept with Archie and Kit, I had often lain awake trembling in the clutches of the terror by night. This attic soon became a hell to me. I thought to see ghosts and fetches slithering in the moonbeams up the wall, and the dark corners seemed full of spooks. I thought to hear my name called from the garden, but on looking out, saw nothing but the ghastly moonlight fluttering in the trees. My face and the palms of my hands were damp with sweat, and in sheer desperation I opened the book-chest, and took out a volume to distract my thoughts.

At first I did not understand half I read by the clear white light of the moon; I realised only that the book was a holy book, and spoke of God and heaven. But soon a sentence arrested me and made me consider, simply because it was so unlike anything I had read before. I had only the vaguest religious ideas—I had been told that there was a God above, Who would certainly thrust me into hell if I continued passionate and unruly. I had also been told that Brede Church was God's house, which did not increase my reverence for my Maker, as the church was dirty and hideous, with walls discoloured by damp and filth, and all view of the altar-table shut out by a huge, unsightly three-decker. But in this book I found God as the God of love. "My son, I am the Lord," I read, "a stronghold in the day of trouble. Come thou unto Me when it is not well with thee."

I paused. The words were sweet. How often and how bitterly had I longed for a comforter! My heart was touched, and my tears splashed on the open page. I read on—"I will come and take care of thee." "Let not therefore thine heart be troubled, neither let it be afraid. Trust in Me and put confidence in My mercy."

I read the "Imitation of Christ" till the sky suddenly flushed with a throbbing flame of light, and the birds sent up a matins through the roar of the wind. Then I put it aside, and lay down and slept on the floor till the sun awoke me. The whole of that day I spent in pouring over my new-found treasure. I forgot that I was terrified, miserable, and hungry; I lived only in the sweet words of the Brother of Common Life. The effects they produced in me were extraordinary. I think that Mr. Wesley would have been glad to know my case—it would have strengthened his theory of instantaneous conversion. I entered that attic passionate, desperate, my heart full of hate and fury. I left it calmed and humbled, with a steadfast resolution to lead a Christian life.

It was very hard—it is always so, and it was exceptionally difficult in my case. I had no loving parents or friends to help me and pray for me. On the contrary, my efforts after holiness often brought on me the ridicule of my family, who could neither understand nor sympathise. Still, I fought on. I fell daily, hourly, but I rose again and struggled forward, learning as much from my failures as from my triumphs.

At first my efforts were directed towards what I called "being good"—that is to say, answering meekly when I was spoken to roughly, obeying even the surliest commands, and banishing all thoughts of rage or unbrotherliness from my heart. But after a while my views widened. I had finished the first three books of Thomas à Kempis, and had begun the fourth—"Concerning the Sacrament." This inflamed me with fresh desires, and my whole being yearned for the Communion. I was sufficiently acquainted with the Prayer Book to know that I could not receive the Lord's Supper without Confirmation, and after some thought I approached my father on the subject, and asked if I might be confirmed.

At first he received the idea with derision, but, remembering that I was fifteen years old and a clergyman's son, granted me my wish. So I was handed over to Clonmel, who kicked and caned my Catechism into me, and one September afternoon my brother and I rode off to Hastings, where the Bishop was about to hold a Confirmation.

It was a still day, and the clouds were dun, but every now and then a gleam of sunlight swept over the fields, faint as the smile of a dying child. Clonmel took no notice of me, as he was sulky at having missed a day's cub-hunting, but rode on in front, his Rehoboam very much on the back of his head, and dismounted for a tankard of beer at every tavern we passed.

We went through Westfield and Ore, and I saw the sea and the cliffs and the little red-roofed town, with the church of All Saints looking down on it from the slope of the East Hill. There are two churches in Hastings, S. Clement's and All Saints', and the Confirmation was to be held in the latter. So Clonmel and I rode down All Saints' Street, and engaged quarters for the night at the New Moon. After a goodly potation of rum-shrub, my brother marched me off to the church, where I took my place in a front seat, while he lounged in a pew at the back.

All Saints', Hastings, was not unlike S. George's, Brede, in point of ugliness. But it was cleaner; there was some beautiful tracery in the windows, and the faded remains of a fresco representing the Resurrection were still visible over the chancel arch. The Confirmation candidates sat in the front of the church, the boys on one side, the girls on the other. The latter were devout enough, and read their Prayer Books till the service began; but the former, who were miserably few, spent their time in whispering, giggling, and ogling the less serious of the girls. I found it practically impossible to pray collectedly, especially as my comrades were laughing at me for remaining so long on my knees. I stuffed my fingers into my ears, and uttered a few disjointed supplications. Then a tear, born of hopelessness, fell on my Prayer Book. I flushed, bit my lips angrily, and rose from my knees to see that the Bishop and the Vicar had just arrived.

Bishop Ashburnham was a fatherly little man, but did not seem much impressed with ideas of reverence. Still, he had some notion of feeding his flock, and before the actual rite of Confirmation, spoke a few words to the candidates. He had a pleasant voice, and his address was practical, if not very spiritual. He told us to obey our parents and pastors, to keep the commandments, honour the King, and say our prayers. He also bade us come frequently to the Communion, though this was a mockery to most of us, who had only three celebrations a year in our parish churches.

As the service continued I began to feel less miserable and hopeless, and when it came to the laying on of hands, peace and devotion had revisited my heart. I went up the aisle like one in a trance, and knelt enraptured with the thin white hands upon my head, while pastoral lips begged the Lord to defend this His child with His heavenly grace.

I returned to my seat, my heart beating feverishly with love and hope. I remember nothing of the rest of the service; I seemed to have soared in vision above that ugly church and slovenly congregation, and to have visited the house not made with hands, and the general assembly and church of the first-born. I was cruelly aroused by my companions pushing past me into the aisle at the end of the service, and rising from my knees I went to where Clonmel was waiting for me at the back of the church.

"What the devil is the matter with you?" exclaimed my brother, when we had passed through the churchyard, and stood in All Saints' Street. "What are you starin' at the sky for, as if you saw spirits, like a damnation Methodist?"

"I am very sorry, Clonmel——"

"Don't answer me like that, you little beast! I won't stand your cant. Hurry on to the New Moon and order me a quart of ale. Make haste, I tell you, or I'll break every bone in your body."

I obeyed him hurriedly, and a few minutes later we were seated at our supper in the coffee-room, Clonmel slowly drowning his ill-humour in his tankard of bitter ale. He seemed to have plenty of friends in Hastings, judging by the number of greetings he exchanged with the other occupants of the room. Our table was soon surrounded by horse-breakers and jockeys in different stages of intoxication, with whom my brother bandied oaths and jests that set me blushing to the roots of my hair. The Reverend Clonmel noticed this, and boxed my ears in his usual brotherly fashion, telling the company that I had just been confirmed, and was already half a Ranter, though, by the hell! he'd flog it out of me before long.

I gulped down my supper and stole out of the room. I was tired, and decided to go to bed. The little bedchamber under the eaves of the old inn was very peaceful after that uproarious coffee-room. I knelt by the window and prayed, while the starlight came down through the space and years, and kissed my shoulders and bent head.

I lay awake a long time listening to the wind as it howled up the street, and thinking over the events of the day. My misery and my happiness balanced each other pretty equally. I was miserable because I was so lonely and unloved: I was happy because I possessed a treasure which God had given, and the world could not take away.

The hours went by, and the noise in the coffee-room increased. Roars of laughter came to me where I lay, with fragments of song, and every now and then an unlovely woman's voice. At last a door flew open, and the shouts and oaths sounded more clearly. The merry company were reeling upstairs. I heard my brother approach my door. Clonmel drunk was worse than Clonmel sober. I lay motionless in a sweat of terror with the clothes over my head. But he took no notice of me, flung himself all dressed on the bed, and was soon asleep, breathing heavily. A few minutes later I fell asleep myself, and thus ended my Confirmation day.

I woke early, and the morning twilight was in the room. I rose noiselessly, dressed, and stole downstairs, and drawing back the bolts of the inn door, went into

7

the street. The little houses were asleep, and my steps rang hollow on the deserted pavement. At the bend of the road, I saw the sea. The water was a soft pearl-grey, the same colour as the sky. Indigo shadows lay here and there on its breast, and from the light into the shadow, from the grey into the indigo, the brown-sailed fishing-smacks glided. The wind came rustling and moaning up the street, and suddenly a blood-red scar appeared in the clouds above the East Hill. I heard a robin sing, and my heart leapt in my breast with peace new-born, and hope revived.

When I reached the inn I found Clonmel and my breakfast waiting for me, for we were to go home early, my brother being anxious to ride with the hounds.

CHAPTER II

OF THE METHODIST AT SHOYSWELL

A soon as we had reached home, Clonmel set off for Doleham, where he hoped to fall in with the hunt. I went into the back parlour, where I hoped to be alone. I found my mother seated at the window trifling with some fancy work. She looked surprised to see me.

"I had no idea you would be back so soon. Your father thought that you and your brother would spend the day in Hastings, so he has hired a man from Doucegrove Farm to help Kit and Archie with the ricks."

"Clonmel has gone a-hunting. Mother," I added suddenly, "when will there be a Sacrament at Brede?"

"A Sacrament!" cried my mother, knitting her brows.

"Yes, ma'am. The Bishop said——"

"Oh, you have been confirmed—I had forgotten it. That accounts perhaps for your extraordinary way of speaking. There will be a Sacrament at Christmas, not a day before."

"That's a long time!"

"Well, how often would your reverence have a Sacrament, may I ask?"

"Once a week."

"You little fool! You don't know what you're saying. Why, the Methodists have a Sacrament once a week!"

"But may we not do as the Methodists do?"

"As the Methodists do! The boy's mad. I've a good mind to tell your father, and, la! wouldn't he beat you! But I shan't tell him," she added more kindly, "for you're only a silly child. Go away now, and learn to keep your opinions to yourself in future."

I left the room and went into the garden. The sun was shining, but the world seemed very grey to the boy who stood with his hands pressed tightly to his bosom, trying vainly to keep down the sobs that swelled it. I do not think that I ever felt so miserable and desolate. But my despair did not last long, for the thought came to me that though there was not to be a Sacrament in my father's church till Christmas, other parsons might do their duty better. Hastings, Iden, Rye, Sedlescombe, I knew to be in the same plight as Brede, but there were hamlets beyond—Bodiam, Salehurst, Ticehurst, and many others—where I should perhaps find what I yearned for. My time was my own that afternoon, as a man had been hired from Doucegrove to do my work. I could not be happier than in wandering from village to village searching for a temple where I might offer my sacrifice of praise and thanksgiving.

The sunbeams flickered in the leafage of the orchard; the wind swept singing over the fields from Lankhurst and dried the foolish tears upon my face. I went into the house, pocketed a hunk of bread and cheese, and thus equipped started on my voyage of discovery.

I walked quickly up the Cackle Street, and came to Broad Oak, where I left the road and crossed the fields to the hop-gardens of Udiam. It was the hopping season, and I passed many a band of hop-pickers, and many an oast with the smoke of the drying furnaces streaming through the cowl. The scent of the vines was delicious, and I sat in their moving shade, ate my bread and cheese, and felt almost happy in the quiet and sunshine.

After I had eaten I stretched myself on the sweet-smelling ground, and slept and dreamed of moaning water and church bells ringing at dawn. When I woke, the sun was at its highest. I rose refreshed, and walked on to Salehurst, my heart bounding to see the world so fair. I forgot that the swallows were flown, that the purple loosestrife had faded from the banks of the meadow stream, and that the scarlet on the leaves I thought so beautiful was like the glow on consumption's cheek, a herald of death and decay.

But my spirits were soon dashed at the sight of the locked doors of S. Mary's, Salehurst, and of the notice which told me that though morning and evening prayers were read there alternately every Sunday, the Lord's Supper was not administered except at Christmas, Easter, and Whitsuntide. It was the same at Bodiam, and before I had come to Hurst Green I was deaf and blind to the beautiful world, and saw only the bare stubble-fields drenched in the tears of the dying summer.

At Hurst Green there was no church, and I set out wearily for Ticehurst. I had now come some fourteen miles from my home, but this would be no obstacle to me were I so fortunate as to find a Sacrament at Ticehurst, for in those days celebrations after Morning Prayer were the accepted rule. Still, the sun was westering, and I knew that I should be punished if I reached home after dark; and as at Ticehurst I was again doomed to disappointment, I started Bredewards with a heavy heart.

The sun was setting fast, and hung low in the sky above Witherenden—a scarlet wafer on the brink of a cloudy chalice into which it was rapidly sinking. I quickened my pace, for I realised that I ran the risk not only of arriving home after dark, but of being locked out for the night. Seeing a lane lead southward through the fields, I turned down it, thinking that it might shorten my road. But this reckless course brought me punishment. The lane merged into a track, and the track gradually faded away and left me on the banks of a stream, with never a bridge to cross by.

I sighed hopelessly, and wandered a little by the stream side. The waters flowed with a moaning sound, and the crimson of the sky was mirrored in them, with the first star hanging on the edge of the glow.

At last I came to a bend where weeping willows kissed the bubbles at their feet, and where the stream looked narrow enough for me to jump it. But I had miscalculated my distance, and this the icy water round my thighs and breast soon told me. With great difficulty I scrambled out at the further side and stood shivering on the bank. That moment the sun went down and the night wind rustled the grass.

I was by this time almost sure that I could not reach Brede much before midnight, when the Parsonage door would be locked. Moreover, I had lost my way, I was dripping wet, and faint with hunger and weariness. I dragged myself across the field, and came into a road. In front of me a lane led southwards, but I would not have turned down it—remembering my former recklessness and its results—had I not seen a light twinkling at the end. I knew that I was near a house, and resolved to go there and ask my way.

The lane was rough and muddy, and the arching trees shadowed it from the dusk as with a pall. I groped my way along the hedge, and suddenly came out of the darkness to find myself in front of an old house with oasts and haggards swarming round it. The farm-house was half-timbered, and roses, passion-vine, and creeper did their best to hide the cracks and gaps in the walls, and to cover the wounds in the old roof, wreathing tenderly about the tottering chimney-stacks, and hanging in festoons from gable-end and eaves.

A light beamed from one of the lower windows, and, passing by, I saw an oak-ribbed kitchen with a table in the middle, at which three persons were seated. I knocked at the door, and the next moment it was opened by a short, thickset man, with kind eyes and curly grey air. He looked sharply at my wet clothes, and when I asked him the way to Brede, exclaimed:

"You're not going there to-night, surely!"

"I am indeed—is it far off?"

10

"If you walked hard from this minute, you couldn't reach it before dawn—and you're soaking wet, my lad Where have you been?"

I told him that I had fallen into a stream, and he shook his head.

"You can't walk far in this plight; you're shivering with cold. Come in to the fire, and dry your clothes."

"You are very kind, but indeed I must not loiter. I I shall get into trouble if I am not home tonight."

"I told you just now that you can't possibly be home before dawn, so come in, my lad. I won't have you leave my door shivering in this way!"

He took me by the arm, and led me into the kitchen. It was a quaint room, and smelled sweet, for great bunches of lavender were hung from the middle beam, and an apple stuck full of cloves stood on the chimney-piece. A man and a girl sat at the table. The man was a tall, thin young fellow, raggedly dressed, but with one of the sweetest faces I have ever seen in my own sex. The droop of his mouth was sad, but his eyes were full of happiness and of a light that was almost divine. He had been talking earnestly to the girl, and his wan cheeks were flushed, as he quoted from the Bible before him: "The zeal of Thine house hath eaten me up," were the words I remember he said.

The girl was of about my own age and dressed in pigeon grey, her hair hanging in a long, thick plait between her shoulders. She was not beautiful, but her eyes were glowing like the sparks which fly from under the smith's hammer, and her cheeks were flushing like the heart of a fire.

They both rose as I came in, and showed no surprise when the grey-haired man told them of my plight, but bade me sit by the fire and dry myself. I drew close to the blaze, and the three took their seats once more at the table, while the ragged saint resumed his reading. Every now and then he paused and spoke a few words to his listeners, and he spoke as I had heard no man speak. His words were rough and ill-chosen, and he gave me the impression of a man who, though educated himself, had mixed so long with the rude and uncultured people as to have assimilated some of the manners and speech. He spoke with force, even brutality, and there was a Biblical ring in his sentences that told of a deep familiarity with the Book before him. His speech seemed too great for his frail body; the thundering words and rolling phrases matched ill with the thin hands and haggard face. What struck me most about his oration was the way he went to Nature for his similes. He had not been speaking for ten minutes before I knew that he could tell the name of every star that trembled on the dun breast of the sky, and of every flower that coloured the grass; that he knew the roosting-places of the birds and the variations of their notes; that he regarded as familiar friends the wild timid creatures of the forest, the conies of the fallow, and the butterflies of the hedge and clover-field.

11

He stopped speaking suddenly, and closed his book. At the same moment a woman came in with three bowls of porridge, but at a word from her master went away for a fourth, of which I was right glad, as I had tasted nothing since noon.

"You shall spend the night here," said the grey-haired man, sitting down beside me on the settle. "You're much too tired to walk further to-night. Besides, you would lose your way in the dark."

"I dare not——"

"Nonsense, my lad! I insist. Your parents wouldn't have you walk through the dark and cold. No,"—and he laid his hand on my mouth "I'll hear no more excuses. You shan't open your lips—except to eat your porridge."

"The night is very sweet," said the girl, who had risen and was standing by the fire. "Father, I shall take my supper to the gable-barn and eat it there. Will you not come too?" she added, turning to me.

Her tone was so frank, so modest, and so sweet that I had neither the will nor the power to refuse. My clothes were by this time dry enough to suit me, for I had been hardily bred, so we left the kitchen and crossed the fold to a barn with tarred wooden walls. The inside was full of hay, which we climbed by a ladder set against it, and found ourselves in a sweet-smelling loft, from which we looked down through a huge window into the fold.

"You have not told me your name," said the girl, when we were seated.

"My name is Humphrey Lyte; what is yours?"

"Mary Winde!"

"What a lovely name!"

"Do you think so? There are so many girls round here called Mary."

"I think it is the most beautiful name a woman can have."

She looked meditative, and cast down her eyes to the hay.

"Does your father own this farm?" I asked her.

"Yes. He used to be a preacher, but his health broke down, so we came to live here at Shoyswell."

"Who is that gentleman with your father? He looks like a preacher, too!"

"That is Mr. John Palehouse, and he goes from village to village preaching."

"You are Methodists!" I cried, suddenly alarmed.

"Yes! Does that shock you very much?"

"No—er no—that is to say——"

She laughed merrily.

"I am sure by your voice that you are very much shocked indeed."

"My father is a. clergyman," I stammered, "and I know that he will be furious when he hears that I have spent the night with Methodists. But after all, he is sure to beat me for not being home by dark, and he cannot beat me harder then he does usually—that is to say," I added, "without killing me."

"You speak as if you would not mind being killed."

"I don't suppose being killed hurts much," I said dreamily; "at least, not more than being alive."

"How wildly you talk!" she cried, drawing away from me. "Life is wonderful and beautiful—at least to me."

"It is," I said, "at least to you."

"There are the fields, the woods, the stars, and the wind," she continued, "and there are books. Don't you love books?"

"I hate them!"

"What a strange boy you are! How do you spend the long evenings if you hate books?"

"I think!"

"And sad thoughts, I'll be bound. Do you know that there are such fierce, frowning lines between your eyebrows? They were the first thing I noticed when I saw you."

"Have you many books?" I asked abruptly.

"Not many of my own, but my father allows me to read what I like of his."

"Tell me about your books," I cried, leaning forward in the hay, and touching her hand. "I love to hear you speak. I never had a playfellow."

"I know nothing of foreign languages, so I can read only English books. But I love them so much that I never wish for any others. Shakespeare, Chaucer, Pope, Milton, and Spenser—I will lend you my Spenser if you like?"

"Thank you! I promise to read it, and it will be the only book, except my Bible and 'Imitation,' that I have ever read of my own free will."

She went on speaking, and I lay listening in the hay. We had finished our porridge, and had set our bowls aside. The night wind blew in on us, and rustled the hay. The stillness was broken by the bleating of sheep, which gradually drew nearer. The fold-gates opened, and the flock poured in, their whiteness tinged to grey in the starlight. All was so dim that sheep from sheep could hardly be distinguished, and an indefinite mass surged between the oasts.

It was like a beautiful dream, which we cry for when we wake. The stars shone mistily, like pearls under a woman's scarf, and farm-lights dotted the country, as if the fields reflected and magnified the stars. A little moon hung between the gables of Shoyswell, and when her light fell full upon the hay, Mary stopped speaking and laughed.

"I have preached of books enough for to-night. Hark! the fold-bells are ringing us to bed."

We climbed down from our nest and made our way through the sheep to the house, Mary going in front of me—grey gown 'mid grey sheep in a grey starlight.

Entering the kitchen, we surprised Mr. Winde and John Palehouse in a dispute as to which room I should sleep in, each declaring that I must have his own. Finding that accommodation at Shoyswell was so scant, I refused both offers, vowing, as was, indeed, the truth, that I would rather lie on a truss of hay in one of the outhouses. By dint of argument and entreaty I at length carried my point, and after we had all knelt for a few minutes in prayer on the warm flags round the hearth, Peter Winde lighted me to my sleeping-place.

It was an old barn and immensely high; but it was warm and sweet-scented. The moon and stars shone on me where I lay, too happy to go to sleep. I had always loved solitude and longed to sleep alone, but my wish had never been granted me—except for the night spent under the haystack on the Rother Marshes—till now, when I lay in the old black barn, and outside the wind-crooned hush-a-bye to the oaks and hazels, and all else was silence save for the groaning cowls of the oasts.

I did not sleep till the morning dusk, and it seemed as if I had only just closed my eyes when I woke to find John Palehouse shaking me by the shoulder. Breakfast was laid in the kitchen, and when it was over, Mary took me into the next room, where the walls were lined with books. She gave me a Spenser from her own little store, and I was delighted, because I knew that I should have to walk over to Shoyswell to return it. On our way out of the room I noticed a number of black-bound volumes in a case by themselves.

"Are those your father's?" I asked, impressed by their size.

"Yes," she said, and added mischievously, "they are Methodist books."

I drew back a little.

"But, after all, if you and Mr. Winde are Methodists, they cannot be such dreadful people as I have been told."

"I wouldn't be too sure of that," cried Mary, laughing. "I am so sorry you must go," she added gravely.

"You are not so sorry as I am. I have been happier these few hours than I have ever been before."

"Poor boy!" I thought I heard her whisper, and I know that there were tears in her eyes as she said good-bye.

14

CHAPTER III

OF THE METHODIST'S CONFESSION OF FAITH

I was not long in reading Mary's Spenser, and when I had returned it she lent me her Shakespeare, and after that her Chaucer. This meant many a walk to Shoyswell, and each visit was sweeter than the last. I found that if I rose very early, I could easily be back by nightfall, and as I was often wont to take long rambles by myself, my family asked no questions. I was much hindered by my duties on the farm, but I enjoyed an occasional holiday, and no one cared to know how I spent it. On my return from my first visit to the Windes I had told my father that, being overtaken by night, I had sought shelter at a farm-house; and as this afforded enough excuse for beating me, no more questions were asked, and the Reverend Septimus Lyte never heard that his son was the guest and friend of Methodists.

John Palehouse had gone on a preaching expedition to Devonshire, and Peter and Mary were alone. They always had a quiet but kindly welcome for me, and my heart began to warm and expand in its new happiness. For this was the only friendship I had known. Though my father and mother occasionally visited or were visited by the neighbouring "gentry," I had never had any other companions than my younger brothers, who were companions only in the sense that we worked, ate, and slept together, and could by no means be called my friends.

My intercourse with the Windes was new and beautiful. Mary and I used to take our books into the hayloft and read aloud to each other, bringing what we could not understand to Peter; and in the evening the father and daughter walked part of the way home with me, as far as Lossenham, perhaps, or Methersham, on the great lonely marsh where the mists were brooding and hanging like streamers on the branches of the willows, where the Rother wound like a ribbon of flame towards the east. Peter would bless me when we said good-bye, and I would walk on to Brede with a light heart, and would dream of Shoyswell.

A great happiness had come into my life with these two friends, but I still had my moments of darkness and depression. These increased as I grew older and my eyes opened wider on the sorrows round me. I soon realised that not only was the Sacrament neglected, but that the Gospel was not preached. The poor people of my father's parish were woefully ignorant—many of them could neither read nor write—and could hear of God and heaven only from my father and Clonmel, who cared for none of these things. These wretched folk lived hopeless, religionless lives, and spent them in bestial pleasures, sin, suffering, and despair. My heart yearned after them—they were like shepherdless sheep on the hills. I resolved to try to better their lot. I secretly visited the old people in their cottages, and I formed a class of lads, whom I taught to read in a kitchen lent me by a cottager of Broad Oak, having only one rule——that each lad I taught should in his turn teach a friend. But my father heard of my undertaking, and if there was one thing he hated, it was to see another do the good works he left undone. He scattered my class, flogged me, and multiplied my duties on the Parsonage Farm, hoping by hard work and hard blows "to knock all the nonsense out of me."

This made me desperate, and I did that which I had been tempted to do some months before, but had not dared. On one of my visits to Shoyswell—they were very few now that my farm-work had been increased—I asked Peter Winde to lend me one of his Methodist books. He had made me a laughing offer once, but I had drawn back horrified, and he looked surprised when I ventured my request.

"Do you really mean it, lad?"

"Yes, I really mean it."

He shook his head, but gave me a volume. It was the smallest of his collection, and during the day I kept it in my bosom, and at night it lay under my pillow. I was in dread of discovery, and read it in secrecy and fear, but when I had finished it I asked Peter for another.

It was sheer desperation that had driven me to this course, and sometimes I paused and wondered at myself, and at the direction matters were taking. It seemed impossible that Humphrey Lyte, the loyal Churchman and devout Sacramentalist, should be reading Methodist books, and becoming each day more favourably disposed towards Methodism. The fact was that my books, and the beautiful lives led by Peter and Mary Winde, had taught me that Methodists were not the evil fanatics and heretics my family believed them. They were truer to Church discipline and to the Sacraments than were most Church people and clergy, and they had a zeal for the Gospel of Christ that made my heart glow with fervour and admiration. With the Calvinistic Methodists, the followers of Whitefield, I had no sympathy, but the disciples of Wesley, with their simple austere lives, their good works, and their enthusiasm, stirred up my highest respect, and respect soon deepened into a wish to imitate.

At first I proposed to go no further than imitation. I fasted and spent much time in prayer and in reading the Bible. I hoped that the Church might be goaded to reform by the example of the noble lives outside her pale. But I soon saw how foundationless was this hope, and began to entertain doubts as to my right to remain in a Church which had fallen so far from her purest ideals.

I angrily silenced my doubts, but they were stronger then I, and tormented me, especially after my failure with my school. I saw that it would be impossible for me to do good in my father's parish. I saw also that no parish in England would tolerate my good works. The Church hated enthusiasm; she preached against it and fought against it. There was no room for the zealous preacher of the Gospel in the Church.

I have told in a few lines of a struggle which raged several months. I shall not enter into the details of that conflict, or describe how my doubts gradually formed themselves into unanswerable arguments and then into convictions. I was about twenty years old when my eyes opened fully on the truth, and I remember my despair when I saw that there was only one course open to me—a secession from the Established Church to the Methodists.

I lay awake night after night in anguish. I said nothing of my trouble to Peter Winde, and he gave me no sign that he suspected it. He had seldom spoken to me of his beliefs, but his life had preached them more convincingly than his lips could ever have done. At last, however, he let me see that he knew of my difficulties. I had managed to find time for a visit to Shoyswell. Mary was out, but Peter received me kindly. He was dusting the shelves of his library, and asked me to amuse myself with a book till he had finished. I remember little of the book—it was "Purchas his Pilgrimage" I think—for I fell a-dreaming over the open page, and was roused only by Winde putting something down in front of me. It was an open Bible, and one verse was deeply scored—

"He that taketh not his cross and followeth after Me, is not worthy of Me."

"I'll walk as far as Reedbed with you this evening, lad," said Peter.

Mary came home from the neighbouring farm-house of Turzes, where she had been visiting some friends, and we had dinner. When it was over, Peter and I set out for Brede. I said good-bye to Mary at the gate.

"You are not coming with us?" said.

"No, not this afternoon!"

"Why not? I should like to talk with you about 'Paradise Regained.'"

"But my father wished to talk with you about something far more important."

Her voice rang serious, and there was a great glow in her eyes and on her cheeks.

"God bless you, Humphrey," and she shut the gate. I hurried after her father, who was half way up Shoyswell Lane, and we walked on side by side for some time in silence. It was not till we had reached the Rothe Levels that he spoke. The March afternoon was drawing to a close, and the country lay round me draped in vesper robes of crimson and grey—crimson on the great sedge-bordered ponds and on the breast of the Rother, grey on the misty fields that huddled, with woods still darker grey, towards the south.

"Well, lad," said Peter, "and will you deny your Lord that He may deny you, or will you confess Him that He may confess you before the angels of Heaven?"

"What do you mean?" I faltered.

"I mean that you must speak—you can't keep silence any longer."

"How do you know what I've got to say?"

"I've studied your face and read a secret there."

"Oh . . . Mr. Winde. . . ."

"You're surprised, are you? But I'm used to studying folk, and though you're reserved enough, I've read the proud young heart that would have nursed its own bitterness."

"I did not care to trouble you," I murmured sheepishly.

"In other words, you were afraid of your secret."

17

"That is true," I cried. "That is true indeed; and, sir, you wish me to tell my family of this?"

"The Lord wishes it, dear lad!"

I walked on beside him in moody silence. The evening was very still, troubled only by the tinkling of a foldbell at Moon's Green, and the splash of our feet on the spongy level.

"It is quite true," I said at last, "that my family do not love me, and that I shall have no heartache in parting from my home, but my father and brother are passionate men, and when they hear——"

"So you're afraid of physical pain! Oh, lad I thought better of you."

"I do not fear pain, but I fear the storm that will break. I shall probably be turned out and disowned."

"That's a light affliction," said Peter, "and 'He that loveth father or mother more than Me is not worthy of Me.'"

"I repeat that I do not love my family, only—oh, I must tell you the truth, sir. I have lived a quiet life until now; I have been unhappy, but I have been in comparative peace. I have lived with thoughts and dreams, and it is hard to come to realities. If my father turns me out I shall starve."

"You can work for your living—you know how to work hard. But I've greater hopes for you, lad. I've hoped and prayed that you should follow in John Palehouse's steps and in mine."

"You mean that I should become a preacher?"

"Certainly, lad. I've noticed before this that the Almighty has given you 'a mouth and wisdom.' So go forth and preach the Gospel to every creature."

We had reached Reedbed by this time, and Peter stood still.

"Yes, go forth 'because of the word of truth, of meekness and of righteousness, and thy right hand shall teach thee terrible things.' Tell your father of your convictions, cast aside your old life of groping, and come into the new life of grasping. 'How beautiful upon the mountains are the feet of him that publisheth peace!' Lad, in this county of Sussex there are hundreds of villages where no one has preached the tidings of great joy. The Lord has called you, Humphrey. He has called you from the pastures of your father's farm, from the herds, and from the sheep-folds and will you say: 'I pray Thee have me excused'?"

His voice rang out over the marsh, and a sudden gust of wind moaned "Amen" among the reeds. I held out my hands.

"I shall do as you wish and as God wishes. My sacrifice is very small, but I offer it with my whole heart."

He smiled and wrung my hand.

"God bless you, lad. Mary will be pleased when she hears this."

"I shall tell my father on my first opportunity."

"And when you have done so come to Shoyswell, and we'll arrange the future. Oh, lad, if only you knew how long I've had this at heart!"

He wrung my hand again and we parted. I looked back after I had come to Hope Farm, and saw him still standing among the osiers of Reedbed. I knew that he was praying for me.

It was always my custom to walk home by the marsh, instead of by the shorter way across the fields, and before I had left the levels the first stars were flickering above the old Kent Ditch, and my lady moon was blushing over Appledore, kerchiefed in the mist. I walked quickly as the twilight deepened and the thoughts chased each other through my brain.

I realised that the sacrifice I was about to make was but a little one compared to those which had been offered rejoicingly by the martyrs before me. I had no dear home-ties to sever; no bitter partings would make me weep. My great fear was that my father would not turn me out of doors, but would shut me up and try to starve me into subjection. However, I thought this most unlikely. Upon one thing I was resolved. I would make my confession to my father alone, and not in the presence of Clonmel.

It was dark when I arrived home, and a storm was blowing up from the west. The raindrops were already on my face when I reached Brede Parsonage, and every now and then the wind raised a mournful shriek among the gables.

On entering the kitchen, where we generally had our meals, I found that my mother, sisters, and younger brothers had finished their supper. Only my father and Clonmel remained at table, and were already in the quarrelsome stage of their liquor, judging by my father's question as to "where the devil I had been all day?" and Clonmel's request to "shut the door and be damned!"

I took my seat without a word, and set a volume of "Tristram Shandy" before me on the table, to read while I ate my supper. I had grown to love books since Mary Winde had introduced me to her favourite authors, and had gone through a course of ridiculously miscellaneous reading, snatching my few spare moments, meal-times, and occasionally an hour in bed. I was far lost in the company of Tristram, Uncle Toby, Yorick, and Corporal Trim, when an extra loud oath from my father made me start.

"Zounds! but the fellow's no better than a Methodist!"

"Confounded Ranter," growled Clonmel, his face hid in a mug of ale.

"A Bible-class!"—and my father pounded the table till the ale leaped and swashed in the jugs. "We'll be having daily prayers soon. What are you staring at, Humphrey, you idiot?"

19

"I was wondering what was making you so angry, sir?"

"The confounded curate at Piddinghoe has set up a Bible-class, and I've turned him off like the knave and Ranter he is. I'll have no Methodist humbugs in my parishes. Those Methodists are past bearing with, and they're not content with their pranks outside the Church, but must needs play Old Harry with matters inside it! Talk of toleration! I'd hang 'em as high as Haman if I had the managing of affairs. Let's drink to their damnation. Fill up your glass, Clon, and here's to their eternal roasting!"

Clonmel swung off his ale. "Damnation to the whole brood!" he roared. "Why, Humphrey, you're not drinkin'!"

"Nor do I intend to," I replied.

"You don't? Then I'll make you!"

He sprang up, and before I could resist, had flung his arm round my neck, and forced his tankard against my teeth. I struggled, but he held me like a vice, half-choking me. At last I managed to wriggle an arm free. I struck him in the face with all my force, threw myself from him, and stood in the middle of the room, with dry skin and heaving breast.

Clonmel swore at me, but he offered no further violence, seeing that I had the fire-irons within reach.

"You young devil!" he screamed. "I'll serve you out for this—you damned Methodist. I'll have your blood from you. I'll make you screech and pant for mercy!"

"By the Lord! What's the meaning of this, Humphrey?" cried my father.

"Clonmel is in a rage because I refuse to drink damnation to the Methodists," I replied, resolving to go on as well as I could with my confession.

"And why won't you drink?"

"Because—because I believe that they are honest and holy men; because I consider them foully and spitefully slandered; because I—I am myself a Methodist."

I brought the last words out with a gasp, and stood silently awaiting their effect.

My father's jaw dropped, and he gazed at me in the uttermost bewilderment and anger. Clonmel started up with an inarticulate oath, and sprang towards me. I darted back, and, seizing a chair, swung it above my head.

"Stand off, if you value your skull!" I cried, and he drew back, still cursing and swearing.

At last my father recovered speech.

"What the devil do you mean, Humphrey Lyte? Are you mad?"

"No, sir, I am sane—and a Methodist."

"And the foulest young devil that ever walked this earth!" roared Clonmel.

"Since when is this folly—knavery, I mean?" cried my father.

"I decided some weeks ago to join the Methodists, but I put off my confession till to-day, and should not have made it even now had I not been forced. I meant to speak privately with you, sir, to-morrow."

"By all the blazes! I never met such impudence. I've a good mind to horsewhip you."

"Stay, sir, I am too old for such threats. I assure you that I have not made up my mind without serious thought. I have found that the Church cannot satisfy——"

"Is this the way you serve the Church that has done so much for you?" cried my father, assuming a clerical air. "You leave the paths of sound doctrine and embrace vapouring heresies. Pah!"

"I ask your pardon, but the Church has done nothing for me, and will, I am persuaded, still do nothing. The Methodists are not heretics; on the contrary, they are more loyal to Church truth and discipline than are Church people themselves. They fast twice a week; they assemble daily for praise and prayer. Wesley and his followers at Oxford used to be called the Sacramentarians, so great was their love for the Communion. My conscience——"

"Dearly beloved brethren, my conscience moveth me in sundry instances to play the game-cock with my betters," cried Clonmel, who was drunk.

"Hold your tongue, Clon, and let me deal with him. Look here, you fool, you are talking stuff and nonsense, but I'll soon see whether you mean what you say, or whether it's your usual damned effrontery. Either you abjure your devil's heresies, or you leave my house."

He was very flushed and excited, but I knew that he meant what he said.

"I was prepared for this alternative, sir, and have already made my choice. I leave Brede Parsonage."

"Go, then, and the devil take you!" he cried thickly.

I went towards the door, but Clonmel, who was still smarting from the blow I had given him, sprang to his feet.

"You young viper and villain, you! You shan't leave this house till I've made you curse the day you were born."

The next moment he had snatched up his hunting whip from a chair beside him, and had sprung upon me, slashing me in the face. I grappled him, but he was too strong for me, and flogged me over the head and shoulders till I thought I should swoon. In mad desperation I seized him by the throat, and he brought both hands to bear at my fingers, dropping the whip. For a moment we swayed together; then he fell heavily to the floor, and lay there an instant as if stunned, before he staggered, cursing most horribly, to his feet. He would have closed with me again, but my father, who, during our struggle had been meditatively swilling, suddenly interfered, thrust us apart, and hurled Clonmel into a chair.

"You young beast!" he cried to me. "Now that you have done mauling your brother, leave my house for ever."

"I am going," I blurted out, half choked with passion.

Clonmel would have sprung up, but my father held him down.

"Let him alone, Clon. We've had enough for a clergyman's household. Be off, you vagabond, and if ever I catch you inside my gates I'll skin you alive."

My heart was beating so hard with fury that I could scarcely breathe, but I strode to the door and flung it open, letting a draught of wind and icy rain into the kitchen.

The next moment something whirled at my head and struck my temple. I felt the blood trickle into my eye, and glared back into the room through a crimson mist. Clonmel had managed to free a hand from my father's grasp, and had hurled a pewter tankard at me as a fitting farewell.

"What are you staggering there for?" roared my father. "Go to the devil with you!"

I gave one last glance at them both. The next moment I was out in the fold, and the night-wind was drying the blood upon my face.

CHAPTER IV

OF THE METHODIST AND RUTH SHOTOVER

I went through the yard, and, as I passed the lighted window of the room where my mother and sisters were sitting, the thought came to me how strange it was that I should have no loving stolen farewells to make before I went out penniless into the world. Kit and Archie were laughing and talking together in the Dutch barn, but they neither heard nor saw the outcast who strode past them into the night.

The wind was barking like a starving dog behind the meadow-hills of Udimore; the clouds ran wildly across the sky, and between them danced the stars, hither and thither, here and there, while the horned moon scudded through the wrack. The rain fell hissing round me, and in a few moments I was drenched to the skin. I had left the Parsonage without hat or cloak; moreover, I had taken off my boots on my return from Shoyswell, and wore only shoes which were in every way unsuited to the rough and stony road I trod. But I thought little enough of these things at that moment, for at first I was mad with rage, and then I was mad with grief. I strode up the Cackle Street, and the light from the cottage-windows burnished the wet road, and bewitched the raindrops into a shower of garnets. Then I left the village, and the angry night threw her shroud round me, and her voices stormed at me, and her winds buffeted me as I half-walked, half-ran over the mud and stones. I felt the blood trickling down my face, so tore off the kerchief I wore knotted about my throat, and tied it around my head, which ached miserably.

I had no exalted feelings to compensate me for my bodily wretchedness. When dwelling beforehand on my confession, I had always pictured myself in some noble attitude, speaking noble words, while my father listened abashed, with "Almost thou persuadest me to be a Christian" written on his face. The dream had been a glorious triumph—the reality was very like a pot-house brawl. Perhaps this was entirely my fault, nevertheless, I felt bitterly ashamed of the fury that had knotted my veins, and nearly burst my heart, and, throwing myself down under the hedge, I sobbed great tearless sobs that tore my throat and chest.

I lay in the wet grass for over a quarter of an hour, then rose shivering, and pressed on to Broad Oak. I realised how useless it would be to try to reach Shoyswell by the fields on such a night, so turned down what I believed to be the road to Sedlescombe, and soon the fitful stormlight of the moon was shut off from me by overarching trees. I had not gone far before I saw that I had taken the wrong lane, but my heart was so numb that the discovery did not distress me, especially as, on coming to Beckley Furnace, I realised that the track I followed would eventually bring me to Peasmarsh, where I knew a cottager who would, I hoped, let me lie in his kitchen during the night.

But the darkness was so great, and the storm so wild, that I soon wandered from my track, and became entangled in a maze of bypaths, which wound up and down and in and out of black woods where the wind whispered, and rustled a twisted undergrowth.

I was hopelessly lost, and faint with cold and pain, for my clothes were as drenched as if I had fallen into the Rother, and my feet were so cut with the stones that I could hardly put them to the ground. My head ached terribly, and a kind of blindness seized me, so that in the glints of moonlight everything looked blurred and confused, and lights danced ahead of me, which at first I took for cottage windows, but which I soon saw were the creatures of my own brain. I cannot tell what kept me from throwing myself down in a ditch to die, for I had no spirit in me. But I struggled doggedly on, stumbling every now and then, and rising and pressing on again. At last the wood grew thinner, then seemed to fall away from me, the trees gliding and curtseying till I became terrified at my delirium—for it was not as if I passed the bushes and trees, but as if they passed me.

I found myself on a track of waste land, half marsh, half wilderness, crossed by dykes, and studded with willows, bent and twisted like the tormented trees of hell. I knew that I must be on the outskirts of the Rother Levels, and that all would go well with me if I could find the river.

But the darkness cloaked the marsh on all sides, and though I pressed, as I thought, northwards, I soon discovered that I was going west, for on a sudden the moon shone in front of me, kissing the horizon and showing me a group of barns and oast-houses about a hundred yards off. The shape of the buildings seemed

23

familiar, and in another burst of moonlight I recognised a ruined farmstead known as Baron's Grange, which I had often visited in my walks. This told me that many acres of marsh must lie between me and the Rother, and that I should find it almost impossible to cross the treacherous swamp of dyke and osier in the dark. I was half dead with fatigue, for I had walked over thirty miles since morning, and it occurred to me that I could not do better than spend the night in a barn at Baron's Grange, and resume my journey at daybreak.

I crossed the waste of rushes and osiers, and went into the ruined fold. All around me the farm-buildings raised tottering gables against the clouds, and their black windows were like sightless eyes. I crept into the oast-house barn, the roof of which seemed fairly watertight, and threw myself down upon a heap of straw. The place had evidently been used as a stable for cattle during the winter, for hay and straw were littered on all sides, with piles of frost-bitten mangolds.

I lay on my back, staring at a ray of light that crept through a chink between the roof and the wall. The wind howled uncannily among the beams, and rumbled in the caverns of the oasts. I shivered. The kerchief I wore round my head was by this time saturated with blood, which poured from under it down my cheeks. My shoulders were horribly stiff and aching, both from the cold and from the lash of Clonmel's whip. My feet were numb, and though I swathed them in the hay, I could not restore sensation.

But my pain of body was nothing to my pain of mind; and I groaned as I lay, and cried to God to end the life of His miserable servant. In my agony and weakness I tossed in the straw, and cursed the life God had given me in His love. At last I found the relief of tears, and sobbed as if my heart would break, and fell asleep sobbing like a beaten child.

My dreams were distressful; I woke in a sweat, and so great was my discomfort that for a moment I actually wished myself back in the low, hot room where I slept at Brede Parsonage. The barn had been in profound silence when I fell asleep, but on waking I noticed that it was full of sounds—rustlings, flutterings, trampings, and groanings. Then a great fear seized me, and I cowered in the straw. I had been extremely nervous and superstitious as a child, and though when I grew older I had fought with my terrors, I had never entirely mastered them, and now, when I lay enfeebled by weariness, pain, and misery, they utterly overpowered me.

All kinds of weird legends, sprung from the soil of the fields and fallows round me, came into my mind—Cicely of Cicely's Farm, who hanged herself on her own barn door, when the sun was red, and the sheep were bleating at the fold-gates, who wanders over the marshes with the suicide's stake in her breast, followed by her wraith-sheep, searching in vain for a fold to pen them in, and silence their bleating: Grey Clement of Stream Farm, who calls his cows home at sunset, even as he was calling them when his shepherd slew by his orders Clement's beautiful guilty wife in Pattenden's field: Colin Clamourne of Winterland Farm, who burned his new-born babe, whose spook wanders screaming through the woods of Ellenwhorne, a fire burning in his heart and shining through his breast and through his eyes. These and many other stories came to me as I lay with the sweat on my face, listening to the ghostly sounds that troubled the stillness of the old haggard. I thought to hear the rustle of women's dresses, the patter of children's feet, and often it was as if something touched me. At length I could bear it no longer. I sprang up, and rushed out into the fold.

At the same moment a wrack of clouds rolled off the face of the sky, and the starlight shone clearly into the barn I had left, showing me a number of rats, scampering and gambolling among the straw and mangolds. These had been the source of my fears, and in my relief I laughed out loud. Still, I did not care to go back to the straw, which was shaking and heaving with its numerous inmates, so, as by a certain freshness in the air I knew that the dawn was at hand, I started out once more in search of the Rother.

The rain had ceased, and the wind was only sobbing. The dawn-star glimmered wan above Baron's Grange, and soon a steely light rode over the sky, and showed me the river not far off. I thanked God, for I had nothing to do but to follow the Rother to Bodiam, whence a lane would take me to Shoyswell. But walking was not easy, for my feet sank deep at each step into the boggy ground, and every now and then I stumbled, and was almost too weary to rise. Moreover, the pains of hunger had begun to gnaw me. I had eaten practically nothing since my dinner at Shoyswell, for the disturbance with my father and Clonmel had taken place before I had done more than taste my supper. I drank greedily of the Rother water, and it refreshed me a little, but I soon saw that I could never hope to reach Shoyswell unless I first had food and rest.

I stumbled on by the sighing river, and gradually the dawn woke, and veiled the stars in her wavy skirts of flame. The Rother valley was yet dusk, but on the hills that flanked it I saw the sunrise lying, and suddenly the mist rolled back from a village on the crest of the southern ridge.

My heart leapt to see the little houses reflect the sun's amber matin-light on their windows, and unconsciously I turned towards that village on the hill. I felt sure that I could find there some kind heart who would let me share his morning meal and rest by his fire.

I toiled painfully up the slope, with a throbbing in my head and a singing in my ears. I met some children at play by a group of pollards, and by the startled shrieks with which they fled, knew what a horrible sight my sufferings must have made me. My shoes had been torn off, and my naked feet were bleeding; my clothes were dripping with rain, and had become so disordered by brakes and brambles that my neck and half my bosom were bare. A bloody bandage was fastened round my head, and channels of blood were dry upon my cheeks.

I went a little further, and came to a garden which sloped from a russet-roofed house on the brow of the hill. As I staggered to the fence, and stood for a moment clutching to it, I noticed that I had passed out of the twilight, and had come into the golden mist of sunrise.

Hardly aware of what I was doing, I climbed the low bryony-tangled fence into the garden. The earth was damp and soft, and smelled sweet, and primroses and dog-violets starred the turf and borders. I went through a kind of shrubbery, nearly hanging myself in ropes of convolvulus, and came out on a lawn which stretched up to the house.

I stood abashed, for a young man was pacing the grass, a book in his hand. He was evidently a parson, for he wore black clothes and shovel-hat, but, instead of the parson's full-bottomed wig, his own pale hair fell about his ears. He walked with a stoop, and looked frail and careworn.

I would have slunk away, for when a Methodist is hungry, it is not to the Parsonage he should come for bread. But at that moment he turned and caught sight of me.

"Who are you? What are you doing here?" His voice, though startled, was not unkind, and I replied, "I had no idea this was a Parsonage when I came into your garden, for I am a Methodist."

"But that doesn't tell me why you are here."

"I have tramped many miles, and am tired and hungry—but I am a Methodist."

He knit his brows and stared at me. He had a good face, but the lines round his mouth were very weak.

"You might tell me more about yourself besides that you are a Methodist. But I do wrong to question you when you're tired and fasting. Come into the house."

I was bewildered. I had not expected this reception from a parson. I staggered as I walked. He noticed it, and bade me lean on his arm.

"You can explain matters afterwards, but you shall rest and eat first."

"You are very trustful," I replied rather bitterly; "for all you know, I may be the worst kind of tramp and thief."

"I don't think so, and I'm good at reading faces. Besides, you are tired, and hungry, and God forbid that I should deny you food and rest."

"Is that your Gospel?" I asked, touched by his simple kindness. "Beware, it may bring you into trouble."

"I think not," he answered gently. "But here we are in the kitchen. Don't be frightened, Rosie"—to a maidservant—"this gentleman has been out all night, and is tired and hungry. Heat him some soup at once"—then to me, "Sit here, my friend, and I shall fetch you some water to wash your feet."

He was gone, and I leaned back on the settle, and closed my eyes. I wondered for a moment if I were dreaming, but the cosy kitchen, the red-cheeked maid, and the hot soup she brought me with soaked bread, were real enough. The voracity with which I devoured my meal astonished my waitress, who refilled the bowl, and stared at me with the profoundest awe as I gulped it down. I had just upon finished when the parson returned, carrying not only a basin of warm water, but stockings and shoes.

He bathed my feet, then examined and bound up the gash on my forehead, and helped me to arrange my dress. While he performed these kind offices I thought it best to tell him my story, and let him know on whom he was bestowing his charity, but my recital nothing altered his goodness.

"I don't agree with you in the least," he said, "but that makes no difference. You are my guest for to-day, and you mustn't resume your journey till you are thoroughly rested."

"You are very good," I said brokenly. For the second time in my life I had found a kind heart, given to hospitality.

"I only do you a decent kindness. How tired you must be! Come, you shall sleep in my bed for a few hours while your clothes are dried." He drew my arm through his, and led me to a small sunlit room in the gable of his house.

"Is this Bodiam village?" I asked, while he helped me to undress, for I was so stiff and cramped that every movement was painful. "I thought old Mr. Henniker was rector of Bodiam."

"This is not Bodiam. It is Ewehurst, and I'm Guy Shotover, the curate-in-charge."

"Ewehurst! What a fool I was not to have recognised it! But I was sick and dazed, and I thought to have come further than this."

"Take courage, you are not far from your journey's end, and you will be another man after you have slept."

He left me, and I fell into a sleep where I dreamed of nothing but green fields, sunshine, and kind voices.

The sun was shining full on my face when I woke, and gazed stupidly round me, wondering where I was. I remembered in an instant, and jumped out of bed. My clothes had been cleaned and dried, so I hastened to dress myself. I had slept off in a great measure my anxiety and despair, and, though subdued, my heart was not so heavy as it had been a few hours ago. I was also physically refreshed, but not to such an extent, for my head still ached and throbbed, and every now and then I shivered, and the next moment I burned.

It was nearly two o'clock, and before I had finished dressing, Guy Shotover came to summon me to dinner.

27

"But before we eat," he said, "I must introduce you to my sister. She was in bed when you arrived, as she sleeps badly, and seldom rises before seven. I have told her about you, and she's most anxious to see you."

"I fear that I am not a very suitable object to present to a lady."

"Nonsense. You look marvellously better after your sleep. There's a brilliant colour on your face."

I followed him downstairs, and through the parlour into the garden.

"Ruth is in the arbour, reading." We went along a path bordered with an array of daffodils, and came to a summer-house at the end of it. Great ropes of creeper hung in front of the arch, and between the leaves I saw the pale blue of a woman's gown. The next moment Shotover caught aside the blushing curtain of young shoots, and my eyes met those of the curate's sister.

She looked little more than a child. Her stature was low, and her figure slight, and she had the dimpled cheeks and soft white throat one loves to kiss in children. But her eyes were essentially unchildlike, though it was some time before I could tell what made them so—whether it was their resolution, their anxiety, or their pathos. Her hair was almost hidden under a scarf she wore wound over her head and shoulders, but a narrow band of it was visible outside the muslin, and it was a rich, ruddy auburn, nearly red.

"Ruthie," said Shotover, "here is Mr. Lyte."

She rose, and dropped me a rather prim curtsey.

"I hope you feel refreshed after your sleep," she said shyly.

"Greatly refreshed, madam, and I am glad to be out again in the sunshine. What a lovely day to follow last night's rain!"

"Lud! It was indeed a dreadful night. What hardships you must have endured!"

"They are over now, and I shall think of them no more, but be thankful that I met such a kind friend in your brother."

"Lud! Guy is good," she said innocently, and I noticed with some surprise that her words brought a look of anguish to the curate's face.

She seemed to realise, in spite of my appearance, that I was not one of the common mumpers and vagabonds to whom her brother loved to give shelter, for the shyness with which she had greeted me passed away, and she chattered merrily as we strolled over the daisies towards the Vicarage. Her voice was musical, and though her speech was full of little schoolgirl affectations, I found her marvellously sweet to listen to, as she told me about the seminary at Peckham she had just left, about "young ladies," her companions, about her "studies"—confined to French, singing, and the use of the globes, it seems—and how glad she was to be back home with Guy. No girl had ever spoken thus to me before. My sisters could not mention their school at Hastings without nudgings, gigglings, and allusions to a certain music-master; Mary Winde had never been to school, and would not have chattered of it so artlessly if she had. We came to a clump of daffodils; Miss Shotover picked one and gave it to me.

"La! how beautiful the garden looks to-day. The tulips are already out in the herb-walk. I'm vastly eager to see Sussex in spring-time. Guy and I came here only in November. We came from Golden Parsonage, in the county of Herts."

"Which is not so fair as Sussex, madam."

"No, faith!" she answered.

Her little hand was in the curate's, and I noticed that he fixed his eyes on her face with a look half of love, half of reverence. She could not have been more than eighteen, and he was evidently over thirty, but his whole behaviour seemed rather that of a child looking up to a parent, than that of an elder brother towards his slip of a sister. He was by no means as handsome as she, though his face was pleasing. He seemed anxious and careworn, and once, when he looked into her eyes, his lips twitched as if he were in pain.

Dinner was prepared in a little brick-floored room, sweet-smelling with hyacinths and violets. Miss Shotover noticed that her brother was depressed.

"Lud, Guy! You mustn't look so vastly glum, or you'll spoil my appetite. What shall I do to make you smile?"

She came up behind him as he sat, and putting her thin arms round his neck, laid her cheek against his. Thought I to myself—he will be a fool if he does not smile now; and he did smile, the cloud of misery passing from his brow, but not from his eyes. Soon we were all three talking together with laughter and friendliness, while a little bird sang in a cage by the window, and nearly drowned our voices in his own.

Suddenly there came the sound of a horse's hoofs on the gravel, followed by a knock at the hall-door.

"It must be Enchmarsh!" cried Miss Shotover, and I saw that every scrap of colour had left her cheeks.

"Surely not," said the curate. "He was here only yesterday."

"But I know it's he. That is his step in the hall, and that is his voice speaking to Rosie."

She sprang up, and I noticed that the sadness of her eyes had suddenly become the expression of her whole face, that she was no longer a little chattering schoolgirl, but a miserable, desperate woman. The impulse of my heart communicated itself to my limbs, and I took half a stride towards her. But the next instant she recovered herself, and tripped gracefully to the door as it opened and the maidservant announced—"Mr. Enchmarsh."

A fine, tall fellow of about three or four-and-thirty came in. He wore a rough and simple riding-suit, which could not, however, hide the grand proportions of his figure. His face was deeply bronzed; his eyes and brows were black as night. He wore his hair cut short against his head, and parted at the side of his forehead, which gave him an additionally manly look. But there was an expression in his dark and restless eyes which repelled, even revolted me, and this instinctive dislike was not softened by the careless way he greeted Shotover or by the familiarity with which he took the sister's hand.

He gave me scarcely more than a nod when the curate presented me, and ignored me almost entirely during the meal which the Shotovers invited him to share. He seemed, though evidently dreaded, on familiar terms with the brother and sister. His manners could not be described as actually bad, though they were swaggering and free. He rattled of his horse, his hounds, his hunt, and his house, called Kitchenhour, on the borders of Wet Level. He pressed Miss Shotover to ride out a-hunting with him, and won a reluctant consent. He snubbed her brother, who wished to go with her, telling him that he could never bestride any mount more spirited than a donkey. He asked me if I ever went hunting, and in the middle of my reply started speaking of something else to Miss Ruth, whom he called by her Christian name.

Soon after Miss Shotover had left the room, Enchmarsh became moderately drunk. The curate seemed anxious that he should not see his sister before he went away, but the squire insisted on bidding her farewell. She was sitting over some embroidery in her parlour, and when we came into the room, started up alarmed.

Her eyes were red, and her cheeks tear-stained. I fell back and so did Shotover, but Enchmarsh strode quickly towards her, and took her rather roughly by the arm. "Here, dry your eyes," and she obediently unfolded a morsel of a handkerchief clenched in her hand, and soaked with tears. Then he whispered something to her, and a strange look crept into her eyes, mingled fear and audacity. I glanced at Shotover, and saw that his hands were both clenched, but his face was more miserable than angry. As for me, I could have knocked Enchmarsh down, and wondered why the curate did not do so.

"Your horse is ready, Enchmarsh," said Shotover at last, in a jerky, nervous voice.

"So'm I," replied the squire. "Don't you play the fool, you two; there's my parting advice," and he flung himself out of the room, Shotover, after some hesitation, following him.

I felt keen embarrassment on being left alone with Miss Ruth, who was still fighting with her tears. I tried to beguile her to talk of her school, but the young ladies' seminary seemed to have lost its attraction, and her replies were monosyllabic. I heartily wished myself elsewhere.

It was nearly three o'clock, and when the curate came back, I told him that I must leave Ewehurst Parsonage. He would have persuaded me to stay the night, saying that he thought me feverish. But though I thought the same, I persisted in my resolution, and at last he gave way, declaring, however, that I should drink a dish of his sister's chocolate before I started.

Either Miss Ruth was a very good actress, or she had suddenly recovered from her depression. "Lud! indeed you must stay for chocolate!" she cried, turning from the window, and showing me eyes once more bright and cheeks all dimpled with

30

smiles. "You shall have chocolate, and cheese-cakes too. I made some this morning. Do you like cheese-cakes?"

"Very much," I answered lamely, somewhat taken aback at her sudden change of mood.

"So does Guy, and so do I—only I like meringues better. I learned to make cheese-cakes because Milly Rogers, one of the young ladies at Miss Wetherbee's seminary, likes them so. Don't you remember Milly, brother, and how beautifully she sang to the guitar when she stayed with us at Golden Parsonage?"

She ran to the curate and kissed him. He patted her hands, and her cheek, and turned away, his lips trembling.

At four o'clock a table was spread under a sycamore on the lawn, and the chocolate and cheese-cakes were served. In spite of her partiality for the latter, Miss Ruth did not eat many; she devoted her energies to forcing them down her brother's throat. He seemed unable to shake off his melancholy, and she seemed resolved that he should. So she fondled and chattered and laughed, and sang little snatches of song in a sweet though untrained voice. But for all her gaiety, I could see that she was in an agony of nervousness. She started at any sudden noise, and the colour came and went on her cheeks.

"Now, Guy, another cheese-cake?" she coaxed. "What, you won't? You horrid fellow! that's because you don't like my cooking. Lud! I shall give it to the chicks, since you're so dainty."

A hen with five chicks had sauntered on to the lawn, and Ruth broke up the cheese-cake, and scattered the crumbs. Shotover sat watching her, his elbow on the table, his chin on his hand. I watched her too, as she crouched on the grass, some crumbs in the palm of her outstretched hand to tempt the timid fools. Her pretty innocence contrasted strangely with the wild eyes, quivering lips, and locked hands of an hour ago. What had given her back her girlhood? and why had Enchmarsh's dark face made her lose it, or rather cast it from her like a garment, and show in its nakedness her suffering womanhood? How was it that Enchmarsh had dared address her with such brutality, and her brother with such contempt? How was it that they had both endured his insults, like children under the lash, who can but weep and writhe in their shame?

A cry of delight interrupted my thoughts. Ruth had risen from her knees, and came towards me, holding a chicken in a cradle made by her two hands—she had the dearest little hands; the spring sun had just begun to bronze them.

"Look, Mr. Lyte! Look! Isn't he a sweet little fellow? Feel how soft he is," and she held the creature against my face. As she did so, her hand accidentally touched my cheek, and at once a strange new divine thrill passed through me and quickened my heart.

The shadows were drawing in; the curate's set face looked grey in the waning light, and I rose to take my leave. Shotover lent me a pair of boots, and he and his sister walked with me as far as their wistaria-tangled gate.

31

"I shall not try to thank you for your kindness," I said to my host. "I am not equal to such a task. But you can guess my gratitude."

"I'm glad I was able to help you," he answered simply. "I like to feel that I can be of use to my fellow-men. Fare you well, Methodist; I hope to see you again soon. If ever you should pass this way, remember that there is always a bed for you at Ewehurst Vicarage."

I wrung his hand, and kissed Miss Ruth's, and they stood at the little gate till I had vanished round a corner of the lane.

I mused as I walked between the blackthorn battlements of the hedges, and the white blossoms against the blue sky made me think of Ruth Shotover's scarf against her gown. I mused on the curate and his sister, and on Enchmarsh, and felt that some mystery bound them together. I mused on the curate's sad face and kind heart, on his sister's merry laugh and miserable eyes, on Enchmarsh's brutality, and on his strange connection with the Shotovers—and the whole perplexed me.

The spring day, lulled by soft winds and tinkling fold-bells, fell asleep. The sky darkened, and the first stars appeared like shining daisies over Furnacefield just as I was beginning to drag my legs wearily. I went down the lane of deep shadows, and came into the light that streamed from the open doorway. I knocked, and the next moment Peter Winde had sprung forward and dragged me into the kitchen.

"Lad, lad, dear lad! You've done it! The Lord helped you!"

"Yes, I have done it, and the Lord have mercy!"

Then the room swam, and Peter's eyes looked at me as through a mist. I cast up my arms, staggered, spun round, and fell in a faint at his feet.

CHAPTER V

OF THE METHODIST AND MARY WINDE

For a time all was blackness and silence, then streaks of flame shot before my eyes, and I gasped for breath. It was as if a huge weight lay on my chest; I thought that I was suffocating, and writhed and panted. Then a sudden light burst upon me, and I found myself lying on the floor, while Peter Winde bathed my forehead with water.

I moaned, but did not raise my head, which was softly pillowed, and lay for a while silent, with Peter's hand on my forehead. Then the room, which had seemed full of fiery mist, became clear again. I turned myself, and saw that my head rested on Mary Winde's lap.

For a moment I gazed speechless into her face, and noticed that there were tears on her eyelashes and cheeks; then I smiled feebly and sat up, gripping Peter's arm.

"Come lad, you're better now," he said; "you were exhausted after your tramp. When did you leave Brede Parsonage?"

"Last night."

"Then why didn't you reach here sooner?"

"I lost my way—oh, it was horrible!"

I struggled up from the floor, and he drew me down beside him on the settle, and while Mary busied herself preparing her supper in the outer kitchen, I poured forth my tale, and found relief in confession, as who does not?

Peter took my hand, and patted it as one would pat a child's.

"Take heart, lad. God measures our love by our efforts, not by our achievements, or we should all be in a sorry way. I've lived fifty years, and have met but two saints—John Palehouse and——"

"Whom?" I asked, as he hesitated.

"She's a woman," he said, "and you can hear her footsteps in the next room."

We sat for a long time in silence, while the firelight leaped on the walls and ceiling, and a great scarlet moon rose from beyond Iridge, and, filling almost the whole of the uncurtained window-pane, climbed up among the stars. Mary's feet sounded ghostly in the outer room, and now and then she crooned to herself little snatches of song which made me think of ruined oasts in a lonely field and spooks in some haunted shell of a farm-house at dusk. I was glad when she came and stood in the doorway, the firelight falling on her, and called us to our supper.

"I cooked it myself, for Jane is gone to visit her parents at Botany." Then suddenly my thoughts flew back to the other girl who that same day had set before me fare of her own cooking, and I realised more than ever that Mary was not beautiful, that her figure was immature, her cheeks were pale, and her mouth was ill-drawn.

But she was so gentle and sweet that I soon forgot her plainness—that is to say if a face which wore such an expression of love and serenity could ever be called plain. She and Peter vied with one another in trying to raise my spirits, and to keep me from dwelling too miserably on the woes of yesterday. Peter spoke many kind words that I did not deserve, and Mary questioned me about Ewehurst Parsonage, the parson, and his sister.

"I have never seen Miss Shotover," she said, "but I have often heard of her from the Cartwrights at Turzes. She sometimes drinks tea there. They tell me she is very beautiful."

33

"She is indeed," I replied, and there must have been more than an ordinary rapture in my voice and look, for Peter and Mary both laughed.

"Her brother's a good fellow, I believe," said the former. "I know very little of him except from hearsay, but he seems to understand his duties as a parson better than many in these parts. Not that he has more than two services a week in his church—I suppose we mustn't expect that of him at present—but he reads them reverently and well, and he visits his poor and cares for them."

"And for any vagrant that he meets," I said.

"I'm rather puzzled," resumed Peter, "at the friendship between the Shotovers and the new squire at Kitchenhour. Enchmarsh is a wild fellow, and his reputation is none too clean; it's strange that I should so often see him riding with Miss Ruth."

"I believe they knew him in Hertfordshire," said Mary, "and perhaps Mr. Shotover thinks that the companionship of such a sweet girl as his sister will make another man of the squire."

"Humph!" grunted Peter, "you look at things from a woman's point of view, my dearie. It isn't likely that Shotover's zeal for souls should make him put his sister to such risk."

He fell a-meditating, and Mary and I had the conversation to ourselves during the rest of the meal.

When Peter had said grace, I asked him if I might go to bed, for I ached with weariness, and my head throbbed painfully. He gave me his arm up the twisting stairs, where the candle-flame cast our shadows uncouthly on the wall, and led me to a room looking out over a field to Shoyswell Wood.

"You slept in the oast-barn the first time you were here, but you shall lie between sheets to-night."

"I shall never forget my first visit to Shoyswell, sir. I have felt better and happier ever since."

"You were a strange lad, then. You made me think of an untamed colt I'd just been breaking in. The young beast kicked and fought with his harness, and hated his life, I'll be bound."

He wished me a good night, and I heard him humming one of Wesley's hymns as he went downstairs. As for me, what could I do but fall on my knees at my bedside and thank God?

I was just about to undress when I noticed that the daffodil Miss Shotover had given me was still in my buttonhole. It was faded, and for a moment I thought of throwing it away, but remembered that I needed a bookmark for my Bible, so put it between the pages, furious with myself because I blushed as I did so.

I flung off my clothes and was soon in bed. The window was uncurtained, and I could see the moon hanging like a crescent of yellow glass in the space, and the stars flashing between the tossed branches of a tree that shadowed my pane. I became conscious of a vague, delicious smell which made me think of September hop-fields and smoking kilns, and I saw in the moonlight that a bunch of dried hops hung above my bed, and swung gently in the draught of the night wind.

My sleep was uneasy with dreams—of Brede Parsonage, my father, and Clonmel, of wet fields and woods, and long twisting roads, down which I trudged wearily on and on, passing only ruined farms and half-burnt cottages, my legs staggering under me, my head swimming. I woke, and the horror and fatigue were still with me. I tried to raise myself in bed, but was helpless, and could only lie and listen to the birds chirruping their dawn-song among the apple-trees, while the stars paled and the sky flushed, and the sunshine crept among the clouds.

It seemed hours later that I saw Peter Winde in the room. He spoke, but his voice came to me only in a confused murmur, and when I myself tried to speak, I found that the words would not do my bidding, but crowded on my tongue without connexion or sense. Then the walls of the room seemed to come together, and I to fall backwards into the dark.

I remember nothing clearly of the days that followed. I spent them sometimes sleeping, sometimes lying awake, every limb racked with pain, sometimes tossing in delirium. I saw faces around me but they appeared and disappeared, changed and wavered like the faces of a dream. I often thought myself at Brede Parsonage and a child once more, smarting and aching under the blows of my father or Clonmel—for the pain was always with me—and sometimes I would fancy myself at Ewehurst, drinking chocolate with Miss Shotover on the lawn. But my most constant vision was that of the endless twisting roads, along which I trudged, sometimes in the sunshine, sometimes in the dark, and sometimes at twilight. Once I thought I felt a woman take my hand and kiss it and bathe it with tears, and to this hour I do not know if it were a dream.

One day I woke out of this whirl of vision, delirium, and phantasmagoria. It was evening, and the sky was soft and throbbing with the sunset. The birds were gurgling and twittering in Shoyswell Wood, the cows were lowing in the stalls, and a girl's voice was speaking just under my window.

"I'm so glad he's better."

I sat up in bed, and saw Mary sewing close by me.

"Who is that outside?"

She started, but answered calmly:

"That is Miss Shotover."

I fell back on the pillows.

"Miss Shotover!" I repeated in a low voice.

"Yes. She rode a-hunting past this farm-house the day after you arrived, and asked how you did; and hearing that you were ill, she and her brother have often been to inquire after you."

"Have I been ill a long time?"

"About a fortnight."

"Was I near dying?"

"We thought so at one time, but you are better now and you must not talk any longer, you must go to sleep."

"I'll do my best, but first tell me, was it you who nursed me?"

"Yes, father and I."

"Thank you, Mary!"

I stretched out my hand, and she came over to the bedside and took it. For a moment her fingers lay in mine, then she drew them abruptly away.

"Go to sleep," she said almost roughly.

I slept during the greater part of the days that followed, and sometimes Mary was with me, and sometimes her father. Once I noticed a basket full of nectarines by my bedside, and was told that the Shotovers had sent them. The same answer was given a short while later to my question as to who had sent the glorious Lent lilies with which my room was decked. I had no doubt but that the brother and sister had taken an interest in me, and the thought solaced my waking hours and sweetened my dreams.

I grew quickly better, and one day, after the doctor had left, Peter came up to my room and said:

"Dr. Hewland thinks that you might come downstairs to-day; and I believe that it would be a good thing, as the Shotovers have promised us a visit this morning, and are very anxious to see you."

I declared myself more than willing to rise, so dressed with the help of Peter. My pulses beat fast with quickening health and hope, and I went downstairs with an agility remarkable in one only just recovering from a severe attack of fever. I told myself that it was the joy of convalescence that brought the flush to my throat and cheek, but in my heart of hearts I realised that my pleasure and excitement were due to Peter's words, "The Shotovers promised us a visit this morning." I heard a girl's voice in the kitchen, and my eyes shone, but it was only Mary speaking to the maid.

"When do you expect the curate and his sister?" I asked Peter, as I sat in an arm-chair by the fire, with a rug over my knees.

"Not for an hour or so. You and Mary must entertain each other till then. I'm going to visit the lambs in the river-field."

He left the room, and Mary drew her chair to the opposite side of the hearth, and brought her sewing—snowy folds of linen on her lap, and the sound of stitching to mingle with the crackle and roar of the fire.

36

"I am sure you will like Miss Shotover when you know her," I remarked, somewhat irrelevantly, after a silence.

"I do know her a little," said Mary, "and I like her very much."

"I am sorry for her. She has such miserable eyes."

"Poor girl! I think she must have had trouble."

"And yet she laughs so often"—I was speaking more to myself than to Mary—"and she cannot have had much sorrow; she is only a little schoolgirl."

Mary sewed in silence, and I watched the hands of the clock move slowly round. A fat, short-legged puppy came sprawling in at the door, and I enticed the little brute on to my knee. The clock struck the hour, and I started. The Shotovers would soon arrive.

"Mary, pray bring me the mirror that hangs by the door."

"No, sir, I will not!"

"That means that I am not fit to be seen after my illness. Bring me the mirror and let me judge for myself."

"I shall not bring it for you, for I value it, and when you have looked into it, you will throw it across the room and break it."

"You can catch it in your apron—but bring it here, I beseech you."

She fetched the glass and I made a wry face at the countenance it reflected—deadly pale, save for the black brows, and an ugly purple scar across the left temple.

"Mary, how can I meet Miss Shotover?"

She would have spoken some comforting words, but at that instant horses' hoofs clattered in the yard and, giving me a smile that made her beautiful, she hurried to the door.

The next moment I heard Miss Shotover's voice, and the sun, streaming suddenly into the room, fell upon her as she stood on the threshold. She wore a dark riding-habit, a three-corner velvet hat and buff chamois gloves with gauntlets reaching half-way up her arm. Her hair was slightly powdered, and tied at the nape of her neck, her cheeks were flushed, her lips parted, and her breath was fast with exercise; her eyes were sweet with kindness.

"Please, please don't move!" she cried, when I would have risen. "Lud! you look dreadfully ill. Oh? Oh! what a sweet little puppy!"—and the next moment the lucky beggar was whisked off my knee into her arms. "I do so vastly love puppies and kittens and little chickens. But here's Guy, looking glum because he wants to speak to you and I won't stop chattering."

Shotover stepped forward and shook me by the hand, and the next moment Peter joined us, and we all sat round the fire. At first our talk was laboured—we spoke of my returning health and of the weather. At last Mary asked Miss Ruth if she were not sorry that the hunting-season was over, and we fell to talking of the hunt. I had

37

sometimes ridden with the hounds—only on rare occasions, for I had hard work to do, and no horse of my own in the Parsonage stables—and my heart leapt with the memory of those days when the woods shrilled with the huntsman's horn, and the fox broke covert through the long grass of Peppering Eye, and my horse, bounding under me, seemed scarcely to touch the earth. The conversation was chiefly between Miss Ruth and me, for the others knew little of our topic, but we soon digressed into a discussion on Fielding, in which everybody joined. The parson held with the new fashion, and vowed that he would never let his sister read "Tom Jones." Peter told him that Mary had read it from cover to cover, and I championed Peter.

It is strange that I should remember the details of our chat so clearly, how friendly we grew over it, and how surprised we were when Jane's appearance with a tray of cake and mead told us that twelve o'clock had struck, and that our visitors must be going. Miss Ruth was full of mirth and high spirits, and her brother smiled at her laughter. Only once her bright eyes clouded, and that was when Peter Winde pressed her and the curate to stay for dinner, and she answered, "My brother and I are promised to dine at Kitchenhour."

The cake was eaten and the mead drunk; Mary, who had made them, was praised, and blushed at her praises; and our friends rose to leave. The next moment I was gazing at the door through which Miss Ruth had just vanished.

"Isn't she beautiful?" I said to Mary.

"Yes, and such a sweet girl!"

Mary Winde and Ruth Shotover had evidently fallen in love with each other, for many were the visits that during the next fortnight Mary paid to Ewehurst and Ruth to Shoyswell. The latter were the most frequent, as Mary could be ill spared from home, and the two girls would sit and talk in the kitchen, where I often joined them.

Miss Ruth's moods varied exceedingly. Sometimes she was all laughter and high spirits; sometimes she was downcast, with the tears not very far from her eyes. She spoke little of her life at the Parsonage, and once she appeared with her eyes red, and told Mary that she had had trouble at home, but begged that she would ask no questions.

The weeks went by, and the swallows came back with May, and I passed through convalescence to perfect health. During the long days when I sat inactive in my chair by the hearth, or walked, leaning on Peter's arm, in the fields or in the garden, he and I had many discussions as to my future. He was just as vehement as ever in his wish that I should be a preacher, and carry the Gospel through broad Sussex, even as Wesley had carried it through broad England. I could earn my bread by working on the farms round the hamlets I visited, and Peter and I mapped out my journey between us. He insisted on lending me five pounds, so that if I could not find work I need not starve.

"This is neither the hay-time nor the harvest, lad, and many a yeoman to whom you offer your services will turn you away, saying that he has enough hands on his farm. And even if he takes you on, what will be your wages? Sixpence a day, or perhaps only food and bed. So take the money, and God speed you with it. I'm not sending you to a soft life, Humphrey, or to an easy one, but I'm sending you to a good life and a great life. Oh, I trust that when you return here in a month's time you will be able to look back on many souls who once sat in darkness, but now see great light."

And I, sitting opposite him in the ember-glow, murmured "Amen."

I shall never forget the last night I spent at Shoyswell. Mary and I sat side by side on the floor in front of the fire, and Peter read to us out of his Bible how Jesus Christ sent out His disciples two and two before His face, bidding them be wise as serpents and harmless as doves. Then we all three knelt on the flags and sang Bishop Ken's Evening Hymn, while outside the wind crooned a low cradle-song to the trees, and the stars yearned through the mist of the spring night.

The next morning we rose early, and ate our breakfast at six. My bundle had been made up the evening before, and, as I had no clothes whatever except those I wore, it contained sets of Peter's stockings and underlinen, as well as the five pounds he had lent me. He also gave me a pistol, which would be useful to the lonely traveller by night. I was heartsick at parting with my kind friends, but life, the world, and labour lay before me, and I was full of good resolutions and zeal.

Peter and Mary walked with me to the end of Shoyswell Lane. The birds were singing gaily, and as we passed under the trees, so beautiful in their spring green, a robin began to trill and twitter. I remembered how that little red throat had brought me comfort on the miserable morning after my Confirmation, and I seemed once more to stand in twilight All Saints' Street, with the cobalt shadows on the sea.

We came to where the lane joined the high road to Wadhurst, my first halting-place, and I turned to Mary to say good-bye.

"Remember me to Miss Shotover," and she promised.

We had been so like brother and sister during the last few weeks that I half thought of kissing her, but something in her face as well as in my own heart forbade it, and I merely put my lips to the little brown hand that shook in mine.

Then I turned to Peter. "Bless me before I go," and I knelt down before him, and he laid his hand on my head and prayed God to bless and keep me, and lift up the light of His countenance upon me, and give me peace "henceforth and for ever more."

CHAPTER VI

OF THE METHODIST AS A WANDERER

The wind that brings the scent of flowers to city gates in May was blowing over the fields as I tramped westward with the tears in my eyes. Awe and zeal and sorrow mingled in my heart. Awe at the life-work laid upon me, zeal for its success, sorrow at the parting which had just taken place. How good they had been to me, that Methodist farmer and his daughter! They had been father and sister to one who was to all intents fatherless and sisterless. They had loved me and helped me, and had pointed through the clouds to the sun.

I trudged on, my bundle slung on a stick over my shoulder, for all the world like a tramp or gipsy, and an evil-looking fellow I was, no doubt, with my thick bent brows and white, scarred face. The day grew every minute warmer and sweeter; the country was waking, throwing off her night-robe of mist and gloom, clothing herself in sweet scents, sweet sounds, sweet sights, sweet sunshine, and laughing a joyous Godspeed to the Methodist.

I went by the farm-houses of Miskyns and Cottenden, with old Churchsettle down in the valley, and came at last to a cross-road known as Shover's Green. This was about two miles from Wadhurst, and as far as I had ever walked from Brede Parsonage, the country beyond it being an unknown land. I stood by the signpost, and gazed down the long white road before me, and began to tremble and shake like a girl. I was to preach at Wadhurst, but what should I say? I had never preached before, might not my tongue falter and fail in its new task? The sweat was on my face; I was like a nervous actor shuddering in the wings, while on the stage his cue is being spoken. But suddenly some words came to me, Bible words: "Take no thought beforehand what ye shall speak, for it is not ye that speak, but the Holy Ghost." I lifted my hat, and prayed as I stood by the signpost at Shover's Green, with the long grass waving round my knees.

Reassured and strengthened, I went on, and came to Wadhurst, a mass of cottages and windmills swarming round a slender spire. It was nearly eight o'clock, and the village was awake and flooded with sunshine. The house doors were open, and the housewives stood in them; children played in the street; girls in brightly-coloured gowns grouped together and gossiped; men and lads loafed against the doorposts, the inn porch, and the lych-gate.

There was a party of yokels chatting and joking in the market-place, where stood a cart from which the horse had been unharnessed. I sat down on the shaft and watched the people. I saw that many of them stared suspiciously at me, especially the group of farm-lads at my elbow. I read a few verses of my Bible, breathed a prayer, and climbed into the cart.

"I have something to say to you," I cried, standing up in the cart.

Every one started and looked amazed; then some laughed, and a man in a smock cried:

"Go on, muster!"

My courage had deserted me, my tongue stuck and stammered, and my knees shook so that I nearly fell down in the cart. I felt utterly unfitted for the task before me. I was not used to speaking to others of spiritual things, for my confidences would have been laughed at by the family at Brede Parsonage, and how was I suddenly to bring my heart to my lips, and pour into indifferent, perhaps hostile ears, the most sacred feelings of my soul?

I stood irresolute, my head held down, my cheeks scarlet. Then a girl tittered, and I was ashamed. I lifted my head, and threw it back, and the next moment a torrent of words rose to my lips.

I have only a faint recollection of what I said. I stammered, I remember, to begin with, but soon my speech flowed more smoothly, and a mad yearning love of those shepherdless sheep before me filled my heart and set my words on fire. I told them of Christ's love for them, of the help He offered, and of the reward He promised. There was no order or method in my sermon; the thoughts ground and clashed against one another like stones in a stream. I spoke for nearly half an hour, then stopped suddenly, for the strange power that had upheld me was gone, and throwing myself down in the cart, I hid my face and groaned.

There was a confused murmur all round me. "A Methodee!"—"Off his head!"—"Take un to the lockup!"—"Quite a boy, and as crazed as Nebuchadnezzar!"—"What rubbidge the poor chap spoke!"

This was not encouraging, and I realised that to lie groaning on the floor of a cart would by no means dispel the idea that I was mad. So I sprang up, and climbed down into the street, pushed my way through the crowd, and hurried out of the market-place.

Some of the people followed me, a few of them interested, but most of them jeering. Well-nigh in despair I turned and said:

"I am not mad, but am feeling very wild and miserable, so please do not follow me. I shall see you again perhaps in a month or so. Think over my words, or rather God's words, which He forced me to speak."

There must have been an unusual look on my face as I said this, for the people slunk away without further badgering me.

I strode forward between the hedges, reflecting on my late adventure. I felt that I had not made a good beginning to my ministry. Perhaps I had left Wadhurst in too great a hurry, perhaps I should have stayed, and reasoned with the people, perhaps I should even now go back to them. But I realised that this would be worse than useless, so sped on, resolving to act more wisely in future.

The next matter was to consider where to find work and wages—for I had resolved not to touch Peter's five pounds till sheer want drove me to it. Fortune favoured me; my first application met with success, and I was given half a day's work among the sheep at a farm-house called Little Pell. I toiled contentedly till sunset, when the farmer's wife called me into the kitchen and gave me and the other farm-hands a supper of bread-and-broth, after which I was taken to a loft full of sweet hay and left there to sleep.

The sunshine on my face awoke me, and I rose singing for light-heartedness. At the farm-house I was given a cup of milk and some rye-bread, and half an hour later set out for Rotherfield, my next halting-place.

The day was sweet and warm, and I reached Rotherfield about noon. There I bought some gingerbread, and ate it by the side of one of the three rivers which are born in the flats near the little town. Then I went to the market-place, and waited for an opportunity to begin my sermon. I did not wait long. In the churchyard close at hand the Burial Service was being read over a child's grave. A curate, with muddy top-boots showing under a surplice well-frayed with his spurs, was hurrying through the Church's sweet words of consolation. The mother sobbed bitterly, and the father, little more than a lad, with a look of dogged misery on his face, groaned aloud during the unseemly gabble. The service came to an end; the curate strode off without a word, though the mother's tears had moistened the grass at his feet. Then I went up to them and to the little group of mourners. The group widened into a crowd, and I ceased to speak of the dead child, but turned to death itself, and told them of the hope beyond the squalid tether of their lives.

Whether it was the solemnity of the occasion, or that I spoke more powerfully and simply than before, I do not know. But my words produced a better effect than at Wadhurst, and when I had finished I heard murmurs of "Thank you," and "God bless you." Happier than I had felt for many a day, I bade the people farewell, and had little difficulty in finding work at a farm-house in the neighbourhood.

I shall not give in detail the rest of my journey across Sussex to the borders of Hampshire. From Rotherfield I crossed the valley of Jarvis Brook to Crowborough, then went on to Cuckfield and Cowfold, and through many a village to Fernhurst, where you can see the Hampshire downs. I preached in every market-place, meeting sometimes with success, sometimes with what seemed utter failure. Since the death of Wesley, eight years before, and the schism of the Methodists from the Established Church, Methodism had fallen into bad repute, and I was often greeted with jeers, even stones and mud. Moreover, my youth was in my disfavour, and at many a market-cross a rude voice from the crowd would exclaim, "Where's yer mammy, my boy?" or, "Yer unaccountable young to be out wudout yer nurse," or, "Yer had better go back to school, or yer'll be whipped for playing truant." In several villages where I preached, the people used to tell me of another preacher who had gone before me "a man of powerfuller words than you, my lad." I wondered who this man might be, and longed to make up with him, for my heart went out to him, hearing that he was a "Methodee." But when I reached Fernhurst, I was told that he had gone on into Hampshire.

In spite of the disappointments and failures that dogged my path, that month of wandering was very happy, almost the happiest of my life. There were, it is true, moments when I would throw myself down and nearly weep in my hopelessness, but there were also moments which will be sweet to muse on when I lie dying. I often had difficulty in finding work, yet this did not disconcert me much, for wherever I was so fortunate as to be given a day's labour the farmer paid me well. So during the whole journey I had no cause to touch Peter Winde's generous loan. It was then that I thanked God that my father had forced me to toil on the farm at Brede Parsonage instead of sending me to school and college like other gentlemen's sons. For I was useful in barn, field, or fold as the oldest farm-hand, and my fame as a labourer far exceeded my fame as a preacher. "De föaks may ferget yer sarmons, lad," said an old farmer at East Mascalls with whom I took service, "but dey'll never ferget wot a fust-rate hand yer wur wi' de ewes, surelye!"

During this month there were moments when I thanked God for the mere joy of living. It was so sweet to feel the wind on my face and to press on over wet roads, my cheeks sprinkled with the soft splashing rain. I loved the twilight and the rosy sleepy dawn. I loved the noontide, when the cows stood knee-deep in the streams, and I loved the solemn nights, when I walked through a great speaking silence. At the beginning of my journey I used to sleep in barns or lofts, but soon I grew to prefer the leeside of a haystack or hedgerow, and often I lay among last year's leaves in the great beech-woods, listening to the scuttle and flutter of the night creatures, and watching the stars that shimmered through the moving tester of the trees.

When I had come to the borders of Hampshire, at Fernhurst, I went southward and preached at the villages of Chidham, Bosham, and Appledram, on the marshy seaboard below Chichester. Then, turning inland, I carried the Gospel to the Down hamlets, and northwards to Fletching. From Fletching I decided to go back to Shoyswell through Maresfield, and Mayfield, revisiting Wadhurst.

It was Sunday morning when I entered Maresfield, and the church bells were pealing a loud *Sursum Corda* over the fields. It had been my custom in villages where there was no Methodist meeting-room to worship at the parish church, and I was soon kneeling in a back pew of old S. Bartholomy's, at rest and at peace in the cool gloom.

There was a gentle footfall on the aisle, and I thought that some woman had just come into the church, but on looking up I saw the flutter of a surplice, and knew that it was the parson who trod so reverently. This surprised me, accustomed as I was to the stride and swagger of my father and Clonmel, and the jingle of their spurs against the pulpit steps. I craned my head to see the clergyman's face. He was Guy Shotover.

I caught my breath. What could he be doing at Maresfield? Had he been appointed to the living? Surely not, in the short time since I had last seen him. Perhaps he was only doing duty there for the day. I really did not trouble to explain his presence, I was too much occupied in looking for Miss Ruth. At first I could not see her, and came with a pang to the conclusion that she was not in the church. But at last I caught sight of her in a side pew, and could hardly take my eyes off her during the rest of the service. She looked pale and worn, I thought, and her head dropped pathetically under her wide hat. She did not notice me, for she kept her eyes fast fixed on her Prayer Book, in which I might have followed her example.

Guy read the service reverently, and preached an earnest, though not very brilliant, sermon, after which we sang the Old Hundredth, and went out into the sunshine. I waited in the porch for Miss Ruth, and in a few moments she appeared, looking very downcast. She would not have seen me, had I not touched her arm.

She started, coloured, and held out her hand.

"Lud, Mr. Lyte! This is an unexpected pleasure for me."

"And for me," I murmured, as I pressed her hand against my lips.

"Are you and your brother staying at Maresfield?" I asked.

"For to-day. Here comes Guy. You didn't expect to meet Mr. Lyte at Maresfield, did you, dear?"

"I'm surprised, but I'm also delighted. You must come and dine with us at Fiveash Farm. We're lodging there, for Maresfield is one of my Rector's livings, and the curate is sick, so I'm in charge of both parishes."

"But they are twenty miles apart."

"Yes, and that means services on alternate Sundays only. But it's the sole thing to be done, as my Rector doesn't wish to pay for another curate."

I readily accepted Shotover's invitation to dinner, and we set off down a bridle-path to a farm-house cuddling in the hollow.

"Have you seen Mary Winde lately?" I asked Ruth.

"Faith, yes! Guy and I spent an hour at Shoyswell yesterday on our way to Maresfield. Mr. Winde and Mary are vastly well, and longing to see you home."

"I shall be at Shoyswell on Wednesday, I hope."

"And at Ewehurst on Thursday," put in Guy. "But here we are at Fiveash. Go, Guthrie, and hasten Mrs. Ferrars with the dinner. The Methodist is starving, I'm sure."

Dinner was served in the outer kitchen, and both brother and sister were in high spirits, and laughed and talked incessantly during the meal. I sat opposite Guy, and whether it was that I had not seen him for so long I do not know, but I was more struck than ever by the weak lines round his mouth; and his laughter, which was nervous, and his conversation, which was excited, confirmed me in the idea that he was even more emotional and high-strung than his sister.

After dinner the curate retired to his room to pore over the afternoon's sermon—he always learned his sermons by heart, and had a final rehearsal a short time before delivering them—and Ruth and I went out into the garden. The farm-house had once been a Manor, and the garden had been a pleasaunce. Tiger-lilies, sweet-william, flox, and peonies still grew among the long grass, and wicker arches smothered in roses yet stood.

From the bottom of the garden the fields sloped upward, dotted with sheep, and on the crest of the ridge was a little wood.

"Let's gather bluebells," cried Ruth; "there's a vast deal in the coppice yonder."

"I should like nothing better, but do you think it wise to go so far? Look at the sky"—and I pointed to some fierce rag-edged clouds that were rolling up from Plawhatch in the west.

"Lud! It won't rain for an hour yet, and I do so vastly want to gather some bluebells for Guy. He loves flowers."

She laid her hand coaxingly on my arm, and looked up at me wistfully with childlike face and unchildlike eyes.

"Come on, then!" I cried, clasping her brown fingers in mine, as if she were a little girl I was taking for a holiday. I suddenly realised what I was doing and dropped her hand, while the colour mounted on my cheeks.

I spoke scarcely a word the whole of our way to Piekreed Wood, though my companion chattered gaily enough. I fear she must have found me woefully poor company, but, after all, I was silent only because I was thinking of her. The woods were full of shadow and peace. Ruth flung herself down among the bluebells and regaled me with an account of how she had once spoiled a new white gown by lying on damp grass, and how Miss Witherbee of the seminary had sent her to bed early as a punishment.

There is a golden chain running through my life, binding me to God, and its links are the happy moments He has given me. The first link was forged on the night I slept by the Rother, the next on the afternoon I gathered bluebells with Ruth in Piekreed Wood. We filled our hands full of flowers, while one of us talked and one of us listened. We never noticed the sunshine fade and the sky become first dappled, then overcast with grey, or heard the first drip of rain upon the leaves. A vivid flash of lightning made us both start, and spring to our feet. Ruth dropped her bluebells, and clapped her hands to her ears as a terrific burst of thunder rocked the trees.

"Oh, Lud! Mr. Lyte! Mr. Lyte! What shall we do?" And she ran to me and clutched my arm.

"We mustn't stay here. We must hurry out into the open."

Her lips trembled. "I'm afraid of thunder," she said plaintively.

"I'll take care of you," I replied, and the words made my heart warm. For the first time in my life I realised the sweetness of having some one weaker than myself to protect.

I drew her hand threw my arm, and we forced our way through the hazel undergrowth, and scrambled over the fence into the meadow. The rain fell steadily in heavy warm drops. Ruth's flimsy dress began to cling about her shoulders. I flung off my coat and wrapped it round her.

"I insist! You shall wear it!" I cried, when she would have objected. "Come, we must run to that little shed in the next field. We shall be sheltered there."

We ran over the grass, the frightened sheep galloping before us, their bleating mingling with the crash of the storm. We were soaked to the skin by the time we reached the shed.

Ruth was shivering as I drew her into shelter. She stood clinging to my arm, and her wet hair dripped upon my sleeve. There was a ewe with two lambs at the back of the shed. The creatures seemed tame, and did not try to leave on our entrance; and one or two sheep, evidently more terrified of the storm than of us, came in and huddled their soaked fleeces together in a distant corner.

"Do you think me very silly to be frightened?" asked Ruth.

She gripped my arm with both her nervous little hands, and I tried to answer her, to reassure her; but words failed me, for the clasp of her fingers and the appeal of her eyes had bound my lips with silence, and filled my heart with a strange humility. "Why was I ever born?" I had often blasphemously flung that cry to God. Now I realised that I had been born for this hour, for this swarming of the blood, this quickening of the heart, for this blessed birth of love and love's twin, humbleness.

"The storm is passing over," said Ruth, and the silly sheep ran out into a sudden burst of sunshine.

"Lud! how silent you are," she added, lifting her eyes to mine.

"I am wondering," I said slowly, scarcely realising what I uttered, "whether it would be safe to venture out."

"The rain has stopped," said Ruth, "and I expect Guy will be anxious about us. Please take your coat back; I don't need it now, and you're shivering with cold."

"I am not cold," I answered, and I spoke truly, though my limbs were numb.

We went out into the field. The thunder-clouds were rolling away; the thunder-breeze swept the grass and sang. I sang, too, as I strode along.

"I never heard you sing before," said Ruth. "What are you singing? Is it one of Mr. Wesley's hymns?" she added, lowering her voice. My Methodism always seemed to inspire her with feelings of awe.

"I don't know what it is. It's nothing of Wesley's."

"I like to hear you sing. You've such a deep voice. But lud! pray don't stride so fast; I can't keep up with you."

I slackened my pace, and ceased my song to listen to her voice, which was sweeter. We soon met Guy, who had come out to look for us, and with him we strolled back to the house, Ruth still wearing my coat about her shoulders.

On arriving at Fiveash I changed my wet clothes in the curate's room. He begged me to stay the night, and I consented, for it would be sweet to sleep under the same roof as Ruth.

All the afternoon and evening I was in a state of exalted happiness, which, I think, must have often shown itself in my eyes and on my lips. Ruth was never absent from my thoughts. I loved her. I did not know if she loved me—but I loved her, and that was all that mattered at present. How blessed it is to love!

We went to Evening Prayer at four o'clock, and afterwards to a children's Bible-class at the village school. Ruth took care of the little ones, and most of my time was spent in watching her as she sat at the back of the room, her arm round one babe, another on her lap, a third at her feet, playing with the ribbons of her shoes. Guy had a rare tact with children, and I was surprised to see how well he taught them. After we had returned to Fiveash and had seated ourselves before the kitchen fire, the curate said:

"What do you think the chief virtue to cultivate in a child?"

I considered.

"Well, after all," I said at length, "I think it is the virtue of love with sacrifice."

"Cannot love exist without sacrifice?"

"Never! Love without sacrifice is like faith without works: it is dead."

"I don't agree with you. I believe—I—I'm sure that love can exist without self-sacrifice."

"Indeed it cannot. For sacrifice is the soul of love, and when the soul has left the body, then the body is lifeless, worthless—carrion!"

I was flushed and excited with my argument and would have pushed it further, but I suddenly noticed that Shotover looked ill at ease, and his sister unhappy, so started on another topic.

I went to bed early that night, and lay awake a long while thinking of Ruth. I was far too happy to sleep. I built a dozen castles in the air. True, I was only a poor tramping Methodist, without home, and estranged from my kin; but the brother and sister had already shown me by their friendship what little account they took of our religious differences, and the day would come, I felt sure, when I should be no longer poor and homeless; then I should have Ruth Shotover for my wife. How blessed it is to love!

I fell asleep shortly after midnight, and woke in a sweat, conscious that some one was in the room. The morning dusk poured in upon a figure standing motionless at the foot of the bed. I held my breath, and felt for my pistol, but suddenly stayed my hand, for no ghost or robber confronted me, but Guy Shotover.

He was evidently sleep-walking, for he was scantily clothed, and his eyes were turned up, showing me only the whites. I had heard that it was dangerous to wake somnambulists, so lay still, wondering what he would do and what I ought to do.

He stood for a while motionless, then bent over the bed-foot towards me, looking so ghastly with his rolled-up eyes that I drew back and shuddered.

"I must speak," he said, in a low, monotonous voice, only less horrible than the soulless cry of one who is terrified with dreams; "I must speak. I can keep silence no longer. There is no love without sacrifice. I——"

He ceased speaking, covered his face, and groaned. At the same moment I saw Ruth Shotover standing in the doorway.

"Guy!" she called softly. "Guy!"

He walked slowly towards her and took her outstretched hand.

"He's walking in his sleep," she said. "I heard his door open and then yours, so I guessed that he had come in here. What did he say to you?"

"Only a few words about being unable to keep silence, or something of the kind."

"Was that all? You mustn't heed what he said. He has the strangest fancies when he's like this. I'm sorry he disturbed you. I shall lock his door on the outside, so it shan't happen again. Come, Guy, come!"

She led him out and shut the door, and I lay for a while thinking of her and her brother, then of her alone, and then I fell asleep and dreamed of her.

The next day I found Guy very penitent at having disturbed me.

"I often walk in my sleep. I should have told you to lock your door."

"You can't be well."

"Oh, indeed, I am quite well," and he laughed rather nervously. "I'm sorry I gave you trouble."

Immediately after breakfast I said good-bye to the brother and sister, promising to visit them at Ewehurst, and started on my journey, reaching Wadhurst that night. Tuesday I spent in preaching in the village and working at Little Pell. On Wednesday I set out again, and at twilight saw the Shoyswell oast-houses against Shoyswell Wood.

CHAPTER VII
OF THE METHODIST AS A LOVER

It would be useless and impossible for me to describe the warmth of the welcome that awaited me at Shoyswell. I was made to tell the story of my wanderings over and over again, as we sat round the fire after supper, and each recital drew out fresh tokens of sympathy and goodwill from Peter and Mary Winde.

My eyes moistened and shone every time I mentioned Ruth Shotover, and I think the Windes must have guessed my love for her; that is to say, if they had not guessed it before—for I now knew that I had loved her ever since I had first kissed her hand.

"Poor Ruth had been very poor-spirited of late," said Mary; "I'm sure that she has something on her mind, but I can't induce her to confide in me. Did she seem dejected at Maresfield?"

"Not at the farm-house: she laughed and was in high spirits then; but in church, where I first saw her, she looked utterly miserable."

"Poor girl! I wonder what is ailing her and her brother, for he often looks as unhappy and anxious as she."

"I believe it's something to do with that fellow Enchmarsh," said Peter; "I can't make out how it is he's always at the Parsonage, or riding with Miss Ruth. He's a man whom every right-minded girl should shun. Even Mary, who sees good in everybody, says that the only virtue she can find in Enchmarsh is that he's a first-rate pistol shot."

I slept that night in the little room where the dried hops still rustled in the wind, and directly after breakfast the next morning I set out for Ewehurst. Ruth was more than usually cordial, and I reached home—I had come by this time to call Shoyswell "home"—in an ecstasy of happiness.

It had been settled that I should stay with the Windes for a week or two before setting out on a second missionary journey, and nearly every day I went to Ewehurst. I came to be regarded as quite an old friend by the Shotovers, and my bliss was complete—or rather, would have been complete but for Squire Enchmarsh, whom I met constantly at the Parsonage. More than once I was tempted to ask Ruth how she could tolerate the continual presence of this man, who treated her brother with undisguised contempt, and herself with a familiarity no less odious. But so closely did she draw the veil over this mystery that it would have been both cruel and presumptuous to try to pluck it away.

About this time my love entered on a new phase. At first I had been satisfied with the mere joy of loving, and would have been content to love without hope of reward. But now all was changed. My love became hungry, and I sighed romantically and foolishly for a word or a look to tell me that I did not worship in vain. This was no doubt owing to the fact that Ruth had suddenly grown very reserved and shy. She had ceased to chatter and laugh, but spoke primly, and seemed to avoid solitary talks and walks with me. I wondered whether she had discovered my love and was displeased at it, or whether she had come to love me, but was not sure if I returned her passion. I pondered and brooded over these surmises; I even thought of speaking my love, but as yet reason held my heart in leash, and I was silent.

Thus the days went by till an evening in early June. The wind was soft, and brought the sound of fold-bells from Marsh Quarter; the red clouds were tossed like burning feathers in the west, and the moon hung above Totease with a star below her nether tip. I had gone for a ramble in the fields, and intended to sup at Ewehurst Parsonage, and walk home under the stars; the lanes at night bewitched me; they were favourable to the dreams of young love.

The Parsonage windows shone in the twilight, and the trees in the garden rustled an accompaniment to the songs of sleepy birds. Fat miller-moths fluttered heavily among the evening primroses, and the violet torches of the glow-worms shone like amethysts in the shade of the leaves. I saw Ruth's shadow against the study blind, and stood for a time watching her while she sewed, and rocked herself as she sewed. A man's shadow leaned over her; she lifted her head, and I knew that she had set her lips invitingly for her brother to kiss. Then another man's shadow came between them; I groaned impatiently, for I recognised Enchmarsh.

I knocked at the door, and Ruth herself opened it. She wore a white dress, babyish, soft, and bunchy, and cuddled a black kitten in her arms. She looked the veriest child and I realised that she must be even younger than I had hitherto thought her—not more than seventeen.

"Good evening, Mr. Lyte; I'm so vastly glad you've come." I could not tell whether her words were truth or courtesy, for there were tears as well as a smile in her eyes.

Enchmarsh greeted me very superciliously when, a moment later, I entered the study. He never took the slightest pains to conceal his dislike for me, and I know that I might have tried harder to conceal mine. Ruth smiled anxiously at us both, and endeavoured to turn and soften Enchmarsh's sneering and often insolent remarks. Guy hardly ever spoke in the presence of the Squire of Kitchenhour, so supper was rather an ordeal, and I felt glad when it was over. Enchmarsh chose to stay drinking and smoking by himself in the dining-room; Guy went off to his study, and I persuaded Ruth—she seemed strangely unwilling—to stroll out with me into the garden.

The moon was high among the stars, and a nightingale was drowning with his rich wild voice the drowsy twitter of some bird yet awake. We crossed the lawn to the shrubbery, and the roses that tangled the path brushed dew on to our cheeks. The spell of the night was upon us, and neither of us spoke for some time.

"I love the moonlight," I said at last.

"I hate it," said Ruth.

"Why?"

"It seems so cold and cruel; it mocks me. Why do you love it?"

"Because it is like—like——"

"Like what?"

"Like you."

She laughed shrilly.

"How can it be like me?"

"It is so beautiful."

She laughed again.

"Lud! How vastly romantic you are to-night! Is it the moon that makes you so?"

I was silent.

"We'd better go indoors," said Ruth abruptly; "my slippers are quite wet."

I do not know what madness prompted me to ask her to stay.

"Wait a moment, I have something to tell you."

"I—I don't want to hear it." To my horror, I saw that she was in tears.

"Ruth, Ruth, you must hear—I love you!"

We were standing in an open space among some bushes; their shadow covered us except for our faces, and I saw Ruth's suddenly become set and white even to the lips. She led her hand over her breast, and swayed back from me.

"Ruth, sweetheart, do not cry. I love you. I——"

My voice died away, for she pushed me from her with a strength I could not have expected in one so frail.

"Go—go; never speak to me like that again. Go right away——"

She stood for an instant motionless, then turned and dashed through the bushes towards the house. The next moment I heard a rush and a scream. I forced my way after her through the thick euonumus, and suddenly found myself face to face with Enchmarsh.

He stood in the moonlight, and I saw clearly the rage burning in his eyes. In his arms he held an unconscious white mass, gathered up against him as one would hold a baby. The white face was thrown back on his shoulder, so that I could see the look of grief and terror it had not lost in unconsciousness.

A torrent of wrath rose to my lips, but Enchmarsh spoke before I could let it loose.

"What the hell are you about?

"What the—what are *you* about?"

"My business."

"You were eavesdropping."

"I was not. But I heard what you said, because, in your cursed effrontery, you spoke loud enough for anyone within ten yards to hear."

There was a rustle in the long grass beside me, and I noticed that Guy Shotover stood close at hand, his cheeks flushed and his head held low.

"And what if you did hear?" I cried. "Is not my tongue my own?"

"You deserve to have it torn out of your head for pestering with your worthless love a lady who is as high above you as heaven is above hell."

"You may be thankful that you have her in your arms at this moment; for if you hadn't I should certainly knock you down."

He did not answer, but suddenly bent his head and kissed the pale face upon his shoulder, and not the face only, but the hair and the extended throat.

I sprang towards him, livid with rage.

"You are drunk, you beast! How dare you insult a helpless girl who, if she weren't unconscious and in your power, would rather blow her brains out than let you shame her so! Guy Shotover, haven't you a spark of manliness left, that you can stand by and see your sister treated so infernally?"

The curate made no reply. The moonlight fell upon him, and I saw that he was shaking from head to foot.

"Coward! Fool!" I cried, and turned from him furiously.

"Stop fuming and ranting!" roared Enchmarsh.

"Not while you hold Ruth Shotover in your arms."

"I shall hold her as long as I please, and kiss her as often as I have a mind to. Stand off, you damned psalm-singing gipsy!"

"As her brother will not protect her, I must."

"Her brother knows that I have a right to do as I please."

"What right?"

He curled back his lips in a contemptuous smile.

"Merely the right of a betrothed husband."

"Betrothed husband!"

I echoed his words blankly, wildly, and staggered back from him, my hands over my face. When I drew them away the stars were swinging, the bushes reeling, and Enchmarsh's face leered at me like a devil's through the darkness.

"Yes, Miss Shotover is my promised wife."

"You lie," I cried hoarsely.

"Shotover, do I lie?"

The curate shook his head.

I looked from one to the other in horror. My rage was dead, my flesh crept and my limbs shook as if with the palsy.

"I—I didn't know. No one told me—I——"

Enchmarsh broke in with a torrent of oaths.

"And why should anyone have told you, you skulking vagabond? Was it any business of yours? Damn you! Do you expect to be told all the concerns of your betters, you insolent fool?"

My fury revived and blazed out.

"If it were not for my vocation, I'd call you out for this!" I cried, grinding my teeth.

"I don't fight with tramps, I kick 'em; and I'll kick you if you come nearer. Be off! This girl belongs to me. She's mine, I tell you be off!" and again he stooped and kissed her cheeks and her mouth, her closed eyelids, and her red hair that streamed over his arm.

I strode up to Shotover and seized him by the wrist.

"You cowardly fool! What devil gives you the power to stand by and see your sister shamed by this villain?"

He turned pale and groaned a little, for in my rage I had nearly wrenched his arm out of its socket.

"Leave Shotover alone!" shouted Enchmarsh. "Why should you maul him? Ought he to have kept his sister for you? Ought he to have rejected all other suitors and kept her for a hypocritical Methodist mumper, that she might share his rags and starvation by day and his ditch by night? But let me tell you that I loved her months ago, before you had begun to poison her sight with your scowling face, when you were washing out the cow-stalls and being horsewhipped on your father's farm."

How he knew of the miseries and degradations of my boyhood I cannot imagine.

"Be off now," continued Enchmarsh, "and don't let me ever see you at Ewehurst Parsonage again."

"The Parsonage is not yours, and I'll not leave it for you."

"Order him off, Shotover."

The curate came forward.

"I'm not going until I've spoken to Ruth," I cried frantically. "I believe that what you have told me is a lie, and that Shotover is only swearing to it because he's afraid of you."

"You may speak to her if you like," sneered Enchmarsh. "Look, she is recovering consciousness."

The limp arm stirred, the head writhed on its support. Her eyes opened, and a quick glance of fear shot into them; her lips parted in horror. She evidently remembered all that had passed.

"Ruth," said Enchmarsh, "are you my promised wife?"

Her dilated eyes looked wildly into mine.

"My darling! My darling!" I cried, unmanned and nearly weeping, "tell me that it is a lie."

"It is true," she said. That was all.

Enchmarsh caught her to him with a loud laugh.

"She's mine—arn't you, Ruth? She loves me—don't you, Ruth? Be off, you tramp; your game is up. Order him off, Shotover."

He caught Ruth to his breast once more, and kissed her; then carried her triumphantly away.

Guy came timidly up to where I stood, speechless and paralysed, and touched my arm. I shook him off with such violence that he went reeling backwards among the bushes. Then I turned and rushed away.

I ran wildly through the shrubbery, tearing my clothes and my flesh among the brakes, often in my blind fury dashing up against a tree, then speeding on afresh, reckless of bruises and pain. At last I came to a fence, and vaulted it without pausing to see what was on the other side. I did not spring high enough, my foot struck against a stake, and I fell headlong.

I rolled over among a mass of dead leaves, which the violence of my fall sent whirling and fluttering round me. Then down I shot for about fifty feet, among stones, leaves, and clods of earth, now my head, now my feet foremost, clutching in vain at every twig and stone, my breath all but dashed out of my body. At last I reached the bottom, and lay battered, shaken, gasping, and bleeding, among the stones of a stream which wound along the foot of the hollow, and which owing to recent drought, was nearly dry.

The trickle of cold water under my head revived me, and I staggered to my feet, feeling very sick, and almost unable to stand. I wondered how I should ever reach home. I was at the foot of one of those glens or "hatches" that every now and then break the peace of the Sussex fields. It was thickly grown with brushwood, but on one side this had been cut away—hence the fruitlessness of my efforts to break my fall. On the further side hazel, ash, and sallow rose almost precipitously, and I despaired of being able, bruised and shaken as I was, to climb out of the stuffy darkness of the hatch into the wind and moonlight above.

However, there was nothing else to be done, so I made the attempt, and toiled upwards on my hands and knees for nearly half an hour. Every moment was agony, and I was covered with sweat by the time I reached the top and found myself in a field where the breeze was rippling the grass into silver moon-shot waves. I threw myself down, and lay there for fully an hour, with the buttercups stretching their Eldorado to where the fold-star hung and trembled. Now and then I writhed, and tore the young grass with my hands and teeth, but it was not bodily pain which caused my throes.

"Betrothed to Enchmarsh!" I cried the words aloud to the mocking wind and sky. How he would make her suffer! He would beat her, perhaps—had I not seen him flog his horse, and kick his dog lame? Oh, how I loved her! Every minute seemed to double the intensity of my love, and to make it doubly passionate, doubly tender, doubly wild, and doubly torturing. If a good man had won her from me I could have borne it, "but not Enchmarsh!" I cried, as I rolled in the rustling grass, "not Enchmarsh! Oh, my God!" I did not for a moment think that Ruth loved this fellow. The idea was foolish and impossible. Again and again I had seen her eyes glow with contempt, dislike, and even horror, when he was near. No, no, no! She did not love him; there was some devilish mystery which I could not fathom. Perhaps the curate was in Enchmarsh's debt. I had heard of women being sold to pay debts.

The night wore on; the moon had set, and a chill mist had risen. I shivered and struggled to my feet, to toil homewards through the rank wet fields, where the grass reached almost to my knees. At last I stood in Shoyswell fold.

The windows were dark; not a soul was stirring; but I found the kitchen window unfastened, and climbed in. The last red gleeds still smouldered on the hearth, and I crouched down before them, for I was trembling with cold. My rage had died suddenly and completely, and in its place reigned a dumb and stony grief. I did not care to go to bed, for I knew that sleep would be impossible. So I crouched there, while the dawn crept grey and quivering into the room, and the wind tossed the trees with a hissing, moaning sound.

CHAPTER VIII

OF THE METHODIST'S JOURNEY INTO THE DENS OF KENT

The sun had just risen between the oasts, and the morning wind was beginning to play with the heavy damp hair on my forehead when Peter came into the room.

"What, lad! you here? I thought you must be spending the night at Ewehurst. When did you come back?"

"About midnight."

"Then why aren't you in bed? Those who don't lie down till midnight shouldn't rise at four."

"I—I haven't been to bed."

I was crouched in the shadow of the settle, and he could see me only dimly, but a movement of mine brought the light on to my face, and he started back with an exclamation of horror.

"Humphrey where have you been?"

"Only to Ewehurst," I muttered, not realising the plight I was in. He took me by the arm, and pulled me from my knees.

"What—good God!"

"I—I had a fall. But I'm right enough."

"Look in the glass before you try to deceive me further."

He dragged me to the mirror, and I saw that my face and neck were scratched and cut and blood-stained, and that my hair was matted with blood. But it was the expression of my face that made it look so changed and dreadful. My eyes were wild and bloodshot, my brows drawn and furrowed, and my whole countenance was lined as if I had grown suddenly to old age. I drew back and covered my eyes.

"Lad," said Peter searchingly, "what's the matter?"

"Nothing."

"That's not true. But there! I mustn't scold you. You're not used to confiding your troubles."

I went to the window and looked out. Peter came behind me and touched my shoulder.

"Won't you tell me, lad?"

"I—I don't know."

"I think you would feel better if you did."

I was silent for a few moments; then I said slowly:

"Ruth Shotover is engaged to Enchmarsh of Kitchenhour."

Peter started back.

"That can't be true!"

"It is true—as God's wrath."

"This is dreadful news."

"It's damnable!" I cried, swinging round upon him, my hands clenched above my head. "It's damnable! It's hellish! Oh, damn him! He's——"

"Lad! lad!" cried Peter.

"Forgive me. I'm half crazy. The Methodist is lost in——"

"The lover," said Peter quietly.

"How did you know?"

"It was an open secret, Humphrey."

"You will keep it?"

"On my honour, I will. But some one else knows it, lad."

"Who?"

"Mary."

I had thought as much.

Peter went over to the settle, and beckoned me to him; and before I had been very long kneeling at his feet, I found the story of my foolish declaration of love, Ruth's terror, Enchmarsh's rage, and my own madness, slipping from my tongue. Peter waited patiently till I had finished the miserable tale, and had thrown myself upon the floor. Then he said:

"Humphrey, is this the way you bear the chastening of the Lord?"

"I can't bear it any other way. I'm mad."

"You're mad with rage. I never met a fellow with a temper like yours, my lad. It ill becomes a Methodist."

I hung my head.

"I can understand and sympathise with your heartbreak, but you're more furious than heart-broken."

"Because I'm sure there is foul play somewhere. Ruth doesn't love that scoundrel. I know she doesn't."

"I must confess that matters don't look quite straight. But we can do nothing, dear lad—nothing but pray, and rage won't help our prayers."

He talked on, and gradually I became calm and humble and bitterly ashamed. I saw how foolish and self-degrading my rage had been, and how that patience under bitterest suffering is "a most commendable and manly thing."

At last the clock struck six, and I heard Mary Winde's step on the stairs.

"I had better go to my room, sir. I'm not fit to meet Mary just now."

He nodded, so I went up, and washed, and changed my clothes. After which I looked a little more presentable, but still very ghastly, with my scratched and bruised face, and my eyes blurred with sleeplessness.

Peter had prepared Mary for my plight, so when I came down an hour later she did not start or draw back from me, but came to meet me with the winning smile and outstretched hand of other days. There was no mention made during breakfast of what had happened at Ewehurst Parsonage. The father and daughter spoke of farming matters, the country, books, and preaching, changing their topic every other minute in a vain hope to interest me. I felt too sick to eat, and rose after having done little more than taste my food. I forgot how the rest of the day passed. All I know is that I prayed for the evening, and when the sun set I cried, "Oh, that it was morning!"

Peter urged me to go to bed early, so I lighted my bedroom candle at about nine. I was half crazy with sleeplessness and I thought sleep would be peace and forgetting. But I could not sleep. I lay desperate and wakeful the livelong night. I saw Capricornus rise above the fog, and Cancer set beyond Starvenden. I saw the first sun-ray kiss the sinking moon, and make her blush. I saw the spume of mist rise slowly from the fields, and hang in mid-air, like a pile of opalescent cloud till the wind tore it, and sent the white shreds fluttering like ghosts against the trees.

I had never suffered from sleeplessness before. It is true that I had passed many a wretched night during my boyhood, but never without one or two hours' sleep. I had heard that insomnia often produced madness, and the horror of madness was added to the other horrors of that night. I cried for sleep; I prayed for it, but it never came. I tossed and tumbled till half the bedclothes were on the floor and my shirt was damp with perspiration. My brain was even more restless than my body, and throbbed with a hundred torturing thoughts.

At last I could endure no more, so rose and went to look for Peter. He was not in his room or in the kitchen, so I sought him in the fields, and found him in a meadow close to the Limden Stream. He knelt by a rift in the hedge, through which the sunlight wavered, red and angry, but bathing his features in a wonderful light. He prayed—aloud in the solitude—and as I drew near I heard him pray for me.

Then I would have turned and left him, and, I hope, gone myself to pray. But he heard the rustle of the grass as I came through it, and rose from his knees.

"Good morning, lad. Are you surprised to find I make the fields my oratory? One prays better under an open sky."

A shower of rain came slanting with the sun, and gently struck our faces.

"I have come to you, Mr. Winde, because I want to tell you of the resolution I made as I lay awake last night. I must leave Sussex."

"Yes, lad."

"You don't seem surprised."

"I'm not."

"I think we had arranged that I shouldn't set out on my second missionary journey till next week. But I cannot stay till then. I must leave Sussex. Where do you advise me to go?"

"Far away, lad. A long journey, with a far-off return."

I groaned, and looked through the mist of crimson rain at the fields around me, at the sun in the east above Scales Crouch, and at the glow of blood on the Limden Stream.

"Oh, Mr. Winde, though I travel all England over, I shall never love a place as I love Sussex!"

"But you must go, lad. You yourself say so."

"Yes, I must—but God help me!"

He took my arm, and we walked down to the bank of the Limden Stream. There Peter talked with me for fully an hour, and we mapped out my immediate future.

I was to go into Kent, and travel through those towns and villages, the names of which all end in "den"—Rolvenden, Benenden, Biddenden, Horsemonden, Bethersden—and northwards to the flat chalk-lands by Rochester and Chatham. Then I was to cross the mouth of the Thames into Essex, and on into Suffolk and Norfolk. I was not to come back till I had learned to suffer in silence, to think of Ruth without wincing, and to bear my loneliness. I felt that these things would never be, and that in setting out to wander till I attained them, I set out to wander till I died.

"And when shall you start?" asked Peter.

"This evening. I shall walk all night, then fall down and sleep from exhaustion—that is the only way I can hope to sleep."

"You shall do as you please. But don't be faint-hearted. Many a man before you has borne your burden, and borne it singing."

"Perhaps I shall sing one day—when I know that she is dead and out of that villain's power. Oh, believe me that it is the thought of her suffering that makes my own so awful."

"Perhaps, poor lad, she's not suffering so cruelly as you think. She must know the fellow's character, seeing that he's her familiar friend; but she may be captivated by his good looks, or by that careless dashing manner of his."

"I know she is miserable. She does not love him; and he will ill-use her—flog her when he is angry, as he flogs his horse and his dogs."

"It may be so. But she's acting with her eyes open. She knows Enchmarsh even better than we do. We can't interfere with her, lad."

"I know that, so I had better go away to where every lane and field does not bring me a memory of her."

The rain had ceased, and the sun had risen higher; the fires in the east flamed no longer, only smouldered, and Peter and I, still talking, sauntered home. Mary and breakfast were awaiting us in the kitchen, and while we ate the latter, we told the former of my plans.

She showed little more surprise than her father when she heard of my resolution to leave Sussex. Only, I thought, she seemed more grieved at it than he.

"We shall miss you, Humphrey," she said simply.

"And I shall miss Shoyswell, and the happy homelife there. You have both been so good to me. I believe I should have killed myself when I was a little lad, if it hadn't been for your kindness."

"Killed yourself! What nonsense!" cried Peter. "You loved God, and a man who loves God will never throw His best gift back in His face. Lad, go through life with a song on your lips and a prayer in your heart, and doubt not but that the song will gladden your brethren and the prayer go straight to your Father."

That evening I made up my few possessions into a bundle, Peter insisting on renewing his loan of five pounds, and I found that Mary had spent the last month in making me some shirts and handkerchiefs. My dear friends did not accompany me, as before, to the end of Shoyswell Lane, but said good-bye to me in the kitchen. Mary cried a little, and for the second time I thought of kissing her, and for the second time her look and my own heart forbade it. The kitchen was red with firelight when I passed the window, and I thought of the evening when I had first come to Shoyswell, and had looked in and seen the two Windes and John Palehouse at the table.

At the end of the lane I paused and glanced back. A ribbon of smoke was rising against the dim sky, and the trees were tossing their branches against a square of red light. I groaned, and bowed my head over my clasped hands as I prayed for Peter and Mary.

Then I went on through the listening night, past Iridge and Bodiam, to where I could see the glint of the moon mingling with the sullen red of the sunset on the Rother. I had left the Sussex fields, and stood on the Sussex marshes. The wind swept moaning through the osiers, and the river moaned. The sunset died as I came to Merstham, and a thousand stars shone among the clouds in the mirror of the overflow. One can ford the Rother at low tide near Ethnam, and from the ford one can see the lights of Ewehurst. I saw them through a mist of tears, and as I stood on the great lonely marsh, a passionate longing gripped me to see Ruth's face. But I fought it down, and stepped into the Rother.

The water at mid-stream came nearly to my waist, and when I saw that another step would bring me into Kent—for the Rother at this point is one with the Kent ditch, and a boundary line between the counties—I stood still, and gazed back at the huddling mass of marsh, field, wood, and waste towards the south. Farewell, Sussex!—my mother, my nurse, my mistress, my home, my goodly heritage! I stood mid-stream, with clasped hands, while the water, sprinkled with mirrored stars, eddied moaning round me. Then I waved my hand to the southward country, and scrambled on to the Kentish bank.

The wind blew fiercely in my face, and tossed the great clouds like feathers about the sky. Turning my back resolutely on the county I loved, I walked to some little houses known as Ethnam, the lights of which I had often seen from the Sussex marsh on my rambles to and from Ewehurst. Here I left the levels and came on to the Kentish weald.

My heart ached madly as I strode on between the hedges, seen dimly through a waving mist of hemlock, chervil, and burnet. I had never longed so desperately for Ruth. I was like a man struck blind and crying for light. My past happiness lay behind me, like the shores of some blessed isle, at which my craft had touched for a moment, but from which it had been rudely driven for ever.

The night deepened; the water-bearer had risen and quivered over Udiam. Charles's Wain hung just above my head, and cast a light on my way. The mist came trailing over the fallows, and it seemed as if the vapour took strange shapes. Now two white girls danced across the grass; then I saw a great lamb standing against the woods of Mockbeggar, which melted into a horse without a head, which in its turn changed into a snow-white bird, that flew with outspread wings into the face of the moon.

I was weak and weary from want of sleep, and I longed to throw myself down and forget my sorrows, if only for an hour. There was a gap in the hedge on my right, and through it I saw the great umbelliferæ waving. I crept into the field, and lay down where a tangle of bramble and bryony shut out the keen little wind that blew up from the Rother. The blessed sleep came almost immediately, born of exhaustion and sorrow. I slept for sorrow. No dreams disturbed my rest, but I woke at intervals during the night, stirred, then slept again. At last a rustle in the grass made me start up fully awake. The dawn lay, a rosy infant, on the breast of the east, and a flock of sheep, their fleeces tinged with rose towards the sunrise, stood a few yards off, staring at me with silly, frightened faces. They scampered away as I raised myself on my elbow, and buried their noses in the rich grass higher up the pasture.

There was a freshness in the air that quickened my blood, and as the sun rose grandly behind the eastern meadows, and the glory of the young day grew more and more dazzling, submission came to my heart, and, kneeling among the spurge, I prayed God to give me strength to endure. Then a robin sang—my little bird of hope.

CHAPTER IX

OF THE METHODIST AT THE VILLAGE OF ROLVENDEN

I preached that morning at Sandhurst, and, buying two rolls and a cake of gingerbread—of which I am very fond—ate them in a wood by the Hexden Channel, then walked to the neighbouring village of Hawkhurst. I preached there, and at Highgate, and towards evening found work on a farm-house known as Mopesden.

I was at this time painfully learning the lesson of resignation, and I felt that my will would be more easily brought in tune with God's if I mortified it by healthy labour. There is nothing like hard work for crushing rebellion. When our bodies are tired, our minds, as it were, grow tired too, and cease to struggle against Heaven; and when we are doing with all our might whatsoever our hand findeth to do, our mind has little time for dwelling on its miseries. I therefore decided to stay a week at Mopesden Farm, and, finding the people kindly and the work congenial, did not repent my decision.

One night, after supper, when I was sitting with the other farm hands by the kitchen fire, the former's wife came in after a ride to Sandhurst market.

"A strange day we've had, the mäaster and I!" she exclaimed. "There's bin a feller preaching in the market-pläace till it seemed as if the very stöans and tiles must be listening to un."

"What?" I cried with interest.

"Oh, he wur a just about grand speaker, and a Methodee, like yourself. He spöake better than you, lad. But döan't 'ee be downhearted; I reckon as he can't mow or stack half as well."

"What was he like?"

"Oh, a tall, slim chap, youngish, but with grey hair."

"Where did he come from?"

"How many more questions, young feller? He came from Sussex and from Hampshire, I heerd tell."

"Why, that must be the man who went before me when I preached in Sussex! Where has he gone?"

"On to Rolvenden and Benenden, I b'lieve. I'm unaccountable glad he's a-gone, for he spöake of hell and death and judgment in a way that mäade one tremble. But let's have no more of un—and to bed with you, lad, for you must be up rath the morrer for the stacking of Yattenden's field, surelye!"

My week of service came to an end a day or two later, and refusing the good farmer's offer for a permanent place at Mopesden Farm, I again set out on my wanderings. I had several reasons for starting thus. I felt that Highgate was too near Sussex for my peace of mind—one can see Ewehurst from Four Throws, close to the village—and continued sleeplessness had so sapped my health that I was physically unfitted for the hard work at Mopesden. I felt also that I had no right to remain in one place when it was my mission to carry the Saving Word through the length and breadth of England. My fourth reason was perhaps the weakest—I wished to make up with the Greater Preacher who went before. I thirsted for company of my own age, condition and faith, and I believed that I should find it in this mysterious Chrysostom, the track of whose conquests I was following for the second time.

I decided to go to Rolvenden by the shortest way—up and down and in and out of a multitude of twisting lanes, where the rose-crowned battlements of the hedges shut out everything but the sky; through fields, where the hay lay mown in great swathes, or where the green corn preached the Resurrection; through woods where every step caused a flutter among the wild creatures that played in the mush of dead leaves; by hangar and bostal, hurst and hatch, cottages and farm-houses, hop-fields, glorious in their summer dress, orchards from which the blossom had withered, and where the shrivelled fruits hung like ruddy fungi among the leaves; through the young fresh morning, till drowsy noon, when, as the sheep gathered on the shady side of the hedges, and the cattle panted knee-deep in the meadow streams, I came to Rolvenden.

The village was half asleep. The bow-pranked team dozed outside the tavern, where the waggoners were nodding over their ale. The old men slumbered on the benches by the inn porch, the women sat idly in their doorways, the children slept in the scanty patches of shade. It was not an encouraging audience, but I resolved to speak, and soon gathered a little crowd round me by the churchyard gate. I think that since the great sorrow of my life had fallen upon me, I had preached with far more eloquence and power. I had noticed that at Sandhurst, Hawkhurst, and Highgate, my sermons had gone deeper into the people's hearts than at Wadhurst, Cuckfield, or Cowfold when I was happy and the world smiled. This day at Rolvenden the sleepy, sordid men and women listened to me almost eagerly. There was no laughing or interrupting, so I gained confidence, and spoke and pleaded with them as I had never spoken or pleaded before. A chapter from Thomas à Kempis came into my mind—"Of the want of all comfort"—and I chose it for my text. For more than an hour I preached of the broken heart, and of the bleeding Hand which alone can bind it. At last I ceased, and at the same moment a voice at my elbow cried out: "Well done!"

I started, and looked for the speaker among the crowd of smocks and stolid faces. The next moment I started again, for by my side stood John Palehouse!

He had altered very little since I had last seen him five years ago, for though he had occasionally visited Shoyswell since then, I had never met him. His hair was streaked with grey, it is true, and he looked thinner and frailer than of old; but the face was the same, with the eyes that shone as if they had once seen the Beatific Vision, and had not forgotten it, and the smile so sad and so wonderfully sweet. He was literally in rags. His shoes were ripped in a dozen places, his shoulder showed through his sleeve, and his neck was bare.

"Well done, lad!" he exclaimed, holding out his hand. "I thank God to meet you thus."

"And I am glad as well as surprised to meet you, Mr. Palehouse. I had no idea that you were in these parts."

"I have only just come into Kent. I have been through Sussex to Hampshire, then back through Sussex to Shoyswell, where I spent a day or two on my way to Kent. Peter Winde told me that the Lord had called you to preach His Gospel, and that you had gone into the sister county before me."

"Why!" I exclaimed, as the truth dawned on me, "you must be the Greater Preacher!

"The what?"

"The preacher who went before me through Sussex, and went again before me through Kent. You passed me while I worked on Mopesden Farm. When did you reach this village?"

"The day before yesterday. I have been nursing a sick boy down at a place called Lambstand on the marshes. A vile hole! The child will die."

"I am so glad that you are the preacher whose praises have been dinned into my ears on every village green. You don't know how I have longed to make up with you and talk to one of my own condition and persuasion."

63

"Stay with me for a while at Rolvenden, and we can talk of Shoyswell and of the labours we have undertaken for the Lord."

"Gladly!" I answered, and we made our way through the crowd to the village inn, where I called for a jug of beer, for I was thirsty after my walk in the dust and heat. Palehouse refused to drink beer, but asked the landlady to bring him a cup of spring water. I ordered some bread and cheese, and when the woman had left the room to fetch it, my companion said:

"I don't think that I should stay here. I have no money, and though I know that Mrs. Edwardes would be quite willing not to charge me for the bread and cheese, I don't think I should let her be so good-natured. I shall wait for you outside."

"Pray do not go!" I cried. "I ordered the bread and cheese for both of us, and should be sorry to eat it alone."

"Why should I presume on your kindness more than on the landlady's? You must not spend your money on me."

"I spend it for selfish reasons. I hate a solitary meal."

He glanced at the table, then at the door.

"Come, Mr. Palehouse," I insisted. "Come, or I shall go too."

Another glance at the table and another at the door, then he smiled and took his place beside me.

"You are very kind, and why should I be too proud to confess that I am starving?"

"Mr. Palehouse!"

"Well, I had my last meal at Sandhurst."

"That was the day before yesterday."

"True. But I have sometimes been without food for longer than that. I can so seldom earn any money. The folks like my prophesying, but not the work of my hands. The last farmer I was with nearly flogged me for my blockheadedness."

"It is just the opposite with me. Folk often laugh at my sermons, but never at my stacking, binding, or mowing."

"You are young, Mr. Palehouse, and your gift is fully developed."

"Young, am I? Do you know that I sometimes forget my own age! I am thirty— no, thirty-one—but I don't feel young. Besides, I am several years older than you, and you are a novice at prophesying."

It was a characteristic of John Palehouse that he always preferred Bible phraseology to that of modern times. "Preaching" with him was "prophesying"; his manner of life was his "conversation"; he had not gone before but had "prevented" me on my journey. He spoke thus without the slightest affectation; it was part of his nature. His mind was saturated in the Holy Scriptures. He seldom read his Bible, for he knew it by heart.

By this time the landlady had brought the bread and cheese, and Palehouse folded his hands and bowed his head in thanksgiving over the coarse fare. Then he smiled gaily, sat down, and ate like—well, like a man who has not tasted food for two days.

As soon as the meal was over, my companion rose, and declared that he must hurry back to Lambstand.

"I left the boy asleep and in charge of a neighbour—his family are at work in the hayfields—but she will soon be obliged to go home and cook her husband's supper, so I must return to my post. Come with me, and we can talk by the way."

I readily agreed. It was blessed to have a companion.

"I shall beg some gooseberries at Sparkeswood Farm for the little fellow," said John Palehouse; "he's in a high fever, and always crying for drink, but the water at Lambstand is warm and foul this weather."

"You will beg for fruit to cool a sick child's fever, but you would not have the landlady of this inn give you food when you were starving."

"The two things are utterly different. I may do for others that which I cannot in all honesty do for myself. Besides, if I once allowed Mrs. Edwardes to give me a meal, she would never take money from me again. These poor folk are often too generous. Again and again a man and his wife would have turned out of their bed that I might lie in there, and the very children on their way to school have offered me their breakfasts when they knew I was hungry."

"You are known in these parts?"

"Oh, yes! I constantly go over my ground confirming weak souls. I have many friends in the southern counties. But come, we mustn't loiter here. Off we go to Lambstand!"

I paid the landlady, and we left the alehouse. The sun had lost his noonday heat, and the cool of late afternoon was in the air. John Palehouse sniffed at the little wind that blew from the west.

"Do you smell the hay? They have cut it in Freezingham meadow."

Lover of Nature that I was, I had not noticed the faint delicious smell till he called my attention to it, and during the whole of our walk it was the same. He saw sights and heard sounds to which I was blind and deaf, and every now and then he would ask me if I did not smell the young hops, or the fennel by the wayside, and I would be obliged to answer that I had never noticed their fragrance. As we went along he talked of the birds, the stars, the rain, and the rustling leaves of the woods. He paused to admire stretches of fallow or cornfield, the windings of a stream, the cobalt of a pillar of smoke against the ultramarine of the sky, the red roofs of the farmsteads against the green of their orchards. John Palehouse had two loves—God and Nature, and two books, the Bible and the green earth.

We went into the garden of Sparkeswood Farm, where the farmer's wife picked us some gooseberries. Half a dozen children trod on our heels, and prattled to John Palehouse. The old shepherd wrinkled up his face with smiles when John's rags fluttered into the fold. The dairy-maids curtseyed and grinned, and the plough-boy was with difficulty sent back to his team. I felt that this was indeed a Greater Preacher.

We set out again on our way, and leaving the road, struck across the fields to where the Rother wound through grey-green marshes. My heart leapt at the sight of old Sussex on the opposite shore. But we were several miles east of Ewehurst, and I looked in vain for the red roofs with the lichen-yellowed spire rising in their midst. I saw Methersham and Reedbed in a golden haze, and beyond them a mass of fields undulating to the south.

Lambstand was a desolate cottage on the edge of the marsh. There was a field behind it, with all attempts at cultivation choked by the rank marsh-weeds that sprang up from the soil. The walls of the cottage were blotched with damp, and huge fungi projected their fat lips from between the clods of which it was built.

There were two rooms inside. The first was filled with smoke; from the second came a sick child's cry. We went in and found a boy of about eight years old tossing on a wretched bed. There were two other beds in the room, and these had not been made that day. The heat was terrible, and the boy's thirst was aggravated by the distant gurgle and suck of the Rother on Maytham weir.

"Water," he moaned, for the cup at his side was empty, and had evidently long been so.

"I have something better than water for you, Dickie," said Palehouse tenderly, and crushed the fruit against the dry lips.

I watched him in admiration. It was wonderful how he brought peace and refreshment into that stifling room. He smoothed the tumbled pillow and bedclothes while he spoke low and tenderly to the child. He brushed back the hair from his forehead and bathed his little hot hands.

"Where's Mrs. Ades?" he asked, when he had finished his ministrations.

"She's a-gone to cook her man's supper. He came home early and flew into a mad rage when he found her here. He beat her, he did—oh, Mus' Pal'us, my head, my head!"

He tossed and writhed in his hot bedclothes, and John took him in his arms, and walked with him up and down the room.

"I should not have left you, poor babe. But I was obliged to visit old Mrs. Harting up at the village, and I wanted to get you some fruit, my poor dear."

He rocked the boy in his arms, and sang to him gently till the flushed eyelids closed. I heard footsteps in the mud outside the house, and a babel of voices. The next moment four lads and a girl rushed in, but stopped and drew back at the sight of John Palehouse and his burden.

"Is Dickie any better, Mus' Pal'us?" asked the girl.

"I'm afraid that he's in a bad way. Where are his father and mother?"

"Father's a-gone to the Fightin' Cocks to drink good luck to the hay-harvest. Mummy's jest a-loiterin'. Surelye!"

"One of you lads go and give her your arm," cried Palehouse; "you know that she is tired and ill. For shame to have left her!"

Again I marvelled, for at these few words from this frail man, the great uncouth lads darted off all four out of the cottage. The girl went into the kitchen to coax the smoky fire, and John laid Dickie back on his bed—or rather, the bed he shared with two of his brothers.

The twilight fell, the stars shone, vapours laden with fever and ague steamed up from the marsh, and the gurgle of the Rother swelled to a moan as the tide rose. The boy lay very still, and the girl moved very softly in the next room. Again there were footsteps in the mud, and one of the lads entered, with a pale woman, her eyes bright with approaching maternity, leaning on his arm. She broke from him and ran to the bedside.

"Dickie! Dickie! Speak to me, my babe!"—and she fell on her knees and laid her cheek against his wasted hand.

"Mummy."

"I've brought yer some flowers, darlin'. I picked 'em in the lane—hemlock, vetch, willow-herb, and campions." She laid the bunch, the stalks hot with the clasp of her hot hands, on the pillow, beside his head.

"Döan't yer remember how yer and me used to pick 'em in Ox Lane, darlin'."

"I remember. Ain't they juastabout fine? We'll pick some more, mummy, when I'm waal."

His head rolled sideways on the pillow, so that his cheek fell on the flowers and crushed them. He was dead.

She threw herself across him, sobbing and praying God to give back her son. Her sorrow did not tear her long, for that night her child was born, and she joined little Dickie at cockcrow.

The episode of the sick boy at Lambstand gave me further insight into the character of John Palehouse, and made me understand more clearly why the poor folk loved him so. He and I lay that night in a barn near Wassall, and talked till the Water-bearer set behind Great Job's Cross. John told me about his visit to Shoyswell and Peter and Mary Winde.

"When do you go back to Sussex?"

"I don't know."

"Where are you going?"

"Oh, on to Essex, Suffolk, anywhere."

"I have been thinking," said John Palehouse, "what if we went together!"

"I should dearly love to go with you. I am very lonely sometimes."

"Then let us go. It is not good for man to be alone."

He leaned towards me in the hay which was our bed, and held out his hand.

"There is my hand in covenant."

"And there is mine. I shall be a better man for your friendship, John Palehouse."

67

We did not talk any more that night, but lay back in the hay and fell asleep. I dreamed once more that I was wandering along endless lanes, and suddenly I became aware that Ruth was in front of me. I did not see her, but I knew that she went on before me. I followed her, calling, but not her name, for I could not utter it. I found myself calling, "Dorothy! Dorothy! Dorothy!" till at last I woke with that same cry of "Dorothy!" in my ears. John Palehouse lay beside me, his arms tossed above his head, his face white and damp, as if in deadly sorrow, while he cried, in the choked voice of one dreaming a horrible dream, "Dorothy! Dorothy! Dorothy!"

I thought it an act of mercy to wake him, and did so. He sat up, still calling "Dorothy!" then gazed bewildered round him, and at the bar of yellow that crossed the eastern sky through the barn-door.

"I've been dreaming. What is it? Did I call out?"

"Yes!"

"A woman's name?"

"Yes."

He took up a handful of hay and bit and tore it with his teeth. Then he threw himself down on his face.

"John," I cried, patting his shoulder, "what sorrow is this, my poor fellow?"

"I'll tell you another time, perhaps but not now, for the wound is raw. Go to sleep—as for me, I will get me to my God."

He went to the barn-door and knelt to pray with the morning dusk upon his face.

CHAPTER X

OF THE METHODIST AT THE VILLAGE OF TENTERDEN

That same day John Palehouse and I found work on Elphee's Farm, for my funds were reduced to sixpence. I was then confirmed in my opinion that, though my friend was a wonderful preacher, he was a vile labourer. Not that he was unwilling or shirking—in fact, at the end of the day he was twice as exhausted as I, who had done twice as much—but he was intensely unpractical and absent-minded, extraordinarily ignorant—there was a rumour, implicity believed at Ephee's Farm, that "Mus' Pal'us had once axed Maaster Doolish by which end he shud 'öald he's scythe"—and had an unlucky habit of deserting his own work to help the women and children with theirs. The result of this incapability was that even the farmers who loved and respected him most thought twice before giving him work on their farms; and in consequence his clothes were always in rags, and his pocket and stomach generally empty.

But though at Ephee's Farm I deplored John's helplessness in the field and fold, at Benenden, a village we reached the next morning, I was struck dumb with wonder and admiration at his preaching. The words of the farmer's wife at Mopesden were true: it seemed as if the very stones and tiles must be listening to him. I had heard him speak before, in the kitchen at Shoyswell; but, in the open air, the breeze buffeting his face, and the clouds sailing above his head, his words were steeped in a new eloquence. It was as if they had borrowed strength from the wind that blew his hair across his cheek, swiftness from the birds that cleft the blue air over the tree-tops, fierceness from the thunder that rumbled sulkily behind the barrows of Swattenden. He was not a soft preacher. Though he himself was mild and tender as a woman, his sermons were stern, rugged, and ruthless as a storm. He spoke of death, hell, and judgment, where I had spoken of Christ and endless life; he warned where I had pleaded; he drove with fear of hell where I had enticed with hope of heaven. He was not a Calvinist, but his creed contained an article—"There are few that can be saved."

In many other ways, besides in power and fierceness, his preaching differed from mine. Though in ordinary speech his language was that of an educated man, his sermons were full of rough, ill-chosen words and expressions, borrowed from the uncultured peasantry he addressed. Moreover, he loved to dwell on Old Testament scenes and characters, whereas I had chiefly spoken of the New: I had preached God as the Father, loving and beloved, showing mercy unto thousands of them that love Him and keep His commandments; John Palehouse spoke of Him as Jehovah, mighty and to be feared, visiting the sins of the fathers upon the children unto the third and fourth generation.

I was struck, also, by another characteristic of John's preaching—namely, the effect it produced on his hearers. Men had listened to me with stolid, unmoved faces; sometimes they had openly jeered. When John preached no one jeered, and every one was moved, even excited. The tears fell down the women's cheeks, the men's faces worked and twitched with their emotion. The silence was a silence of bated breath, broken only by the rush and sough of the wind up the street, and the mutter of distant thunder. John spoke for two hours of wrath and judgment, then suddenly ceased, came down from the cart where he stood, and was no longer the fierce and ruthless prophet, with his message of fear, but the mild and tender brother who had nursed a sick child at Lambstand, and bore a message of love.

"John," I cried, as he came to me through the silent and motionless crowd, "your life and your gospel ill agree."

"My conversation is not all that I could wish, friend, and as for my Gospel, it is given me of the Lord; yea, woe is me if I preach not the Gospel."

69

"Gospel means good news—why do you speak of death and hell?"

"Because I would have folk flee from the wrath to come, when He shall shake earth and also heaven."

He bowed his head and seemed greatly exercised in his mind. I thought it best to say no more for a time, so took his arm and led him to the outskirts of the crowd. Here he shook off some of his depression, and insisted on returning and greeting his friends among the throng of smocks and print aprons. His friends seemed numberless, and he greeted them all. He inquired after sick husbands and children, after black sheep that disturbed the home fold, and after lost sheep that had deserted it. The people had trembled at his preaching, but they evidently realised that the preacher and the man in him were two different personalities. Women brought him their children, and he kissed them and patted their heads; the young men told him of their work in field and barn; the young women spoke of their sweethearts, and some of an approaching marriage-day. He chatted with the yokels and with the old men, who held out shaking hands to clasp his. He joked with the young labourer and his pretty wife; he comforted the mother whose son had run away to sea; he cheered the desponding lover; he had kindness, smiles, and sympathy for all.

Towards evening John and I left Benenden for Tenterden. We did not take the shortest road, but walked as far as a cross-roads known as the Brogues, in a field near which we passed the night. The next day at sunrise John visited the tenant of an old farm called Rat's Castle, and also some cottages at the hamlet of Castiswell. Wherever he went he was welcome, and we breakfasted at Rat's Castle off bread and cheese, cherries and curds.

It was still fairly early when we reached Tenterden, a little market-town in the midst of the hop-gardens of Kent. The sun lay hot on the cobbles of the High Street, and on the steep roofs of the houses, above which rose the church-tower, buttressed and crocketed.

"I am hot and tired," said Palehouse, when we entered the village, "and so are you, lad. Let us put off our prophesying till the afternoon, and rest till then in the cool wind."

"I'm sure I should like that, for my eyes and throat are full of dust. Where shall we go?"

John pointed to the tower of old St. Mildred's, round which the swallows were wheeling. "Right up to where not even a tree can screen us from God's wind."

I readily agreed, and we went to the church. It was locked, but John knew where to find the key, and we were soon in the cold aisles, with the smell that haunts damp old churches in our nostrils.

Tenterden Church was ill-kept, dirty, and dark, with cattle-pen pews, a hideous three-decker pulpit, and a neglected sanctuary. John Palehouse sighed, but knelt down to pray in a pew near the door, and I knelt beside him. A few minutes later we rose, unlocked the tower-door, and went up a dark, twisting flight of steps to another door, which opened out on to the leads at the top of the steeple.

The wind blew on us, rich with the scent of hay-fields. John and I sat down on the parapet, and gazed over the giddy brink at the red roofs swarming below. All round us lay the wonderfully contrasted yet wonderfully blended colours of the weald—red and yellow farm-houses, with their white-capped oasts and black barns, emerald pastures, olive-green hop-fields, green-bice woods nearly black, glorious variegated patches of garden, brown and purple commons, where the gorse-fires flared, and above all the blue sky across which the clouds were scudding. Due south stretched a strip of apple-green, with a blue ribbon winding along the centre. It was the Rother Marsh, with the Rother. And on the further side huddled the fields and woods of Sussex. It seemed as if I could never escape from the county of my birth and love and sorrow. I saw her meadows and marshes from every hill-top, and each sight brought the intensest longing.

John and I sat silently, and feasted our eyes on the green beauty below and the blue beauty above us, while the wind cooled our hot necks and faces, and the throbbing in our tired limbs died gradually. At last John spoke.

"This is a glorious spot. We look down on the world, and yet are not of the world; we see its loveliness and are spared its dust and heat. This is an ideal place for——"

"For what?" I asked, as he hesitated.

"For confidences, lad."

He touched my hand and smiled.

"I am fond of you," he said simply.

"How can I help you, John?"

"By listening to me—I should like to tell you about—about—Dorothy."

I flushed with pleasure. Short as the time of our comradeship had been, I had become much attached to John Palehouse, and was deeply touched by this token of his love and confidence.

"Yes, lad. I decided last night that I would tell you when I had opportunity. A sorrow loses half its bitterness when told to a friend, and you are my friend, Humphrey. I have not known you long, but I have grown to care for you more than I ever cared for any man, so I shall tell you what I never told any man."

"Not Peter Winde?"

"Not even Peter, though I love him dearly and trust him implicity. I don't know why I feel so drawn to you. Perhaps it is because we are fairly of an age, because we are working together in God's vineyard, because we have shared bed and board—the stream-side stone our board, the field our bed—or because we are both wanderers and have lost or estranged our kith and kin. But, be the reason what it may, I am fond of you, and would feel much relief in telling you what I have never told any man."

"Tell me, then, John. I wish that I could help you."

"You cannot help me except by your sympathy. You cannot bring the dead to life. But your sympathy will be help indeed."

He was silent a moment, and sat swinging his legs against the parapet, gazing at the roofs beneath. At last he lifted his head and spoke.

"You may be surprised to hear that my father was a gentleman of wealth and position, and my mother a high-born lady."

"I'm not surprised. I always thought you were of good birth."

"In spite of my rags and vagabond ways? Come, now, you will surely be surprised to hear that I have been well educated?"

"I—I don't think I am—but——"

"You may well stammer and falter; there are few traces of my education left. I have not opened a book, except this"—and he touched the Bible in the ragged bosom of his shirt—"for years, and I have forgotten nearly all I once knew.

"My father was a squire of good family and fortune, and we lived in an old house called Mackery End, in one of the Midland counties. My mother died when I was fifteen, and the same year my father and I heard a sermon by Charles Wesley, and joined the Methodists. Fired with the zeal of the Lord, my father sold his house and lands, gave the money to the poor, and one morning led me by the hand into the lanes, that we might preach the Gospel to those who sat in darkness and had no light.

"We tramped through the whole of England with the good tidings of great joy. We slept in fields and sheds; we hungered and thirsted and fainted. The years went by, and one day my father laid himself down on a truss of hay in a haggard, and died with the name of JESUS on his lips.

"This was a terrible blow to me, for I loved him dearly, but my heart did not break, because lately it had begun to throb with a new happiness. In the course of my wanderings my father and I had often visited our native village of Harpendeane, and had always found a welcome at the house of the Methodist minister, Charles Grimsdale. He had two daughters, Dorothy and Katharine—and I fell in love with Dolly."

He paused a moment and bowed his head. I waited silently till he continued.

"She was as beautiful as the flowers and the young grass. Her eyes had the glow of a forge in them—you know Scullsgate forge, when the glare streams over the fields of Great Nineveh on a summer night? She was a mischievous witch, and a dozen hearts lay at her feet. She laughed at them, played with them, and sometimes broke them. Half the county sighed after her. Her eyes were like the burning fiery furnace of Shadrach, Meshach, and Abed-nego, slaying all who approached them.

"I had reason to think myself the most favoured of all her lovers, and though she often flouted me and drove me desperate, I had good hope of success.

"Kitty Grimsdale was not so beautiful as her sister, neither was she such a little minx and flirt. She was a sweet, rather quiet girl, engaged to a good young clergyman of a neighbouring parish. I often went to visit the sisters at the cottage by the meeting-house, and as time went by I noticed that my wild, beautiful Dolly was growing tamer, and I often thought that her proud spirit was passing under the yoke of love.

"On one of my visits to Harpendeane I was surprised to meet my cousins Harold and Robert Macaulay. I had seen very little of them during my boyhood, and had heard no good. Still, I was glad to renew our acquaintance, for they declared that they had sown their wild oats, and had resolved to spend the rest of their lives in quiet and innocence. With this object in view, they bought a house in Harpendeane, a few doors below Grimsdale's Manse.

"They were fine-looking men, and the younger had the most pleasing manners. The elder I found a surly fellow, with little good-breeding, though he would occasionally put on a rough dashing air that captivated the hearts of silly women.

"I introduced my cousins to their neighbours, the Grimsdales, and the next day, when I met Doll in Harpendeane market-place, she scolded me so prettily that I could have kissed her then and there, for presenting her to such a bearish fellow as my cousin Harold; and a few minutes later I met Kitty, who reproached me for having brought under her notice an affected coxcomb like my cousin Robert.

"However, the sisters did not long remain so dissatisfied with the Macaulays; I often met my cousins at the Manse, and soon found out that they were welcome there. I fear that there was for me more wooing than prophesying in the summer months that followed. I shall never forget how Dolly and I used to sit in the Manse garden, where the rose-petals lay like blood-drops in the grass; how we used to walk in the lanes and gather wild flowers, and speak in the language of smiles and glances; how I used to say good-bye to her at her father's gate, and watch her go singing up the path under the rose arches, the colours of the roses painted on her white gown by the sunset. Well, it is all over now, as a dream when one awaketh.

"At the end of the summer the Spirit drove me to carry the word into Kent, and when I returned the leaves were brown and dying and the swallows flown. But this death and decay could not cloud my happiness as I trudged through the lanes under the misty stars. I lay that night in a field near Harpendeane, and my joy kept me awake. Poor preacher as I was, I felt sure that Dorothy loved me, and next day I would come with the sun to her window, and offer her my heart in the dewy silent dawn. She would blush and hang her head, and stammer and falter—and plight her troth with kisses.

"I rose at cockcrow. The day was sweet, and the clouds flocked like doves into the east, where they blushed as red as Dolly's cheek. I had nearly reached the Manse, when I saw a man coming to meet me, wild in look, disordered in dress. He was Charles Grimsdale.

"'Minister!' I cried, my heart sickening with fear, 'what is wrong?'

73

"His lips twitched, but he could not speak.

"'Speak, for God's sake!' and I shook him by the arm.

"'My girls are dead!'

"'Dead! What do you mean? Both dead?'

"'Dead in trespasses and sins!'

"My jaw fell, and I groped for his meaning.

"'They have run away with your cousins, the Macaulays!'

"'Impossible! You are raving.'

"'Listen, before you decide that I am raving. My daughters' room was found empty this morning, and their bed had not been slept in. We searched for them and called them; then I came across this letter on my writing-table. Read it.'

"He took a letter out of his pocket, and I read it, though a mist swam before my eyes.

"'Forgive us, we beseech you. But we cannot help ourselves. We love Harold and Robert Macaulay with all our heart and soul and strength, and would go to hell for them.'

"I reeled, and clasped my hands to my head. I could scarcely believe my eyes and ears. But it was all true—my cousins' house was found shut up and empty, and I never saw them or my poor sweet Doll again."

John Palehouse was silent, and I gazed at him with all the love and pity of my soul in my eyes. For fully five minutes we remained thus; then I broke the stillness with:

"Is that the end?"

"The end of my happiness, boy."

"Did you ever hear anything of Dorothy?"

"Yes; she died a year ago, after seven years of a life worse than death. My cousin deserted her at the end of a few months. She was afraid and ashamed to come home, and sank deeper and deeper into the slough. We lost all trace of her, and it was through a mere chance that I heard of her death last June. Katharine caught a fever, and died only three weeks after her elopement. Her lover, the young clergyman, is happier than I."

"And your cousins?"

"I know nothing of Harold. He may be alive or he may be dead. Robert died only six or seven months ago. He returned to Harpendeane with his brother for a few days' secret visit, and the vengeance of the Lord overtook him. He fell from the topmost window of his house, and perished even as Jezebel. I heard this from Mr. Grimsdale, for I was away at the time. I have never visited Harpendeane since my heart was broken."

"You tramped and preached?"

"Yes. I had neglected my prophesying for lovemaking, so the Lord thrust sore at me. I struggled to atone. For the last eight years I have tramped, starved, sweated, and prophesied. I have cried the name of the Lord through the length and breadth of

England. I have nursed the sick, rebuked the wicked, comforted the comfortless. In ministering to others I have done much to heal my own wound. My heart has often been vexed within me. But although the fig-tree shall not blossom, neither shall fruit be in the vines, the labour of the olive shall fail, and the fields shall yield no meat, the flocks shall be cut off from the fold, and there shall be no herd in the stalls; yet I will rejoice in the Lord, I will joy in the God of my salvation."

We both sat motionless, gazing at the peaceful cloud-flecked sky. Some cattle were lowing on Forstal Farm, and children's voices rose and fell in a meadow near the church. I held out my hand to John Palehouse.

"Thank you for your confidence. I will try to be worthy of it."

"I felt sure that I could tell you, for—for——"

"For what?"

"I am not the only one of us to dream of a woman and cry her name."

I bit my lip.

"It was when we were lying in a field near the Brogues," he continued, "you moaned in your sleep, and cried——"

"Ruth?"

"Yes, lad—three or four times."

I bowed my head over my clenched hands.

"After that I felt sure that I could count on your sympathy, and—and—Humphrey, if there is a load on your breast that might be eased by—by confidence——"

"Not yet!" I cried, starting up; "not yet, John. My heart is still bleeding, and—and I'm trying to forget her. John, if you love me, do not mention her name."

CHAPTER XI

OF THE METHODIST AT THE VILLAGE OF BIDDENDEN

The friendship between John Palehouse and me, begun at Rolvenden, and confirmed at Tenterden, grew stronger and deeper as we tramped through Boar's Isle and High Halden to Biddenden. We were admirably suited to each other by the law of contraries. Besides, there is nothing that draws men closer together than the sharing of afflictions.

John often spoke to me of his Dorothy—when we worked together on the Kentish farms, walked together in the Kentish lanes, or slept together in the Kentish fields. He seemed to find relief in talking of his sorrow. I steadfastly nursed mine. I was far more reserved by nature than he; my wound was fresher than his, and I felt a strange pleasure, often experienced by young men, in suffering alone. I did not realise that a wound untended by sympathy will often fester. I would tell my friend some day, I resolved, but not just yet, for every thought of Ruth was torture.

John sympathised with my silence, and did not seek to break it. He tried to distract my thoughts, and it is wonderful how entrancing he made that ramble from Tenterden to Biddenden. I had long known his devotion to the green earth and her children, but it was during that week, when we tramped the convolvulus-netted lanes, or worked with rake and scythe in the scorched hay-fields, that I gauged the full depth of this love. I was never tired of hearing him speak of Nature's beautiful things—of the wind among the larches, of stars, of the dawn, of the sweet rain he loved, of the rabbits that play in the beech-woods, of the squirrels that dart across the lane, and of the birds that praise God from daybreak to darkness.

Moreover, he knew all the wild legends of the country through which we roamed. He told me about Norah Powlare of Omenden, whose spook tempts women to starve their babes; about the Field of the Unbaptised near Hareplain Wood, where the souls of the unbaptised wander and wail; about Feverden House, where lived one who had committed the sin against the Holy Ghost; and about the woman-spirit that carries a light, and is always searching and never finds. The weirdness of these tales was increased as he told them by his implicit belief in them. He believed in ghosts and fetches, elves and evil spirits, and only smiled and sighed when I chid him for his superstition.

We did not travel fast—we took a week to cover the few miles between Tenterden and Biddenden. We worked on two farms—Pigeon Hoo and Duesden—and preached at two villages—Boar's Isle and High Halden. It was John who first brought me into contact with organised Methodism. I had worshipped in the chapels when I had found them, but had never spoken to the ministers, or acquainted myself with their methods. Organised and settled Christianity is apt to look down on that which is unorganised and itinerant; and this I found to be the case at High Halden, where John introduced me to the minister, and where we spent the night at the minister's little house which he called Wesley Manse. He was very superior in his manner, criticised our sermons, and found fault with our methods, which he termed "too free and easy." He told us to our faces that John was a dreamer and fanatic, differing but little from the Puritan Nonconformists, and that I, in my like for the Sacrament, was very like a Papist. "I may also remark," he added, "that you will find the respect of the populace rather difficult to win in—er-your—er—ragged costume!"

It was at High Halden that I first noticed signs of decay and disunion in Methodism, and my glimpse of Minister Browne's parochial organisation opened my eyes to many defects in the Methodist system. I have never cared for chapel life, for the petty interests, ambitions, and quarrels of Salem and Little Bethel. I am a born wanderer—vagabond, if you like—and always preach badly within four walls. And though at the present time I am in charge of a chapel in the suburbs of London, that is because my health will not suffer me to lead my old roaming, roofless life— and I long madly to have the market-cross for my pulpit, the tree-stump for my table, and the green earth for my bed.

On a grey day towards the end of June John Palehouse and I left Wesley Manse for Biddenden. We were prepared for some danger and difficulty at this village, for Mr. Browne had warned us that the curate of Biddenden was a vigorous opponent of the Word. Hitherto, we had often found the clergy scornful and indifferent, but never hostile.

There was a rumble of distant thunder as we went up the village street on our way to the inn, for we were thirsty after our walk through the dust. John asked for a cup of cold water, and I a mug of beer, and we were seated drinking in the inn porch when a young clergyman came up and spoke to us.

He was fair, tall, and walked with a slight stoop. The epithet "vigorous opponent" seemed inappropriate to one who looked so indolent. He stared at us fixedly, and I saw that he had a cast in his eye.

"Are you the two preacher fellahs come up from Halden?" he drawled.

"Yes, friend; what would you have with us?" replied John Palehouse.

"I merely came to tell you to pack off. I won't have your demned ranting in my parish. Will you leave it?"

"No, friend."

The curate's fixed stare became a trifle more insolent.

"You won't? You may regret that decision, my good fellah."

"You can't interfere with us," I said, "if we don't make any disturbance in the village."

"Ain't preaching a disturbance? Demmit! I've heard of ranters being put in the stocks."

"I trust, friend," said John, "that you will not resist the Spirit. I—I mean to preach here."

The curate answered nothing, but, taking off his hat and bowing low in mock courtesy, turned on his heel and left us. The landlord was standing close by.

"Ye're in for an unaccountable vrother wud Curate Kitson," he remarked. "Mäay the Old Un fly away wud me if that feller sticks at anythink whatsumdever, fur all he looks so sheep-like. I advise you to mäake off, young men."

"We are not afraid of their terror," said John, rising; "we have regard unto the recompense of the reward. Come, Humphrey, fear not nor be dismayed, for behold He is with us alway, even to the end of the world."

His face shone with an intense exultation, such as a martyr's features might have worn. He took my arm, and we went down the street to an open space of common-land, orange with gorse. The clouds had parted above our heads, and the sunshine struggled through the rift and kissed John's hair as he took off his hat and knelt down to pray among the thyme and the restharrow. I prayed too, chiefly for him. I felt sure that we were in danger, and that we might count ourselves lucky if we escaped unharmed from the village of Biddenden.

A large crowd of people soon assembled. They looked far more brutal and depraved than any congregation we had hitherto addressed. In the villages where the parson was lazy and negligent we had found the people squalid, hopeless, and miserable, but here was something more terrible than hopelessness stamped on the dark faces before us. John had hardly begun to speak when a chorus of hoots and hisses rose from the crowd. I could easily tell who prompted the disturbance, for Curate Kitson was lounging on the outskirts of the throng. He was speaking to some rough, ferocious-looking fellows, and my heart beat wildly and fast.

Suddenly my worst fears were realised. A stone was thrown at us. John, who had been appealing passionately to his surly hearers, and had forced attention from more than one of them, stopped speaking, and stared in amazement. The next moment another stone whirled at his head; he ducked, and avoided it. Another and another came hurtling at him; they struck him, and the blood poured down his face. I dashed to his side and tried to ward off the missiles, but they came thick and fast, and though some fell wide, the majority struck us. John seemed to be the chief butt, no doubt because he had been the chief withstander of Curate Kitson. He made me think of Stephen, as he knelt, bruised and blood-stained, the stones crashing round him. Only, unlike Stephen, he never spoke.

It could not last long. Already I saw the sun through a mist of blood, and a horrible feeling of nausea almost overpowered me. I still tried to shield John Palehouse, though he made feeble attempts to push me away. Then, suddenly, he stretched out his arms and fell forward without a complaint or a cry.

He lay with his face buried in the thyme, the blood trickling from his head, shoulders, arms, and sides. The crowd rushed on us, and I thought that the end had come.

Suddenly there was a loud shout, and the mob swayed and parted, as a gentleman and three stout grooms, all armed with hunting-whips, flogged their way through.

"What is this?" cried the gentleman, who looked like a country squire. "Kitson, do you know anything of this?"

"I'm sure I can't tell what made 'em so furious," drawled the curate. "I warned these two fellahs not to preach here, but they were too demned pig-headed to take my advice."

"Gad! this is a matter for a magistrate. I'll look to it later. Meantime, these poor wretches must be taken to Ihornden Hall. Can you walk as far as my coach?"— addressing me—"my grooms will carry your friend."

Two of the lads picked up the unconscious John Palehouse, and I followed, leaning heavily on the arm of the third. The squire strode on ahead, for he had ladies in his coach, he said, and must prepare them for our arrival. He declared that they could easily walk home across the fields, and insisted that John and I should drive.

It was all swift and sudden as a dream. The crowd fell back sulkily, and we came to where a coach and four was standing. A stout, comely woman, whom I took to be the squire's wife, had already alighted, and a younger lady stood upon the carriage-steps. My heart gave a sudden, fierce bound, then every pulse in my body seemed to stand still. My eyes met the eyes of Ruth Shotover.

She stood in the carriage doorway, clad in a simple white gown, her curls straying from under a little black velvet hood. Her lips were parted in mingled wonder and pity, her eyes were full of tears. The sight of her sickened me more than the blows of a minute past—I fainted.

CHAPTER XII

OF THE METHODIST AND ONE WHO SUFFERED MORE BRAVELY THAN HE

I opened my eyes in an old oak-panelled room, through the windows of which I saw trees and sky, pale and vague, like the landscape of a dream. I had no idea where I was or what had happened, but I was full of a nameless misery, the cause of which I could not determine—as when one wakes and is conscious of sorrow before remembering the exact source and nature of it.

At my side stood the squire. He was a short red-faced gentleman, with kind blue eyes, and rather a loose mouth. His boots, hair, and finger-nails showed that he cared little for the niceties of the toilet. For a moment I lay staring at him in bewilderment; then suddenly remembrance came, and I stared up with but one thought in my heart.

"Where is——" I was going to say "Ruth," but recollected myself, and bit my lip.

"Your friend? He's in the guest-room. The doctor is putting him to bed."

"Is he badly hurt?"

"He has been finely drubbed by those rascals, but there's little danger, I reckon, though a good deal of pain. Begad! You must be feeling pretty sick and sore yourself, Mr. Lyte. You see, I know your name. Miss Shotover told me. She said you were very friendly with her and her brother in Sussex."

I smiled grimly, and glanced at my tattered clothes and bloodstained hands.

"I do not look like a friend of Miss Shotover's."

"You've been tramping the roads, and can't be expected to look as if you'd just taken leave of your valet. Gad! I wish we had more of your kind in Merry England.

The parsons are a very sorry herd, and we need an honest man or two to show 'em their duty. I must apologise for the way those knaves treated you at the village. They shall suffer for it, you may be sure. But, come, you ought to be in bed like your friend."

"Indeed, I would rather not——" I thought with horror of the wakeful hours I should be sure to spend, and of the thoughts that would torture me as I tumbled and tossed.

"Take my advice, and go to bed at once. You've been infernally knocked about."

"Pray do not press me. Let me wait till my friend is able to see me, then allow me to watch the night by him."

The squire shook his head, but seeing that I was obdurate, at last gave in.

"You can sit quiet here till the doctor is ready to overhaul you. Then, if he allows it, you can go to your friend's room."

"May I ask," I said, as he was leaving me, "to whom I am indebted for all this kindness?"

"My name's Wychellow, and this house is Ihornden Hall. Begad, sir! don't speak to me of kindness; my wife and I are only too pleased to do all we can for you."

He left the room, and I drew my chair up to the fire, for though the month was June, old Ihornden was damp and cold enough; besides, I was shivering with fever. I was miserable and spiritless, my limbs ached wearily, and I felt horribly sick. It seemed as if fate had pursued me, and overtaken me at Ihornden Hall. To escape Ruth Shotover I had torn myself from my friends and the county of my birth—and here she was under the same roof as I. How had she come to Ihornden, and why? Surely heaven was unmerciful to cast such a snare on my path. Oh, but I would flee from it! I would insist on removing John to some farm-house in the neighbourhood; I would not stay another hour in this house of temptation. But who would nurse John at a farm? He would have to lie hard and be roughly tended. I had no right to sacrifice him in such a way. After all, my strained relations with both Ruth Shotover and her brother would induce her to avoid me as much as lay in her power. I could have my meals with John Palehouse, and so escape even a glimpse of that torturing sweet face.

I sat miserably while the glow of the afternoon paled, and evening came with pink and golden lights on the oak floor. The fire was an inert crimson mass, except where in one corner a solitary flame writhed its singing horn. Sometimes I dozed, and dreamed again of the forsaken roads along which I was bound to tramp, in spite of dizzy weariness. I never slept for more than five minutes at a time, and would wake with a groan. The birds were chirping and gurgling in the trees outside, and every now and then a swift flew screaming through the air, and—such were my depression and weakness—made me start.

At last the doctor came. His examination was short, and, though he advised me to go to bed, he finally gave in to my entreaties, and, after an application of ointment and bandages, allowed me to go to my friend's room.

I went down a long passage, smelling of old wood, and was just about to lift the latch of the door pointed out to me, when it opened from the inside, and I stood face to face with Ruth Shotover.

The blood dyed her neck and cheeks, and my own tingled and throbbed in every vein.

"You've come to see Mr. Palehouse?"

The words roused me out of the trance into which I had fallen.

"How do you know my friend's name?" I asked, rather abruptly, and the colour left her face at once.

"We met in Hertfordshire," she answered shortly, and I saw that my question and the manner of it had been rude.

"You must forgive me my rough speaking. It is evident that my manners as well as my senses were knocked out of me this morning."

She smiled in her old sweet way.

"Lud! how terribly you must have suffered under that cruel stoning!"

"Not half as terribly as my friend. Tell me, is he better?"

"Faith, I can't say. He's conscious, but in great pain. You're in a fearful plight yourself."

"It is nothing. Is your brother at Ihornden?"

"Yes. He was in Mr. Palehouse's room a minute ago. Sir Miles Wychellow was a friend of our father's, and when he heard that poor Guy was sick, he asked him to Ihornden Hall."

"Then has your brother been ill?"

"He's ill now, and it's vastly necessary that he should have rest and change. We've been here nearly a week, and I've no idea when we shall be able to go back to Ewehurst."

Her voice trembled with tears. She curtseyed hurriedly, and left me gazing after her as she sped down the corridor. For an instant I stood motionless, while the bitterness of death nestled in my heart, and made it almost stop its beating. I recovered myself with difficulty, and went into John Palehouse's room.

Lady Wychellow was at the bedside, but she slipped out when I came in, and left me alone with my friend. The room was dim, for the curtains were drawn, though a red shaft of sunset streamed through the narrow slit between them. The walls were ribbed with oak, and two handsome, gilt-edged mirrors reflected the furniture, which was heavy and luxurious. It was then I realised that, had it not been for Ruth's recognition, John would doubtless be lying in the servant's quarters instead of in the chief guest-room of Ihornden Hall.

I went softly over to the bed—a huge four-poster, with green hangings. John's eyes were shut, but he opened them at my approach, and said feebly:

"Well, my lad, you see me in a pretty plight. I hope you escaped with less bruises than I."

"Indeed, I have only some trifling hurts. It makes me wretched to see you thus, John."

"They did it in ignorance," he said earnestly; "they are sorry enough for it now, I'll be bound. Oh, poor shepherdless sheep!"

"You think more of them than of yourself."

"They are in a worse plight than I. Oh, lad, my heart aches for the poor things."

He spoke with difficulty, and as I knew that every word must mean torture, I implored him to be silent, and for some time he lay with no other sign of life than the wandering of his large, restless eyes. I watched beside him till the patch of ruby light on the floor had faded to yellow and to pearl. Then I was called away to a futile attempt to eat, while Lady Wychellow and Ruth Shotover watched by the bed.

I resumed my post at about nine, and though Sir Miles Wychellow came several times and begged me to take some rest, I remained till morning in an armchair by my friend's bedside. I longed to ask John about his acquaintanceship with Ruth, but shrank from disturbing him; besides, he was delirious, and raved for the greater part of the night.

I did not sleep, and was sure that, even if I had been in bed, I could not have slept. I felt glad that, instead of tossing alone, I was sitting by my friend; for, though unconscious, he was, nevertheless, a companion, and his ravings were not wild and horrible, but gentle as the voice of a little child who talks in his sleep.

He spoke of the old days at Harpendeane, and of his evenings with Dorothy Grimsdale in the Manse garden. That name was on his lips the livelong night—"Dorothy! Dorothy!"—and I wondered if it would be the same with me if I fell ill, and whether I should lie from roosting-time to cock-crow crying, "Ruth Ruth!" The thought horrified me, and I resolved to fight desperately against the sickness I believed was at hand.

My poor friend's sufferings were awful, and between his cries of "Dorothy!" and gentle wanderings in a happy time long past, he comforted himself from the Book of Job and from the Psalms: "'Why dost thou strive against Him? For He giveth not account to any of His matters.' 'He will deliver my soul from going into the pit, and my life shall see the light.' 'Why art thou so cast down, O my soul, and why art thou disquieted within me? Hope in God: for I shall yet praise Him, Who is the health of my countenance and my God.'"

These words, uttered in a semi-conscious state, stole like drops of healing oil into my heart. A sudden realisation of my ingratitude and rebellion came to me. I had railed against Fate for bringing Ruth Shotover and me together at Ihornden Hall, forgetting that Fate is only another name for Providence. "'How should a man be just with God? If he contend with Him, he cannot answer; he cannot answer Him one of a thousand. He is wise in heart and mighty in strength. Who hath hardened himself against Him and hath prospered?'" said John Palehouse from the bed. I had been murmuring against God, questioning His will, kicking against His commandments. "'Be ye not like to horse and mule,'" said John Palehouse, "'which have no understanding, whose mouths must be held with bit and bridle lest they fall upon thee.'" If God's will was being fulfilled in my greatest misfortune, I had no right to do otherwise than rejoice. "'God is faithful,'" said John Palehouse, "'Who will not suffer you to be tempted above that which you are able, but will with the temptation also make a way of escape, that ye may be able to bear it.'" I knew that He would help me to bear the tormenting presence of Ruth Shotover day after day, even week after week. I went over to the window and fell on my knees, and the tears in my eyes were not of misery, but of contrition.

The dawn was in the room, and I drew aside the curtain and looked out. A beautiful park sloped from the house, and beyond it lay twilight fields, and a range of blue barrows on the horizon. The sky was pale, and the morning star was wan. A sudden flush of light throbbed in the east, the wind swept up and shook the trees, and the birds began a drowsy whimper. I heard myself called from the bed.

"Is it morning?"

"Yes. The sun is just going to rise."

"Is the dawn grey?"

"No, red as blood."

"Then we shall have mist and rain. How sweetly the birds are singing! I love their voices; they teach me, 'Fear not; ye are of more value than many sparrows.'"

I crossed over to the bed.

"Are you better, dear John?"

"Better in mind, if not in body. I feel sure that God has heard my prayers, and has forgiven those poor misguided souls."

"Can I do anything for you?"

"No, thank you, boy. Humphrey, I have seen a ghost."

I knit my brows.

"I meant to have told you before this, but the Lord thrust sore at me, and I could not speak. You remember the young clergyman I told you of, who was engaged to Katharine Grimsdale?"

"Well?"

"He is in this house."

"You don't mean Guy Shotover?"

"Yes. Do you know him?"

"We—we—knew each other in Sussex. But I had no idea that he and the unfortunate young man of your story were the same."

"I didn't know that he was in these parts, and was surprised to see him yesterday. I called him a ghost because he is the shadow of his former self. In the old days he was a stalwart, healthy young man, full of life and gaiety. Now he is a wreck in body and mind."

"No wonder, poor fellow! after all he has suffered."

I lapsed into silence. For an instant I thought that I had grasped the secret that cankered the lives of Ruth and Guy Shotover, but the next moment I saw that such a cause could not have produced the effect I had witnessed. The curate's love-affair could only be a matter of sorrow and regret, not a present and pregnant anxiety, mysteriously bound up with Enchmarsh of Kitchenhour.

"Did you know Shotover's sister at Harpendeane?" I asked Palehouse.

"Very well. I dined more than once at Golden Parsonage. Her name is Ruth."

His eyes met mine suddenly, and I quailed. For a moment I thought of telling him everything, but my reserve and sentiment were too strong for me.

"It is a common name," I said abruptly; and with his accustomed tact he never again alluded to the subject.

I sat by my friend's side while the daylight grew, and when the sun rose I sang to him Bishop Ken's Morning Hymn.

CHAPTER XIII

OF THE METHODIST AND THE MAN HE HATED

As soon as breakfast was over, I went to bed, and rose much refreshed after a few hours' sleep. I spent the rest of the day in my friend's room—I dared not mix with the household and meet Ruth.

Time wore on uneventfully. I quickly recovered from my bruises, and John Palehouse began slowly to mend. It was a beautiful summer; the days were long and golden, the sun rose early and dawdled over his setting. I seldom went out of doors, though the sunshine and the scent of the flowers invited me, for from my window I often saw a white-gowned figure moving in the garden, or standing like a solitary patch of snow in one of the great fields near Ihornden. We rarely met, and then it was only a bow and a curtsey, a "good day, madam," and a "good day, sir." Guy Shotover I saw oftener. He seemed disposed to forget what had passed between us at Ewehurst Parsonage, and now that Enchmarsh was no longer present to rule him was friendly enough with the man he had but a short time ago ordered from his house. I fear that I met his advances surlily at first. I could not help thinking that he had a great deal to do with Ruth's unhappiness. But, after all, he had once been kind to me, and had befriended me when I stood in sore need of a friend. Besides, the poor fellow looked so ill that it was impossible to nurse enmity. I felt sure that he must be in a decline, and his scarlet cheeks, shaking hands, harsh cough and hysterical laughter confirmed my opinion. He occasionally came to see

John, and would sit by the bedside, jerking his head as if he had St. Vitus' dance, twisting his pocket handkerchief round his fingers, and starting if anyone spoke loud, if a chair creaked, or if a bird flew crying past the window.

Towards the middle of July, John was well enough to leave his room, and often walked in the garden, leaning on my arm. Sometimes we roamed along the twisting lanes to Kalsham or Stede Quarter or sat together in the fields of Plurenden, or lay together in the scent and shade of Dashnanden Wood. We each bought a new coat in the village, for those in which we had arrived at Ihornden were rags, unfit for a gentleman's house. I do not know whether it was the new coat or the sickness from which he was recovering, but I began to notice a change in John Palehouse. He lost his look of tramp and vagrant, and I saw in him the high-born squire of Mackery End. His hands were no longer brown and coarse, but white and transparent, so that one saw the blue veins through the skin; the sunburn had faded from his cheek, and left it as softly tinted as when his mother used to kiss it. Sir Miles Wychellow took a great fancy to him, often sat in his room, and surrendered to his entreaties that no notice should be taken of the rough usage he had received at Biddenden. However, in spite of the kindness and consideration with which he was treated, I noticed in him an ever-increasing desire to resume his wanderings.

"While I am idling here," he said, "hundreds may be dying without the Lord. Oh, pray, my lad, that you and I may soon be preaching on Frittenden Green."

One afternoon, after a shower of rain, I went out into the garden. The flowers smelled so sweet, and the wet grass and trees were so beautiful, that my heart bounded with joy in spite of its load of sorrow, and I realised that God would still leave some happiness in my life if He left me the earth and sky. From my childhood I had found comfort in Nature. The trill of a nightingale would soothe the misery of the little beaten child who lay and sobbed in the long grass of Spell Land. The overworked boy, full of disappointment and vain longing, would look up with a smile when he saw the sun burst from behind the meadows of Ellenwhorne and turn the Brede River to blood. And this day the sorrow of the despairing man was blown to heaven with the incense of the flowers.

The lane looked even more inviting than the garden, and I strolled down the avenue towards the channel of moving shadows. At the gate I heard a horse's hoofs beating a gay presto on the road, and the next moment a horseman trotted up and entered the grounds. My cheeks flushed and my blood warmed angrily at the sight of him. He was Enchmarsh of Kitchenhour.

He looked wonderfully handsome. His eyes were bright, his cheeks ruddy with exercise, and his parted lips showed his fine, white teeth. He recognised me at once, and his brow darkened.

"Hello! Where the devil do you come from?"

"From Ihornden Hall."

"What are you doing there?"

"That's no concern of yours."

"Isn't it, though? What about a certain lady I have forbidden you to have anything more to do with?"

"I don't care a jot for your commands."

"You don't! I'll make you."

He raised his crop, but I sprang forward, twisted it out of his hand, and hurled it far away among the bushes. For a moment we faced each other, our eyes blazing, our bosoms swelled with fury. At last Enchmarsh broke the silence.

"What hell's reason brings you here?"

"That's my business." My voice shook with rage, but suddenly my heart smote me for such an unchristian spirit, and I added:

"I am with a fellow-preacher who had some rough usage in these parts, and is staying at Ihornden till he recovers."

"Confound you! And look here, you Lyte, keep clear of Miss Shotover, and keep clear of me. The sight of you makes me want to eat grass like a sick cat."

He cantered past me, then turned in his saddle and cried:

"By the by, my engagement to Miss Shotover is no longer a secret. We are to be married next month." He burst into a fit of triumphant laughter, and left me confounded.

I stood gazing after him, gnawing my lips with anger. Surely God did not expect me to bear this fellow's insults. In that moment of fury I half thought of challenging him. At last, however, I grew ashamed of myself, and as the afternoon was so soft and sweet, decided to ask John Palehouse to come out and share it with me.

I reached John's room without encountering Enchmarsh. He had evidently not heard of the visitor's arrival, and as I still felt angry and sore I did not mention it. He took my arm, and we went out into the lanes together, and strolled as far as Brakefields Farm. The summer swale was dusking into night; the sun had set, the violet clouds were veiling the red scar he had left behind him. A little cold breeze blew up from Bettenham, and I advised John to go home.

We took a path through the fields, for it was the shortest way, and John loved the fields. We paused at a hedge, and watched the moon rise out of the purple mist, while the fold-star shone timidly over haunted Omenden. Suddenly I heard voices on the other side of the hedge, and my heart thrilled while Ruth Shotover spoke.

"Miss Shotover has also come out to admire the evening," said Palehouse. Then his voice trailed off, and his face whitened, as Enchmarsh answered Ruth.

"Who is that?" he asked sharply. "I know the voice."

"That is her betrothed, Squire Enchmarsh of Kitchenhour in Sussex."

"Enchmarsh!"

"Yes. Do you know the name?"

"No, but I know the voice. Let me look."

He pulled aside a rope of bryony, and peered through the hedge, then drew back with white lips.

"You may know the man as Enchmarsh of Kitchenhour, but I know him as my cousin, Harold Macaulay!"

I stared at him stupefied, and the blood was like ice in my veins with horror.

"The scoundrel who ruined Dorothy Grimsdale?"

He nodded.

"Are you sure that the fellow is your cousin? As far as I know he has never borne any name but Enchmarsh."

"As far as you know. But I am certain he is Macaulay" he looked again. "Yes, I am too familiar with that dark face to mistake it. For some reason or other he has changed his name. Woe betide him! What has brought him here?"

His cheeks were hectic with excitement. He bit his lip, and one thin hand wrung the other till the joints cracked.

"He arrived here an hour or two ago," I said, forcing myself to speak calmly. "He has evidently come to visit Miss Shotover"—and I writhed.

"How long will he stay? If he stays I must go. I hate him! I hate him! No, no, no! I must not hate him. The dear Lord prayed for His enemies. But I can't pray. My tongue is dried up like pots-herd."

His teeth gritted together, and his limbs trembled. I had never seen him so passionate.

"Come, dear John, do not fret yourself. You are far too weak and ill to leave Ihornden and why should you go away? You need never meet him, and he probably will not stay long. Take my arm, and let me help you back to the house."

He grew suddenly calmer.

"I am forgetful of my calling. The Lord's preacher should not hate or rail. God must forgive me. I am very weak and unprofitable, though there are many years since my conversion."

He took my arm, and I led him back by the way we had come. He was silent for a long time, then he said suddenly: "But how is it that he is betrothed to Miss Shotover? I can't understand such a state of affairs."

I struggled with a tempest of bitter thoughts.

"Perhaps she does not know," I said faintly.

"That is impossible. Her brother was engaged to Kitty Grimsdale."

"What can we do to save her," I cried hopelessly.

"Perhaps my cousin has repented and been turned to the Lord. Surely she could not have accepted him as he was."

"He's no more converted than the devil!"

"Then what can have induced her to accept him?"

87

"I can't say. Sometimes I think that she has sold herself to pay her brother's debts."

"That is possible, but hardly probable. What is her attitude towards Macaulay—Enchmarsh, I mean?"

"As far as I can see she hates him."

Palehouse shuddered.

"Poor girl, we must pray for her."

"We must do more than pray."

"What more can we do?"

"Speak, entreat, conjure———"

I stopped suddenly in my wild talk. Our eyes met, and there was in his a strange look of interest and of pity.

I lay awake all that night in misery. My bed was soon hot and tumbled with my tossing, and once or twice I rose and went to cool my forehead at the window. The night was very black. I could feel no wind on my face, but I heard it moaning and roaring in the trees. One word was borne me on the wind's wild cry—one word formed the burden of the owls' wail in Ihornden Park—"Ruth!"

How could I save her? She seemed beyond my reach—beyond the reach of all save God. She had made her choice in the light of knowledge; she was under no delusion, and believed no lie.

Towards morning I ceased to writhe and groan, but began to consider. I lay still and pondered while the sky reddened and the birds woke, and suddenly, as the first sun-ray kissed me healingly, came to a decision.

It was a bold resolve, but I was desperate for Ruth, and courage is strong when born of desperation. I decided to go to her, tell her all I knew, and entreat her to give up Enchmarsh.

She might rebuke me—and a rebuke from her would be terrible; nevertheless, I would face it. I commended my resolution to God, rose, and went to John Palehouse, that I might fortify myself by conversation with him; for he was one of those whose mere presence consoles the afflicted and strengthens the weak.

CHAPTER XIV

OF THE METHODIST AND THE WOMAN HE LOVED

I did not have an opportunity for speaking to Ruth till evening. Then I found her alone in one of the quaint old sitting-rooms in the west wing of Ihornden Hall. The oaken walls were hung with prints and strips of tapestry; the ceiling was ribbed with heavy beams, on which the firelight danced ruddily; the polished floor reflected the legs of the tables and chairs—old-fashioned, twisted, and carved. There were a couple of candlesticks on the table, and a hundred candle-flames flickered and throbbed in the mirror-like panels of the wall. The window was only half curtained, and through the open space could be seen the branches of the trees, wildly tossing against the moon, the stars scudding in and out of the storm-clouds, and a silver shower of rain.

Ruth sat before the fire, some needlework on her lap, her hands folded idly over it, while her eyes gazed into the embers. She started at my footfall, and rose. She was all in white, but the firelight made ruddy smears on her dress and a red carnation was fastened in her bosom. She curtseyed stiffly, while her eyes questioned me. My tongue stuck, and I moistened my lips again and again before I could speak. I dare say that I ought to have approached my subject circumspectly, but I am a fool at the little artifices of speech, and blundered out:

"Miss Shotover, forgive me if I seem rude, for I must speak, even if I offend you."

"Lud! I shall never think you rude, Mr. Lyte. I know you too well for that."

"Thank you. You give me courage."

I sat down opposite to her.

"You knew John Palehouse in Hertfordshire, I believe. He has just told me the truth about Enchmarsh——"

"And Dorothy Grimsdale?"

"Yes. I felt sure that you knew it too."

"My brother was engaged to Katharine Grimsdale."

I leaned forward in my seat, and our eyes met. Mine were burning, hers were full of tears.

"Miss Shotover, you will think me the most insolent dog on earth, but I have come to you this evening to implore you to break off your engagement——"

"Mr. Lyte! I——"

"I speak abruptly—it's my failing. I have no aptitude for mincing and biting my words when my heart is full. Miss Shotover, Enchmarsh is a villain—you know it—and you do not love him. No doubt you have a reason for accepting him, but believe me, nothing can justify your marriage with that beast. I—I have a sincere regard for you, and it would break my heart to see you united to a man who would make your life hell with his brutalities and intrigues. I speak to you as I would speak to a sister I saw in danger and wished to save, so forgive me as you would forgive a brother."

She sat absolutely rigid, her hands locked together, her cheeks and eyes glowing as if a fever had stricken her.

89

"I had to speak," I cried desperately.

"I know—I know; but it's all useless."

"Useless, madam!"

"Useless. I—I can't unwrite the past."

"You can blot it out, and, oh, I entreat you, blot out that man's name from your life."

"You don't know what you ask," she cried, covering her face.

I groaned.

"You've done your best," she continued more calmly; "but your best is useless. I must marry Enchmarsh. I can't tell you why—but I must."

"Oh, don't drive me desperate. My life will be all hell if you commit this act of madness. It's indeed madness, I assure you, to cast away in your youth all hope and happiness, to break your own heart, to—to——O God of Mercy! Who knows? It may drive you to self-murder!—damn your own soul."

She did not speak, but two tears glittered on her face. I lost all self-control, and, sinking on my knees before her, cried:

"Ruth! Ruth! For the sake of the God Who made us——"

She sprang up, but I caught her dress—it was hot and scorched by the fire.

"I shall not let you go till you have promised to give up that brute——"

"Humphrey—for God's sake."

"Hush, sweetheart, hush—don't cry. You are mine, Ruth. I love you! I love you! Neither God nor Satan shall part us. Do not cry. The world has treated us infernally, but we'll defy it together. We'll laugh at it, Ruth—we'll laugh at the whole miserable farce that tried to keep us apart, but failed, darling—failed! For I love you, Ruthie. You are all mine, and I shall never let you go."

Then I started to my feet, caught her to my breast and devoured her thin face with kisses, the mad, hungry kisses I had so often given her in dreams.

That embrace lasted for an instant, which seemed eternity. She did not struggle or scream, but lay against me as if lifeless, while the tears poured down her face. All the love with which my heart was throbbing was on my lips as I pressed them to hers, and in my eyes as my tears mingled with hers. We forgot the past; we ceased to dread the future. Love veiled all except the present—which was Paradise. We threw back our heads and laughed aloud; then our lips pressed again and more rapturously.

The spell broke. She sprang from me with a scream, and I threw myself on the floor. The past flashed back to us with its misery; the future loomed before us with its dread. The present was once more anguish.

We crouched opposite each other for several silent minutes. The clock ticked on, the fire crackled and spluttered, and an owl was crying far away in Ihornden Park. A dog howled, and I started, and, raising myself on my elbow, gazed across at

Ruth. She half sat, half huddled, on the settle, her hands over her face, her hair, dishevelled with our embrace, pouring over her shoulders. Now and then a great sob convulsed her.

"After all," I said at last, misery making me cruel, "I suppose you have an excellent reason for all this."

She started, looked at me, and shuddered.

"I say you doubtless have a good reason for the blasting of two lives."

"Don't, Humphrey, don't!"

"Why shouldn't I speak? This is so—so extremely unpleasant that I should hope there was some reason for it all."

"Humphrey, don't look at me in that way."

"But I—oh, sweetheart, tell me why we should suffer so."

I had risen and taken her cold hand.

"You're so vastly cruel. I can't tell you."

"You must tell me. I have a right to know. A poor fellow going to hell has a right to know why he's sent there."

"I—I can't tell you. We shall be undone."

"Why should you be undone?"

"Because, because——Oh, Humphrey, have pity——"

Her eyes were so beseeching that I cursed my selfishness.

"Don't tell me, then, Ruthie."

"That's kind of you."

She sat silently for a time, her eyes big with thought. Then she said suddenly:

"But I don't see, after all, why I shouldn't tell you You won't betray me."

"My darling, I'd rather die in torture."

"Don't call me 'darling.' It's cruel—and it's wicked, too, Humphrey."

"I know it is, but, before God——"

"Hush hush! I'm going to tell you a story—my story. I can't bear to have you misunderstand me, and when you've heard, you will see how it is that I can't give up Enchmarsh, though it is true, as you have guessed, that I—I don't love him."

"Oh, if you would only tell me, Ruth!"

"But you must promise—no, you must swear—not to breathe a word of what I am going to say. Oh, pray don't think me distrustful, but this is a matter of life and death. A day or two ago torture wouldn't have dragged this confession from me, but to-night your soul and mine have met, and I know that you would rather die than injure me. So I shall tell you my life's secret; you will understand—and you will go."

"Go, Ruth?"

"Yes—go for ever."

"Oh, my God!"

"You must go—ah! but I forgot your poor sick friend; it might rouse suspicion if you left Ihornden without him—but you must go, Humphrey, or I must."

"You can't leave, and it is I who have brought this misery on our heads by my uncontrolled passions. I can tell part of the truth to John Palehouse—that I am in hopeless love—and easily find some excuse to offer Sir Miles."

"It will be kind and generous of you to do so. You and I are best apart after this."

"I shall go to-morrow."

"Thank you. And now for my story—and your oath."

She took a small Bible from her pocket and held it out to me.

"Swear on this."

She looked like a child in her simple white frock, with her soft, sweet face and loose hair. The gravity of her eyes only enhanced the babyishness of her dimples and the full curves of her lips. I felt for her the devotion touched with awe, which one so often feels for a child.

I took the Bible in my hand, and said over the sacred words, "so help me, God!" and she bowed her head with the simple reverence of a babe.

We drew our seats close together, so that she could put her lips to my ear. Then came that conversation in whispers, which still haunts my dreams.

"John Palehouse told you the story of Kitty Grimsdale and Robert Macaulay?"

"Yes."

"He—he told you how Macaulay met his death?"

"Yes."

"How did he say it was?"

"He fell out of an upper window and was killed."

"That is all John Palehouse knows. I know that Macaulay did not fall out of the window—he was pushed out."

"You mean that he was murdered?"

"Yes, by my brother."

It was as if my heart had stopped beating, and a dimness clouded my eyes. I saw Ruth's face through a mist, and her voice seemed to come from far off.

"My brother," she repeated, her eyes wide with dread.

"Poor, poor sweet Ruthie! Is this the secret you have been nursing all this while?"

She began to cry hysterically.

"Yes my secret, my awful companion and bedfellow. Humphrey, I've told you— no one but you. You—you won't betray me?"

"Ruth!" and I pointed to the Bible on her lap.

"Forgive me. I'm crazy with grief. I know that you will keep your oath. You're honourable, and you love me. But I haven't yet told you how Robert Macaulay's— m-murder led to my betrothal."

"Tell me, dear."

"It was like this. I was only a little boarding-school girl when my brother lost Kitty Grimsdale. I had a vague idea of what had befallen him, but, of course, he wouldn't allow a child to know much about his misfortune. It was not till many years later that I heard the story—and I may here tell you that I had never met either of the Macaulays.

"When I was sixteen I went to stay with a school friend, Milly Rogers, in London. Two young men were constant visitors at the house. Their name was Enchmarsh, and they had some fine property in Sussex. It was not long before the elder began to pay me attentions, and one night, when we were brushing our hair, Milly made me flush scarlet by whispering, 'I vow Mr. Harold Enchmarsh will ask you to marry him, Ruthie.'

"A week or two after our first meeting he did just as Milly said, and told me that he loved me madly. I know you'll think me vastly wicked and foolish, but the idea of being engaged at sixteen—of showing my ring to the young ladies of the school—together with his handsome face and dashing manner, turned my head. I promised to be his wife. He begged me to keep our affair secret for a few days. I loved secrets, and consented. About a week later he came to me and suggested a run-away match. This made me suspicious, and I asked him why he wanted an elopement, considering that my brother would doubtless be only too pleased at our marriage. He gave me an evasive answer, but my fears were not to be so easily soothed, and at last he told me that his name wasn't Enchmarsh. He and his brother had inherited some property from a relation, and had been forced by the requirements of the will to adopt his name. Their real name was Macaulay, and his brother was the wrecker of Guy's happiness.

"I tell you that I'd never really loved him, and can you wonder that at this revelation I came to my senses, and ordered him away? 'Do not let me see your face again,' I cried; 'your brother ruined my brother's life, and you sinned with him. You're a scoundrel and a deceiver. Do not let me see your face again!'

"The next day I went back to Guy at Golden Parsonage, and told him all that had happened. He said that I'd done right, and that his heart would have broken if I'd married Enchmarsh. So I took comfort, and soon afterwards I left school and came home to live with my dear Guy.

"We heard nothing of the Enchmarshes for about three months. Then a sudden rumour flew through Harpendeane that they were in the village. They were in their old house, which they hadn't yet managed to sell, and when Guy heard how near his enemy was to him I saw a terrible look creep into his eyes, and though I kissed him, and sat on his knee all the evening, I couldn't drive it away. His manner became vastly strange; he spoke wildly of the past and of all he had suffered, and he used some dreadful words with regard to Robert Macaulay. I'm sure that he was half mad with grief, and that he wasn't really responsible for what followed.

"I cried myself to sleep that night, and the next morning I rose early and plucked him a salad for his breakfast. I wanted to show him, just by a little thing like that, how much I loved him and wanted to make him happy. Breakfast-time came, but he never appeared. I went up to his room, but couldn't find him. I looked for him in the church—he's such a devout man, and I thought he might have gone to ask God's pardon for his anger of yesterday—but he was nowhere to be seen. I began to feel vastly anxious, and questioned the villagers, and at last heard that a little boy had noticed him leave Golden Parsonage early in the morning, and take the road for Harpendeane.

"A terrible foreboding seized me. I ordered my horse, and rode after him. I made inquiries from time to time on my way, and traced him to the Macaulay's house. Then I felt sick with fear, and my legs shook under me as I dismounted. There was an atmosphere of dread all round that house. I trembled in every limb, and—I shall always swear it—so did my horse.

"I didn't knock, but went straight upstairs to a room which I knew the brothers used as a study. For a moment I thought that there was blood on the doorhandle, but it was only the sun streaming through a pane of red-glass in the staircase window. I opened the door, then fell on my knees—because of what I saw between me and the light.

"Two men were standing, and one lay on the floor with a dark stream oozing from his hair. The men who stood were Harold Enchmarsh and my brother, while it was Robert Enchmarsh who lay bleeding between them.

"The thud of my fall made them start and turn round, and my brother threw his arms above his head, and staggered against the wall. Enchmarsh came to me and lifted me to my feet. But I could neither speak nor walk; I could only stand staring at that dreadful Thing on the floor.

"Then Guy spoke, but I couldn't answer, so he ran up to me, and fell at my feet, and, clinging to my gown, cried: 'Little sister! little sister!' and sobbed with his face against my knee. He told me how he had gone hotfoot to the village with murder in his heart, how he had gone into that awful house, into that very room; how he had found Robert Enchmarsh leaning out of the window, and how Satan had entered into him. He had stolen across the floor like a panther; he had seized his enemy, they had struggled together; Enchmarsh had bitten him—he showed me the bleeding place on his hand—he had thrown Enchmarsh out of the window.

"'Then as I turned round,' said my poor Guy, 'expecting to find the devil standing behind me, I saw this man, Harold Enchmarsh, in the doorway. I shall not tell you what passed between us. It's enough to say that his servant is at this very moment saddling a horse to ride off to S. Albans and fetch the constable. Ruthie, Ruthie, your brother will be hanged!'

"Oh, Humphrey, I can't help crying when I think of the awful minutes that followed—how I shuddered and cried and clung to Guy, praying God to have mercy on us and strike us both dead. Enchmarsh stood by in silence, and suddenly I threw myself on my knees before him and caught his arm.

"'Pity me, pity me, and spare my brother! Oh, be merciful and spare us both!'

94

"He didn't speak, but gazed down on me, then tried to move away, but I clung to him, praying him to pity me for Christ's sake. He swore, and struggled to shake me off, but I only gripped more fiercely, and he dragged me half across the room before I fell at his feet.

"Then he spoke—for as I lay before him, I begged him to pity me for his love's sake.

"'It's true that I love you.'

"'Then spare my brother for your love's sake!'

"He caught me up from the floor, and I could see the pulses beating in his throat, so close was his face to mine, as he whispered:

"'Ruth, if you marry me, I'll spare your brother!'

"'No, no, no!' and I sprang from him, sick with horror.

"'I would rather die!' cried my brother, who had overheard the whisper.

"'As you please,' said Enchmarsh, biting his lips with vexation, for he wanted me more than he wanted his revenge.

"At that moment there was a trample of hoofs in the yard. The servant was starting for S. Albans. I saw Guy turn pale, and shiver from head to foot, and my love for him overcame my hatred of Enchmarsh.

"'Stop him! stop him!' I shrieked. 'I will marry you!'

"'You shall not,' cried my brother. 'I'd rather die at the torture stake!'

"'Stop him! stop him!' I could cry nothing else till Enchmarsh had called to the servant to wait a few minutes. Then he turned to me.

"'Listen, both of you. Though this is the corpse of my only brother, I'm willing to forgive his murderer if the murderer's sister will become my wife. Ruth, during these past months I have loved you, and you only——'

"'He's a lying scoundrel!' interrupted Guy. 'Don't listen to him, Ruth.'

"'Hold your tongue, and let me settle this matter with your sister.'

"He took me by the hand, and led me aside.

"'I love you,' he said, 'and if you will marry me, your brother shall be safe. I give you my solemn oath.'

"I gazed from one man to the other in hopeless misery. In spite of all he said, I knew that Guy was really in mortal fear. He's always been afraid of death, and his lips were white and his limbs were shaking. I loved him more than my happiness— more than I hated Enchmarsh. You may call me weak and wicked, but I couldn't help myself. I promised to marry Enchmarsh if he would spare my brother. If at any time I went back from my word he might go back from his. Guy protested vehemently at first, and vowed that life would be hell if bought at such a price. But my arguments overcame him.

95

"The servant waiting in the yard was told to unsaddle the horse. He was privy to the murder, as he had seen Robert Enchmarsh fall, and had helped carry his body upstairs. He's still alive, and has sworn to give evidence against Guy if Enchmarsh should require it. He has sworn, also, to keep silence until commanded to speak, and never shall weakness of mine cause that command to be uttered.

"Our engagement was kept a secret. It would have filled the village with dangerous gossip if it had been known in Harpendeane. A few months ago we came to Ewehurst. The curate was dead, and Enchmarsh induced the Rector to appoint Guy in his place. So my future husband has us what he calls 'under his eye.' We didn't publish the betrothal even in Sussex. Secrecy was still advisable, and Guy would never have agreed to our compact if Enchmarsh hadn't promised that the marriage should not take place for a year. The year is not over yet, but my lover thought it right to declare our engagement a few weeks ago."

"Why?"

I interrupted her almost rudely, for I knew what she was about to say.

"Because—because you loved me, Humphrey."

She began to cry, and I bit my lip. There was a long pause. Then I said:

"Do you think Heaven approves this devil's bargain?"

"I can't say, and it doesn't matter to me. I shall carry it through—I shall pay the uttermost farthing."

"But he is a scoundrel, a rake, a brute! You would be happier in hell than at Kitchenhour."

"He's better than he used to be. He has had no—no intrigues since he left Harpendeane."

"But he's a beast, a gambler, a swaggerer, a drunkard. What worse could you have?"

"Oh, don't tempt me; it's all for my brother's sake."

"Your brother!" I cried, grinding my teeth. "Your brother is a coward, and unworthy of your sacrifice."

"I love him," she sobbed piteously. "You can't understand. You never loved a brother."

"No. But I am sure that Guy Shotover is unworthy of your love. Even Enchmarsh despises him, though he gains by his cowardice. I know I'm speaking brutally, but no brother with the slightest spark of manly feeling would allow his sister to marry a drunken rake in order that he might save his own skin."

"Guy withstood me obstinately at first. I had the greatest difficulty in persuading him. Besides, suppose that he had refused my sacrifice and had gone to his death, should I have been in a happier case? I should have found myself alone in the world at sixteen, helpless, homeless, and friendless. Enchmarsh would have taken advantage of my helplessness, and I should have met a fate so horrible that I hardly dare think of it. Guy knew all this, or he would never have given in to me."

Was an abject craven ever half so well defended? I looked at once admiringly and despairingly into her brave eyes, while my bosom ached with unshed tears.

"I told you my story," she continued, "that you might understand—and go."

"You told me your story," I cried harshly, "that I might love you a thousand times more than ever. Before this I loved you because you were so beautiful and sweet, because you were—O God!—so child-like. Now I love you because you are a thousand times better and braver than I. You are no child to be pitied and protected. You are the noblest woman that a man ever looked into the eyes of and called blessed."

I sank on one knee before her and kissed the hem of her little gown.

"Humphrey! Humphrey! don't kneel"—and she tugged frantically at my hand to pull me to my feet. "Why won't you stand up? Why won't you leave me? Don't you see that it's because I love you so much that I want you to go? I love you too well to let you be an occasion for sin to me. You can't help me except by your prayers. Go and pray for me."

I rose wearily to my feet. "I am going," I said, but I did not move.

"That br—— Enchmarsh told me you and he are to be married soon," I muttered, after a pause.

"In a month. He's here at Ihornden till next week, when he goes back to Kitchenhour."

"Do you see much of him?"

"Very little, as he practises pistol shooting nearly all day. Go, now, Humphrey, please go."

"I am going. To-morrow I leave Ihornden. Oh, that I could help you, dear! What a useless coward I feel! Why must I flee when I long to fight?"

"Go and pray for me."

I went towards her and held out my hands. Her own hung heavy at her side.

"Let me kiss you."

"No . . . for God's sake! . . ."

A terrible, haunting stillness pervaded the room. Both the candles flickered out, and in the dusk of mingled firelight and moonlight our hands met. Then I turned from her and went to the door mechanically. On the threshold I paused and looked back.

97

She was standing by the window, her little hands clenched in anguish, her hair falling over her face and sparing me the sight of her tears.

CHAPTER XV

OF THE METHODIST IN PLURENDEN QUARRY

I could not speak to John Palehouse that night, for when I left Ruth he had already gone to bed. But I was resolved to have an interview with him the next morning, and on the whole I was glad of a few hours' meditation before I attempted to leave Ihornden. My heart was torn with conflicting passions. I had promised to leave Ruth—but could I fulfil my promise? It seemed dastardly to desert her in her hour of need, yet my presence was a torture to her rather than a relief.

I went to my little room and lay down on the bed. I could not sleep, but I did not wish to. I had grown accustomed to my malady of sleeplessness, and though I realised that my health was surely failing under it, bore it with resignation. Besides, it gave me more time for thought, and I felt that this night at any rate would be better spent in thinking than in sleeping.

What was I to do? I pondered a dozen mad schemes, but dismissed them one and all as hopeless. I thought of appealing to Shotover, but entertained the idea only for a moment. The curate would listen to me, certainly; he would shed tears, perhaps, but fear of death would prevent the great sacrifice that alone could save us. I thought of appealing to Enchmarsh—the next moment I laughed out loud. Were my sufferings crazing me that I should for an instant cherish such a scheme? Should I appeal again to Ruth? Why, fool! She is the most obstinate of the three.

There they stood between me and all hope—the girl, the man, and the coward. The coward was chained by his fear, the man by his hatred, the girl by her love, and it would be difficult to say which was the fastest bound.

There was no help for it, I must leave Ihornden. I must abandon Ruth to her fate. No! That should never be. Ruth's fate was my fate, and I would never leave her to it. There was still a month to elapse before her marriage, and during that month I should not cease to labour for her deliverance. But how could I labour, how could I deliver, shackled as I was by my oath of secrecy? I gnashed my teeth in hopeless frenzy. Then into my own mind came Ruth's own words: "Go and pray for me." I believed in prayer and in the God Who hears it. Surely He would help me and Ruth. I had realised by this time that nothing could save us but a re-arrangement of circumstances, the happening of the unexpected. I would trust God for that. I rose from my bed and knelt down beside it. "O Thou that hearest prayer, to Thee shall all flesh come."

A sleepless night is not the best preparation for a troublous day. I could eat no breakfast; my head ached, and my limbs throbbed with fatigue. The morning was grey and cold, and a fierce wind blew from Frittenden. Nevertheless, John Palehouse was eager for a walk in the fields.

It was wonderful how his sweet temper and serenity smoothed the furrows between my eye-brows, and softened the lines of rage and pain about my mouth. He seemed in an unusually peaceful mood. He was even joyful, and took my arm with a smile, and a quick upward look of happiness.

"Where shall we go this sweet morning?"

"Do you call this a sweet morning? I call it dull and unlike summer."

"The sky is grey, but it is beautiful as a woodpigeon's wing, and see how an occasional flash of sunlight rests on the fields. What a delicious wind is rustling up from the west, and the birds, it is long since I heard them sing so merrily. Oh, it is a wonderful, wonderful day."

His delight was infectious, and I felt a vague comfort in the thought that though I lost Ruth for ever I should still have the green trees and fields, and that even on my death-bed I should see the sky.

We went through Ihornden Park to Brakefields Farm, and struck out across the meadows towards Heartsap. It was then I told Palehouse that I must leave Ihornden because I loved Ruth Shotover.

He listened attentively, and said:

"I knew all this, lad."

"You knew it?"

"Yes. It was plainly written."

"There is one thing, then, that I have learned—a man can't hide his love. I am in love, and Peter Winde, Mary Winde, and John Palehouse, all find out my secret."

"It was not much of a secret. You are a strange lad. Where many a man would tell his thoughts you lock them up in your heart, yet you can't keep them out of your eyes they're written on your face, and he may run who readeth them."

"I wish I was not in love. But no, I can't say that. Better to have loved hopelessly than have never loved at all."

"My poor boy! I know what it is to love in vain. So you want to leave Ihornden? You are right."

"But I must find some excuse to give Sir Miles."

"I have a good one for you. I have long been anxious about the poor folk at Frittenden. There is a family at Whitsunden Farm the thought of which kills sleep. Tell Sir Miles that I have asked you to continue your journey, to preach at Frittenden, Horsemonden, Bethersden, and to wait for me at Headcorn. I shall soon be able to follow you."

"I shall wait for you at Bethersden," I said. I was resolved not to go further than that from Ruth.

"As you will, lad; but why not at Headcorn?"

"I hope that you will join me before I have time to reach Headcorn."

"When do you start?"

"This afternoon."

"Won't Sir Miles think that rather sudden?"

"I don't care if he does. I must go."

"Perhaps it would be best. I wish that I could go with you;" and he sighed.

"Does your cousin know you are here?"

"He must. But we never see each other, which is fortunate, for if we did I could not stay at Ihornden. You see, Humphrey, that I am very weak and unworthy. Do you still insist on leaving me this afternoon?"

"I'm afraid I must."

"And I do wrong in trying to keep you back. Go, and God bless you. Oh, lad, you will often be downcast and weary of your groaning, but believe the words of one who has suffered—there is joy in the world, even for a broken heart."

We had entered a chalk quarry in the corner of a high meadow known as Plurenden. The wind swept it, rumpled our hair over our brows, and danced the poppies on the chalkstone cliffs. The sun burst suddenly through a cloud rift, and John stood in the full glare of it, his hands clasped over mine.

"Yes, lad, joy for the broken heart. God is good, and the earth is green; life is wonderful, and death is sweet. The girl you love is in stronger, tenderer hands than yours, and though you be parted like two meadow streams, remember that all waters mingle in the sea and all lives touch in eternity. 'Although the fig-tree shall not blossom, neither shall fruit be in the vines, the labour of the olive shall fail, and the fields shall yield no meat; the flocks shall be cut off from the fold and there shall be no herd in the stalls, yet will I rejoice in the Lord; I will joy in the God of my salvation.'"

His hands closed more tensely over mine, and his eyes looked into mine, full of love and hope and joyousness. Then a cloud veiled the sun, and a wave of darkness rushed over the fields. I heard a footstep behind me, and a voice I knew and hated well.

"Good morning, my handsome cousin! This meeting is as opportune as it is unexpected."

John turned very pale. Enchmarsh stood with his arms folded, his face flushed, his eyes dangerously bright. In his hand he carried a pistol, well grimed with recent use.

"I've been shooting down in Ihornden Park, but it's as hot as hell in the valley, so I took some wine and came up here to cool myself."

He had evidently been drinking heavily, so I pulled John's sleeve, and we moved off.

"Don't leave so hurriedly. Stay and speak to me, coz. To think that you and I should have spent forty-eight hours under the same roof, and never have met, though we love each other so dearly. But you have been in the wars, my swashbuckling Methodist, and have tasted a little of the stoning of Stephen."

"Let me pass," said John. "It is not right or safe"—the outraged man in him triumphed over the preacher—"that you and I should speak together."

"Not right? Not safe? Shall you kill me, then, my valiant singer of psalms? Oh, a happy life you would have led my Dolly! She was no Methodist."

Palehouse was silent, and this maddened Enchmarsh, enflamed with wine.

"You won't speak? Then I'll tell you a piece of news. Dolly vowed that she was happier as my mistress than she ever could have been as your wife. There, does that warm your fish's blood?"

"The Lord rebuke you!" said John Palehouse; and I wondered at his calmness, till I saw the mark of his teeth on his nether lip.

"No; Dolly was never made for virtue, nor virtue for Dolly," resumed Enchmarsh; "so they were best apart."

I could restrain my fury no longer, and would have struck the brute down, but John Palehouse seized my arm.

"Do not strike him—he is made in God's image."

Enchmarsh sneered, but the next moment drew back uneasily, for John strode up to him and grasped his wrist.

"Silence, wretch! You have slandered the woman I loved, that I still love, though she died a sinner. You seduced her and betrayed her, and now you smear her name with the filth that should be daubed on yours before the whole world. It was through you that she took the first step in sin, which led her to the bottomless pit. Before you decoyed her she was pure as snow. The Lord rebuke you."

His mouth quivered with righteous fury; he still held Enchmarsh by the wrist. Then he dropped his hand and his proud head. The squire stood motionless, panting with rage; suddenly his eyes flashed. He seized John Palehouse by the shoulders, and shook him as a dog shakes a coney; then he struck him furiously with the butt of his pistol.

John fell to the ground without groan or cry. His face was white, his lips were a little parted; and as I gazed at him, petrified, I saw the blood rush under the skin of his temple, and form a little grey bruise there.

"My God!" I cried, and fell on my knees beside him. I thought him only stunned, but an impulse bade me put my hand on his heart. There was no throb.

101

I felt no grief—it was all so sudden and like a dream—but something seemed to snap in my breast and freeze my eyes. I lifted John's head on to my knee, and gazed down at his peaceful face. Then I raised my eyes to Enchmarsh.

"You are a murderer!"

He did not answer. His nerveless hand had dropped the pistol, his lips trembled, and his eyes were fixed on the dead man's face. For a moment or two we remained silent, gazing at the marble features and limp, lifeless form. His eyes were wide open, and stared up at us, so I closed them gently.

My movement startled Enchmarsh out of the trance into which he had fallen. I saw a look of terror leap into his eyes, and the next instant he would have rushed from the place, had I not caught him round the legs and held him like a vice. He writhed and struggled, and fell on the ground beside me. Over and over we rolled together, silent except for our panting. Enchmarsh fought like a wild beast, but, though by no means so powerful as he, I was more agile, and contrived to keep uppermost in the struggle. At last I managed to pin him beneath me, and he lay helpless, with my knee on his chest and my hands on his throat.

"This shall be your last crime, you blackguard! You have betrayed the innocent and oppressed the helpless, and no man gave you your reward. But your career is ended with the murder of John Palehouse."

"Take your hands off my throat!" he panted. "You're choking me."

"I shall keep my hands where they are till I see you in custody. There are some labourers working in Coarsebarn field. I shall shout for them, and if you move an inch I'll throttle you."

"Shout, then, you beast! But, remember—if you have me arrested, I'll have Guy Shotover hanged. I have power to hang him——"

"I know that."

"How do you know?"

"Never mind how I know—and you may hang Shotover as high as Haman for all I care. He's nothing to me."

I paused a moment after I had said this, for I remembered that, though Shotover was nothing to me, he was the brother of the girl who was all things to me, and into my mind came her words: "I loved Guy more than my happiness—more than I hated Enchmarsh." I should show myself unworthy of Ruth if I sacrificed her brother to my revenge. My dearest friend had been brutally murdered, but I had no right to demand vengeance at such a price. Into Guy's grave would go his sister's youth, hope, and happiness. She had given up all that makes life sweet in order to spare him the doom to which I, who swore I loved her, was about to send him to gratify my ungodlike passions.

I meditated with my hands on Enchmarsh's throat, while the wind sang in the grass, and suddenly I remembered the bargain my enemy had made with Ruth over Robert Enchmarsh's body at Harpendeane, and I realised that if I followed his example, it was in my power to free her from this scoundrel she hated, and yet spare her another drop in the cup which was already overbrimming with tears.

"Listen, you blackguard. I said that Shotover was nothing to me, but for his sister's sake he must not be allowed to perish. If you set Ruth Shotover free from her engagement and at the same time hold your tongue as to the curate's affair, I'll keep silence as to what you did for John Palehouse."

"Ugh-gh—you're choking me——"

"Nonsense. Do you accept my offer?"

"I'm damned if I give up Ruth for you to marry her."

"You'll have to give her up, anyhow. It's only a question of whether you and Shotover go scot-free, or whether you both hang."

"It's a devil's bargain!" He writhed, and the grip of my hands tightened on his windpipe. He was soon lying quiet as a lamb.

"You'd better not struggle," I said grimly. "Come, give me a straight answer. Will you lose Ruth Shotover and your life together, while enjoying your revenge, or will you lose her and live—without revenge?"

"I suppose life's better worth having than vengeance," he said sulkily.

"That's for you to decide and be quick about it."

"Then I'll live and hold my tongue; and now, for God's sake, take your hands off my throat."

"We must settle matters more definitely first."

"Oh, anything you like—I'll swear—Ugh-gh——"

"I want something more trustworthy than your oath. You shall write out a full confession of your crime."

"Yes—at Ihoraden."

"No—here."

"Why not at Ihornden?" The fellow knew that he could easily give me the slip once we were out of the quarry.

"Because I intend to have it here."

"But I've not even a piece of paper."

"That's a lie. You have a notebook in your pocket;" and I pulled it out. "I can lend you a pencil."

"I can't write it lying on my back, while you're half strangling me, you beast!"

"Sit up, then."

I relaxed the grip of my hands and the pressure of my knee sufficiently to allow him to raise himself.

"There, you can write now, and, remember, I'll throttle the life out of you if you move an inch."

He began to write in the notebook at my dictation:

"I, Harold Enchmarsh———"

I had seen his handwriting on several occasions, and knew that the round, bold letters he was forming were merely an attempt to make the document valueless. I pressed my fingers on his windpipe, and the next moment he had dropped the pencil and paper, and was writhing between my knees.

"You scoundrel! I'm not the fool you think me. Write in your usual hand—I know it well—or I'll shout for help, and deliver you over to justice, come what may."

He sat up, looking very white and ill, and wrote, his hands trembling because of the grip of mine:

"I, Harold Enchmarsh, hereby declare that I murdered my cousin, John Palehouse, by striking him on the temple with a pistol in Plurenden Quarry, on the fourteenth of July, 1799."

I bade him tear out the leaf; then I took my hands from his throat, leaving blue finger-marks on the skin, and thrust the paper into my pocket.

"You can go now."

"What shall you do with that?" he said hoarsely, pointing to John Palehouse.

I considered.

"I can account for his death in a fall from the top of the quarry, and for the bruise on his forehead in one of the stones scattered round about———"

I ceased speaking suddenly, for the grief which had been waiting outside my heart till rage had left it now stole in, and choked my voice. Enchmarsh stood by me in silence, his hands clasped round his throat. As I looked at him, I was seized with an unholy joy that I had punished the villain so well.

"What are you going to do?" he asked faintly.

"I shall run to Coarsebarn Farm and tell the folk that my friend had had a fall into Plurenden Quarry, and is dead. As for you, you had better be off at once"—it was my great ambition to get the brute away. "On your first opportunity release Ruth Shotover from her engagement, and remember that if you move a finger against her or her brother, I produce my evidence—and many a man has been hanged on less."

"Ruth Shotover"—he stood repeating the name and biting his nails—"Ruth Shotover—Ruth Enchmarsh—Ruth Lyte. Oh, damn you!"

"Be off!" I cried. "Remember that I carry your death."

He threw me a fierce glance of hatred; then he looked towards the dead man, turned very white, and hurried away in a sweat.

I went to John Palehouse, and stooped over him. He lay as he had often slept— one arm across his breast, the other stretched out among the grass. Surely he rested well.

I sat for about a quarter of an hour in Plurenden Quarry, while the wind waved the poppies on the cliffs. At last I rose and went softly from the place, as if I feared to wake John Palehouse.

I shudder to think how terrible my grief would have been had not joy come to me hand in hand with my sorrow. In John's death I suffered my first bereavement, and to those who remember the anguish of their first bereavement I need say no more. But his death opened the gate of happiness to two lives against which it had long been barred.

Once in the lane outside the meadow, I began to run. The oast-houses of Coarsebarn Farm rose in front of me above the hanger of Heartsap Hill. I hoped—indeed, I prayed—that I might be able to utter my lie with firm lips; for on that lie Ruth's happiness depended. If the murder were discovered, and Enchmarsh proved to be the murderer, then Guy Shotover would perish, and his sister's heart be broken. But if all were kept secret and John Palehouse believed to have met his death through a fall into Plurenden Quarry, then—oh, blessed thought! it sent the blood to my cheeks and the tears to my eyes.

Suddenly, as I ran, I became aware of footsteps following me, and of voices calling me to stop. I turned my head. The little lane was steep and rough. I stumbled in a rut, and fell prone. The next minute a pair of hands were on my shoulders, pinning me to the ground, while my legs were seized and held forcibly, and a voice I seemed to have heard before exclaimed:

"Now we have you, my fine fellow!"

What with the violence of my fall and the unexpectedness of all that had happened, I lay for a second or two utterly bewildered, without power of speech. At last, however, I managed to turn my head, and looked, dumbfounded, into the face of Curate Kitson.

"What—what the devil is this?" I stammered.

"Yes, indeed. What—what the devil is it?" mocked Kitson.

"Will you let me get up?"

"All in good time. Leave go his legs, Pitcher; he had better stand. He can't very well speak with his mouth full of dust."

The grip on my ankles was relaxed, and I rose painfully to my feet. Kitson stood before me, with two farm labourers. One of these, as soon as I was upright, pinned my arms to my sides. I was evidently regarded as a dangerous subject.

"Will you do me the favour of explaining all this?" I cried hotly.

"Oh, certainly," drawled Kitson. "We have just discovered the corpse of your fellow-Ranter Palehouse, in Plurenden Quarry."

"He fell over the edge . . . he is dead. . . . I'm on my way to Coarsebarn Farm for help."

"Yes, you seemed in a demned hurry."

"I suppose you think I murdered him?" I cried angrily, for by this time I had guessed the reason of their violence.

"Well, such an idea did cross our minds, I must confess."

"It's a lie! My friend fell into the quarry, as I've told you, and dashed his head against a stone."

My lips were accustomed to speak the truth, and stammered horribly over the lie. Kitson grinned.

"I should be quite ready to believe you if it were not for this," and he took a pistol out of his pocket.

I turned pale. I had forgotten the pistol, and must have left it on the ground beside John Palehouse, fool that I was—oh, thrice a fool! Thanks to my idiocy, everything would be discovered. The pistol would be recognised as Enchmarsh's; he would be arrested, Shotover hanged, and Ruth's heart broken—oh, fool, fool! A hundred times a fool.

Suddenly I started, and looked closer; then my jaw dropped, and the sweat beaded out on my forehead. The pistol was MINE.

How had it come into Enchmarsh's hands? Was it indeed my pistol that had killed John Palehouse? I stood absolutely dumbfounded, but saw that I must rise to the occasion. My first impulse was to betray Enchmarsh, but I thought of the consequences, and refrained. There was surely some other way of clearing myself of this hateful charge. If I did not think of it now I should think of it later. I had no right to wreck Ruth's happiness simply because I was in danger.

"Well," drawled Kitson, "how much paler, and how much redder, and how much more sweat?"

I saw that my emotion was damning me, so fought it down.

"Well," continued the curate, "how do you account for the pistol?"

"I must have dropped it."

"Yes—and fractured the butt."

He held out the pistol and showed me a deep crack across the butt. With such force must Enchmarsh have struck John Palehouse.

"Do you still deny that you are a murderer?"

"I do."

"Perhaps you deny that this is your pistol?"

"No, I don't deny that." Such a course would have been useless, as my initials were engraved on the butt, and every one at Ihornden knew the weapon to be mine.

"It is just as well not to tell more lies than you can help. We won't keep you here any longer. Your reverence shall see the inside of a jail for once in your saintly life. But we must have a warrant of commitment first. 'Let all things be done decently and in order,' as the Apostle says. So off with you to Sir Miles Wychellow."

I was quite ready, for I felt sure that I should easily be able to clear myself before the kind magistrate, who knew of my love for John Palehouse and the good character I had hitherto borne.

The two farm men instantly gripped me by the shoulders and marched me up Heartsap Hill. They were great rough fellows, and seemed to relish their work. They had doubtless been among the rioters on Biddenden Common, and rejoiced to wreak their spite on the hated Methodist. The curate walked beside us, his lip curling slightly. He, too, delighted in the hour of revenge.

I held my head high, for I felt confident. In fact, the only thing that perplexed me was—how had Enchmarsh come by my pistol? Had he been using it in mistake for his own? Had his own been damaged, and had he taken mine, rather than ask a favour of me? Or—desperate thought!—had he intended to murder John Palehouse, and deliberately made use of my pistol, so that he might avert suspicion from himself and fix it on me, and thus kill two birds with one stone—his cousin and his rival?

We had reached Ihornden before I could answer any of those questions. The servant who opened the door fell back in surprise at the sight of my escort, but neither I nor Kitson vouchsafed any explanation. The curate asked for Sir Miles, and on being told that he was out, requested to be shown a room where he and his prisoner—a slight accent on the word "prisoner," which made the servant stare yet more blankly—could await his return. We were ushered into a small room looking out on the terrace. Kitson and the two labouring men sat at the table, while I flung myself on a bench near the window.

My spirits were somewhat dashed by an hour's waiting—in fact, they soon fell very low indeed—for after some thought, I came to the conclusion that I should not find it so easy to clear myself as I had imagined. I was resolved not to speak a word that might lead to Guy Shotover's arrest, and it seemed as if only by such word I could be saved. I spent the hour that followed in imaginary conversations with Squire Wychellow, every one of which ended in my betraying Enchmarsh—and with him Shotover. My only safe course seemed to be to hold my tongue.

The sky grew greyer, and gusts of rain beat against the windows. A dog howled to the accompaniment of the wind, and every now and then a door slammed in a distant part of the house. Kitson and my guards talked in low voices, as if cowed by the uncanniness of the day. A cart had been sent to fetch the body of John Palehouse, and the men who drove it had gone forth pale and wide-eyed, starting at every sound. Horror was in the wind and in the house. A gust blew the leaves off the trees as if autumn had come, and they danced on the terrace a dance of death.

At last the horrible wind brought us the sound of coach-wheels, and Sir Miles's coach rolled up to the door. From the window I could see Lady Wychellow dismount, followed by her husband, Guy Shotover, and Ruth.

Kitson rose, and went to meet the magistrate in the hall. I still gazed out of the window, for Ruth was still standing where I could see her.

Sir Miles entered in great perturbation, rubbing his hands, as was his habit when excited.

"What the devil is all this?" he cried. "Surely there's some mistake!"

I was at a loss what to say, so fixed my eyes on the floor, and answered him not a word.

Sir Miles looked mystified.

"Give your evidence," he said abruptly, turning to Kitson.

The curate gave his evidence, which was confirmed by the working men Pitcher and Green.

"Do you wish to contradict anything these gentlemen have said?"

"No."

"You confess that you killed Palehouse?"

"No!" I cried sharply, lifting my head.

Sir Miles knit his brows.

"Begad, Mr. Kitson! your evidence is clear enough, but I'm loth to disbelieve this young man."

"Why, he's as big a liar as Ananias!" cried the curate, roused by hatred out of his usual state of insolent calm. "He has already told us several lies. You don't deny that, do you?"—turning to me.

"No."

Sir Miles glanced at me impatiently.

"Begad, sir! I'm sick of your 'no.' What has come over you?"

My heart was too full for speech, so I only stared at the ground. The squire shrugged his shoulders.

"He looks hang-dog enough. But when I first met him he was risking his life and limb to save the man you say he has just murdered. He and Palehouse loved each other like brothers——"

"No doubt it was a sudden quarrel. These Ranters are always as hot-tempered as Old Harry—and who killed Palehouse if not this fellah?"

"Perhaps he fell from the top of the quarry?"

Kitson grinned. "Mr. Lyte did not make that statement with—er—sufficient calmness for me to believe it. Besides, what of the pistol?"

"Is this pistol yours, young man?"

"Yes, Sir Miles."

The squire shook his head.

"I've sent for a doctor from Cranbrook to examine the body; and, of course, there will be an inquest, when we shall be told whether the bruise on Palehouse's forehead has anything to do with Mr. Lyte's pistol. In the meantime——"

"He must go to jail," drawled the curate, who evidently enjoyed heaping every insult on me.

Sir Miles flushed.

"I fear so. The charge is serious. Young man, I am oth to commit you, but you leave me no choice."

He stood for a moment in thought. "Come, Sir Miles, the warrant," said Kitson sweetly.

Swearing under his breath, the squire moved slowly towards his writing-table. The warrant was made out, and I was locked into an attic till the constable should arrive from Biddenden to take me in charge.

Here I had ample time for reflection—the constable was a leisurely man—and I cannot say that the hours passed pleasantly. Hitherto I had been racking my brains for some way of clearing myself without involving Enchmarsh. I had realised that this would be difficult, but now I saw that it would be impossible. I could not establish my innocence without sending Enchmarsh—and with him, Guy Shotover—to the gallows.

I saw that even now it would be comparatively easy to put matters straight. Enchmarsh must be somewhere in the house, the marks of my fingers must still be on his throat, no one would question the authenticity of the confession in my pocket, and the presence of my pistol in Plurenden Quarry could no doubt be satisfactorily explained. I could certainly save myself if I pleased—but ought I to do so?

The question rose stern and baffling, and I trembled before it. Shotover's arrest would certainly follow my betrayal of Enchmarsh. I thought of Ruth's face as I had last seen it, her eyes full of pleading, her lips quivering with unselfish love. She had given up all that makes life worth living to save her brother. Had I the cruelty to make her sacrifice of none effect?

"Ah, but it is because I love her!" I cried in answer to my own thoughts. "Surely she had rather lose her brother than lose me—surely she loves me more than that abject coward."

"True," replied the inward voice; "doubtless she loves you more, but she has loved you all these past weeks and yet she has sacrificed you to her brother. She could any day have banished Enchmarsh and have given herself to you, but she would not, because to do so would have meant the death of her brother, who loved life."

"She naturally shrank from uttering his death-sentence with her own lips, but if he perished through words of mine——"

"She would despise you for ever."

"But I should be dooming him only indirectly. He would owe his death to Enchmarsh——"

"And to you. If you speak you speak with the full knowledge that your words will hang him."

I groaned. A year ago I should have been glad to die. But this day happiness, love, and heart's desire had been put within my reach, and it was cruel to have them snatched from me. Oh, I must speak, I must live, come what may!

Then I pictured my meeting with Ruth after I had spoken. She would look at me with sad, reproachful eyes.

"Dear," I should cry, "I did it all for your happiness."

And she would answer kindly, perhaps, but sadly:

"No doubt you did it for the best, but that makes it no less hard for me to lose my brother—and my confidence in my lover."

I sat in silence, my head sunk on my breast, my hands clasped between my knees. Whatever course I adopted, Ruth was bound to suffer. The question I had to consider was—which would cause her least misery? Surely she would rather lose her brother. But not through me, for that way she lost me too. If I betrayed Shotover I could never be to Ruth what I had been before. All her faith in me, her trust, her reverence, would be gone.

Then there were other considerations. I had told Enchmarsh that Guy Shotover was nothing to me, but now I realised that at the bottom of my heart lurked a sort of sneaking affection for the fellow. It was true that his weakness and cowardice stood between me and all hope, but I could not forget that he had befriended me when I was friendless, and taken me into his house, fed me, washed my feet with his own hands, and had made me sleep in his own bed. Besides, I could not deny that the man was lovable, that he was gentle, simple-hearted, and devoted to holy things. But the chief point in his favour was that he was my benefactor. One had scruples about sending one's benefactor to jail.

So love and honour bade me be silent, to suffer death rather than speak. After all, the evidence against me being purely circumstantial, it was possible that the county magistrates might not think it safe to give a petty jury the chance of convicting me.

But if I betrayed Shotover I sent him to certain death and what would become of Ruth when he was hanged? I should be too poor to marry her for years to come, and she had no relations living. Doubtless the Wychellows would care for her; nevertheless, her lot would be a hard one. I had no right to condemn her to it.

No. I must be silent. I saw my way plainly—the way of silence. Love and honour tied my tongue, bade me suffer, and, if need be, die. So I fell on my knees and commended my resolution to God, asking Him to help me, who, without Him, was helpless.

After that I felt calmer, and sat listening to the sweet songs of the birds, till a step outside my prison made me start. The next moment the door was unlocked, and Sir Miles Wychellow came in.

"The doctor has arrived from Cranbrook," he said abruptly. "He has examined Palehouse and he has examined your pistol, and swears that the death of one is due to a blow from t'other."

There was dead silence. I had risen, and stood shuffling my feet uneasily. Sir Miles laid his hand on my shoulder.

"Come, my lad," he said, very kindly, "I'm sure you can explain all this if you choose. Make a clean breast of it. Did you kill Palehouse?"

"No."

"But, young man, there's little use in saying 'no.' You must give us facts."

He waited for a moment, then, as I remained silent, continued: "Did you and Palehouse meet anyone near Plurenden?"

"No."

"You and he were alone together the whole of your walk?"

"Yes."

"That's bad! If Palehouse and you were alone the whole morning, why——" he hesitated.

"Yes," I replied, "the conclusion is natural enough."

"I can't understand you," said Sir Miles; "you are either a fool or a liar."

I was both, but I would not tell him so.

"Come, lad, why so proud and silent? If you're guilty, confess. Perhaps there are extenuating circumstances."

His voice was so gentle, and he patted my shoulder so kindly that I was cut to the heart, and could not answer him.

"You won't answer me? Well, so be it," and he went off, shaking his head.

I paced miserably up and down the room, now and then singing a verse of "Jesu, Lover of my Soul" to comfort my fainting heart. Rain began to fall, and the clouds rolled back from the face of the sun, so that an angry copper glare streamed upon the rain. The west was bloody and ragged as if the sun were setting in wrath. In about half an hour my prison door opened, and Sir Miles came back to tell me that the constable had arrived from Biddenden, and would take me off to the village lock-up.

I followed the magistrate to the hall, where the constable was waiting with gyves. I winced at the sight of these, but schooled myself to submission and held out my hands. I noticed that Guy Shotover was skulking at the further end of the hall. When we were about to leave the house, he came forward and whispered a few words to Sir Miles.

"Egad! I had forgotten," said the baronet. "Wait a moment, my man, the prisoner has had no food since morning."

I had been so highly wrought that I had not noticed how hungry I was. My needs had occurred to no one but Guy, and his solicitude was characteristic of him. The constable made no objection to waiting while I had some supper. I ate in silence, and had soon finished. Guy shook hands with me, and asked if I had any money. I told him that I had enough, and he begged me to borrow of him if ever I should be in need.

The sun was sinking fast when we left the house, and went down the avenue. We were nearly at the gate when a white figure suddenly flashed into the copper glare of the sunset. It was Ruth. I do not know whether she was out on purpose to see me, or whether I had come upon her unawares. She did not speak, but drew aside to let us pass, while she stared in horror at my gyves. Her eyes were red with crying, and the sight of her was as hot iron on a raw wound. I looked into her face and tried to speak, but the words froze on my tongue. Did she believe me guilty or innocent? I longed to ask her, but had not the courage.

In a quarter of an hour we reached Biddenden, and I spent the tramp in racking my brains for a safe way of disposing of Enchmarsh's confession, for I knew that as soon as I reached the lock-up I should be searched. The paper was in the breast-pocket of my coat, and I wondered if I could slip it into a safer place without the constable noticing me. He did not seem a very observant fellow. He walked beside me half asleep, his eyes nearly shut.

"Wot yer doing, young man?" he cried suddenly.

"Tying my shoe-lace," I replied, as I slipped Enchmarsh's confession from my pocket into my stocking.

"I can't have no loitering, come on!"

I obeyed, well satisfied; and a few minutes later we entered Biddenden. The men had not yet come back from the fields, and the street was deserted, save for a few women and children who stared curiously at me and whispered among themselves. I was marched past the church and the inn to the village lock-up—a tiny dark cell, the floor rough and dirty, the walls trickling with damp.

I had not expected a very thorough search, and the constable did little more than bid me turn out my pockets. Having satisfied himself as to their contents, he went off, locking the door. I groped my way to a bench set against the wall, which was the only furniture the place contained, and gave myself up to thought. I decided to let Enchmarsh's confession stay where it was for the present, as I might be searched again.

The stars came out, and the hush of night fell on all things, but I was too sorrowful to sleep. My heart was full of bitter longing for John Palehouse. I had hitherto been too much engrossed in my difficulties to pine for him; but now that the questions which had tormented me were answered, now that I had taken the roughest of the two roads before which I had stood hesitating, my heart was open to grief and craving, and I brooded miserably. It was terrible to think that all men believed I had killed him, my dearest friend, for whom I would have willingly laid down my life. To be charged with such a crime was only a degree less awful than to have committed it.

Day dawned after what seemed an eternity, and about nine o'clock the constable appeared with a bowl of gruel for my breakfast, and told me that the inquest had already taken place, and that a verdict of "wilful murder" had been brought against me. At noon I appeared before the local magistrates, who, after hearing the detailed and conclusive evidence of Kitson, Pitcher, and Green, committed me for trial at the Maidstone Assizes. I was taken back to my dirty little cell, and there I sat, hot and depressed, till at twilight the bolt was shot back and the constable, muffled in many wraps, bade me tumble up, for I was to go to Maidstone by the night coach.

The fresh air was sweet after the stuffiness of my prison. It fanned my hot cheeks gratefully; it soothed me into a happier frame of mind.

We reached the cross-roads near Three Chimneys after a few minutes' walk. Here we were to wait till the Maidstone coach went by. The sun had set, and the sky was blue-grey, except for dark masses of cloud, and for a faint glow of red and orange in the west. It had been raining, and the hedges, fields, and trees were wet, and great pools shone on the road in the twilight. The fold star hung above Chittenden, and the wind crept with a moaning whisper over the fields, and rustled the grasses by the wayside. Every now and then a burst of summer lightning showed me the meadows and spinneys lying in their night stillness, showed me High Tilt and Hareplain, and the roofs of Castwisell, and all the dear places where John Palehouse and I had roamed together. I thought of my friend lying silent and peaceful at Ihornden Hall, his white hands folded on his breast; and the thought no longer tortured, but soothed me. "They shall hunger no more, neither thirst any more." His sufferings were over, the chastening hand was lifted from his back and sides, the cup of deadly wine was withdrawn from his lips. No longer would he sorrow for the beautiful unworthy woman he had loved, no longer would he travail in prayers and tears for the thankless souls of men, no longer would he starve, and tramp, and toil. "Yea, saith the Spirit, for they rest from their labours."

A rumble of wheels drew near, and at last the coach rolled into view, and pulled up at a signal from the constable. The outside was crowded, so we were forced to go inside, which I hated, for the summer night was glorious, hot and still, and the interior of the coach was stuffy, and full of noise and smell. Moreover, my fellow-passengers had little relish for travelling with a man who wore gyves on his wrists; and though the constable assured her that I was "perfectly tractable, madam," one old lady removed herself and her belongings to the further end of the coach, and declared that she would not be able to sleep a wink all night, for she was sure that I should murder her if ever she closed an eye.

I sat in a kind of stupor, while the coach lurched and jolted over ruts. A lamp hanging from the roof swung with every roll and cast weird shadows on the faces of my companions. Near Headcorn I fell asleep, and dreamed a strange, jumbled dream about Ihornden and Shoyswell, Ruth Shotover, Mary Winde, and John Palehouse. Then I dreamed that I was dead, and stood as a disembodied spirit in Shoyswell fold. I woke with a shudder. The wheels were jolting over cobbles, and houses reared their gables against a sky yellow with moonlight. We had reached Maidstone.

The coach drew up at the Star Inn, and the constable, swearing that he had never been so thirsty in his life, led me into the bar. He was a kindly fellow, and offered to stand me a glass of ale, for which I was grateful, as both my soul and body were faint enough.

In spite of the late hour the bar was crowded to overflowing. I sat in an obscure corner, the constable's burly figure shutting out the rest of the company, whose talk, songs, and laughter came to me as in a dream. I had soon finished my ale, and leaned back with closed eyes. I had nearly fallen into a doze when I heard close by me a feeble twitter, the ghost of a lark's rising song. I lifted my eyes and saw above my head a tiny cage in which a lark was imprisoned. There was barely room for him to turn, and every now and then he dashed his little body against the bars with the force of desperation. Occasionally he tried to sing the old glad song with which he had flown up into the face of God but the notes were piteous, and died off in a haunting cry. Poor little heart! How I pitied it with its ruffled breast and round, frightened eyes. I had seen larks rise from the Sussex fields; I had been awakened by the stirring of their wings.

Then the thought came to me that in an hour's time I should be even as this lark a prisoner, beating in vain against iron bars. Poor little heart! You and I are brethren.

The constable interrupted my reverie.

"Come, young feller, no more starin' at that tedious bird, but off with yer to jail!"

With that he marched me through a crowd of curious mocking faces into the fresh air and moonlight. A few minutes' walk brought us to a huge grey building with shackles hung over the door. Before the constable had told me I knew this was the jail, and my heart sank.

The formalities that preceded my admission were short, and, owing to the time of night, sleepy. Shackles were no longer worn by the prisoners, so mine were struck off, much to my relief, and I was led down a series of dark, stuffy passages to an iron door.

I held my breath, but the next moment gasped it forth in horror. The opening of the door revealed a terrible sight—a room in which sleeping men lay together like beasts. The window was unglazed, nevertheless the atmosphere was noisome. Accustomed as I was to living and sleeping in the open air, the idea of such quarters chilled my blood. For a long time after the jailer had locked the door, I stood motionless, with covered face, shivering like a girl.

At last I managed to control my disgust, and started to pick my way across the room, warily and shrinkingly, like one who crossed a battlefield the day after the fight. I touched a man's head with my foot, and he swore, but did not wake. At last I reached a spot where there was room for me to lie down. Fortunately, I was exhausted after two nights' sleeplessness, for it would have crazed me to lie wakeful in that hell.

CHAPTER XVII
OF THE METHODIST IN PRISON

The sound of laughter mingled with my dreams, and I awoke. A number of men were standing round me, and they laughed again at my mystified face; for at first I had no idea where I was. Remembrance came all too soon, and with a groan I struggled to my feet.

"When did you come here? Answer civilly," said a tall, thin fellow, who seemed to be the leader of the rest.

"About midnight."

"What's your name?"

"Lyte."

"What are you here for?"

"On a charge of murder."

"Just as I told the lads while you were sleeping. You've a reg'lar murderer's phiz. Think you're likely to get off?"

"I can't say."

"Are you one of us?"—and he addressed me in a strange jargon I could not understand, evidently thieves' cant.

I shook my head.

"Then what are you? Anything in the smashing line?"

"No; I'm a Methodist preacher."

A roar of laughter burst from my audience.

"A Methodee! A Methodee! The devil! but we'll be having daily prayers now. Are you saved?"

> ng hey for the Methodist
> n;
> ng ho for the Ranter bold!
> ɛ kissed my wife——"'

"Hold your damn noise, will you?" cried my questioner. "I want to find out something more about the cove. Where's your little Bethel?"

"I have no chapel. I'm a travelling preacher."

"How old are you?"

"Twenty-one."

"You're young for holiness." Then he put his face close to mine, and winked. "Any pretty girl to love you?"

I flushed angrily, and was silent.

"Come now; won't you tell us whether she's dark or fair."

"I refuse to answer any more of your questions. What right have you to pester me in this way?"

"I advise you to be civil, young feller. We lads aren't over gentle with the young and insolent. But never mind; you've said your catechism like a good boy, and I'll leave you alone till I've had some beer."

With that he went off to the other end of the room, or "ward," where a bottle was going round.

A church clock close by struck nine, and I realised that I was very hungry. But I had rather starve than mix with the rough, profane crowd, devouring and swilling meat and beer a few yards off. I lay down in the cleanest spot I could find, and gave myself up to thought.

I took advantage of my comparative solitude to slip Enchmarsh's confession out of my stocking—by no means a convenient hiding-place—back into my pocket. I had been searched, in a very perfunctory manner, on my arrival at the jail, and did not expect the ordeal to be repeated till I was brought up for trial.

The sun rose higher, and fell with such fierceness on the stones where I lay that I was forced to creep into the shade. Here three men were stretched, talking so foully that I hurriedly left them for the crowd, who, I felt sure, had not viler tongues than they.

I found every one drowning their cares, and was invited to join them. But I suffered no less from hunger than from thirst, and asked for some food.

"Have you any coin?" was the immediate question.

"Yes; but why?"

"Why? Because you can't have any prog till you tip us the blunt."

"I thought rations were provided by the prison authorities."

"Do prime tripe and ham pie look like rations provided by the prison authorities, as you're kind enough to call a pack of blessed old fools and knaves? No, my man this 'ere tripe and this 'ere pie have come from the Lock and Fetters over the way, and must be paid for in cash down."

"What does the prison provide in the way of food?"

"Not enough for you to live on. No one lives on prison rations unless they wants to escape hanging. So which will you have, young feller, tripe or pie?"

"I'll have some tripe. But I shall be ruined at this rate."

"Haven't you any pals to keep you?"

"I don't wish to be kept by my friends."

"Oh, we're a bit of a game-cock, are we? Never mind; starvation will soon lower our crest."

I did not answer, but fell to my helping of tripe, supplemented by a mug of very bad ale. For this meal I was obliged to pay just double the price I should have paid under ordinary circumstances, which made my heart sink, as I had only a few shillings left, and hated the thought of borrowing.

The sun rose higher and the room grew hotter. By noon the atmosphere was suffocating, and men lay stretched on the floor, panting like beasts. My lips were cracked with thirst, for the ale was finished. Outside in the street a girl was selling fruit, and every now and then her voice floated into the stifling room and mocked us—

pe cherries! I cr
ho'll buy, who'll

I opened my Bible, and tried to find comfort, but my head ached, and I felt deadly sick.

At last the evening came and the horrible sun left us for a bloody setting. Darkness fell and the stars glittered. Far away in the fields the dew was shining and the wind was rustling the grass. I thought of the beech-woods where I had so often spent the night, of the rabbits that used to waken me by scampering over my body, of the toadstools, orange, yellow, and speckled, that used to spring up round me while I slept. Perhaps I should never see the fields and woods again, perhaps I had enjoyed my last of singing birds, rustling grass, falling dew, and scampering conies.

117

I was seized with a desperate longing for the open air. I could have rushed at that stern iron door, shaken it, kicked it, beaten out my brains against it. Why, because a fellow-man is a murderer and a coward must I lose all that makes life sweet? I can endure this horrible captivity no longer; I must go back to the fields and the wind. Next time the jailer comes round I shall ask to see the governor; I shall show him Enchmarsh's confession; I shall demand Enchmarsh's arrest; I—get thee behind me, Satan! I am here for love's sake, and God is love, and God has said: "Whosoever shall lose his life for My sake shall keep it unto life eternal."

There were no beds in the ward, only a few rugs, and these were dirty and verminous. I shuddered at the thought of spending a night under one of them, but an icy wind sprang up, and seemed to pierce my very bones.

I was standing watching my miserable companions lie down and huddle together like cattle in winter, when some one touched my elbow. I looked round, and saw a young fellow of ragged yet genteel appearance, whom I had noticed very drunk that morning.

"Excuse me, but you seem to have no friends in this place. May I offer you a share of my rug?"

"Thank you kindly, but I must not put you to such discomfort."

"There will be no discomfort; on the contrary, I shall be all the warmer for an extra bedfellow."

"An *extra* bedfellow?"

"I have one mate already, but he's so dirty that I daren't lie closer to him than I can help. Do accept my offer. Rugs are scarce, and you can't sleep without one, for the nights are as cold as the days are stifling."

I was grateful for his kindness, and availed myself of it. We lay down under an exceedingly filthy rug, and soon were joined by a dirty foul-tongued wretch, who plagued us for an hour or more with stories of the various bedfellows he had had in Lewes Jail, which were neither amusing nor edifying. About eleven o'clock there was silence, and we all tried to sleep.

I hardly closed my eyes. All round me men snored and shivered, moaned and cursed. Every now and then a fellow would scream, and some of the younger ones sobbed in their sleep. In spite of the cold the atmosphere was stifling, and we lay so close that I could not stir without touching the flesh of other men. One of my bedfellows was, as I have already said, filthy in the extreme, and even the other was far from clean—I was not clean myself; it was impossible to be clean in such a place.

Oh, the indescribable wretchedness of that night! I panted and shivered at one and the same time; I longed and prayed for morning, though I knew it would bring only a change of evils. The lad at my side moaned, tossed, tumbled, and raved. Every now and then he would, to my surprise, murmur a sentence from the English Prayer Book: "That it may please Thee to have mercy on all prisoners and captives, and on all who are desolate and oppressed"-"We do earnestly repent, and are heartily sorry for those our misdoings. . . . Have mercy upon us, most merciful Father."—"Thou hast laid me in the lowest pit, in a place of darkness and in the deep. . . . Free among the dead, like unto those that are wounded and lie in the grave, who are out of remembrance." He talked louder and more frequently than anyone else, and occasionally a restless prisoner would wake him with a kick or a blow, and bid him hold his tongue and be damned.

Surely sleeplessness and suffering would eventually drive me mad! But God is very merciful, and just as my brain was reeling and my heart breaking under my burden of loneliness, pain, and longing, He sent sweet thoughts of my dead friend to cheer me. I realised how near he was to me, though death divided us, how he was now one of the cloud of witnesses who gazed on my struggle and helped me by their prayers. And when the white, trembling dawn showed up the prison bars, a strange, half-fearful peace crept into my soul and whispered, as the light grew stronger and stronger, and showed me plainer and plainer the dirt, degradation, and misery in the midst of which I lay: "Though ye have lien among the pots, yet shall ye be as the wings of a dove, which is covered with silver wings, and her feathers like gold."

So in spite of the horrors of that night, I rose in a fairly peaceful frame of mind. Most of my companions lay till a late hour, for to many the sleep which had been denied them in the darkness came with the dawn, and by the reddening light I saw them lying in the stillness of exhaustion, their sorrow-stamped faces showing how bitter were their dreams.

About eight o'clock the ward was too noisy for any more sleeping. The sleepers awoke, stretched, cursed, groaned, and staggered, half-blind with drowsiness, to where an early jug of ale was going from mouth to mouth. I would have none of it. My stock of shillings was very low, and as I was not hungry, I resolved to live that day on prison fare. This, which consisted of a small loaf and half a pint of water, was brought to me half an hour later, and I sat down to breakfast in a distant corner.

Here I was joined by my friend of the night. He brought a bowl of porridge, which he insisted on sharing with me. He evidently wished to make friends, and though at first I was inclined to be reserved I soon began to take an interest in him. He seemed to have had some education, and his language was clean.

"I hope I did not disturb you much last night," he said. "I fear that I rave terribly in my sleep."

"You talked a good deal especially about the Prayer Book."

He flushed scarlet, then said in a low voice:

"I was once a clergyman."

I was too much taken aback to reply.

"Yes," he continued, "for eighteen months I was Vicar of Rowfant."

"Why, that is in Sussex! I come from Sussex too!"

"I knew it—I knew it by your speech. You have the Sussex drawl."

"Which is not pretty."

"No. But it is like home. It was that which made me take kindly to you at once. You reminded me of the old days."

I did not care to ply indiscreet questions, so was silent, hoping that he would of his free will tell me more. I was not disappointed, for after a few minutes' silence he said:

"Yes, I was ordained very young, and appointed to a living in the gift of a friend of my father's, Harold Macaulay——"

"What! You know Macaulay?"

"Yes. Do you?"

"Too well."

"So do I—too well."

"You do not speak as if you loved him."

"I hate him—I had a little sister, and——"

"I understand. Have you heard that he has changed his name? He is now Squire Enchmarsh of Kitchenhour, in Sussex."

"I know it, and I shall give Sussex a wide birth, or I may one day find myself in jail for murder. But to go on with the story there's not much more of it. Soon after my appointment to Rowfant Vicarage, some terrible sorrows came upon me. I lost my sister—not through death—and my mother, whom I loved above all things, died of sickness brought on by grief. I was half crazed with misery, and I did not seek comfort in God—I sought it in wine. My parishioners found me drunk again and again, and at last I grew so ashamed that I sent in my resignation to the Bishop, and went to live where I could no longer offend Christ's flock by my evil example. I soon fell into want, and one day I faced starvation. I fought with the anguish for twenty-four hours, but my better nature was weakened by indulgence, and in the evening I stole a piece of bread."

"And you were caught?"

"Caught in the act, and I remember that when they arrested me I wept, not because I was a prisoner, and likely to suffer cruelly, but because they had taken the bread away."

"How long have you been in this place?"

"Nigh two years—a more lenient sentence than I expected. I have only five more weeks to go through. Oh, it has been worse than hell!"

"Poor fellow!"

"You must not pity me," he said simply; "I do not deserve it. You are here on a charge of murder, are you not?"

"Yes. What do you think of me?"

"I am very sorry for you. Nowadays the guilty often fare better than the innocent."

"Then you believe me innocent!"

"Certainly I do."

The words were quietly uttered, and were called forth by nothing more reliable than a few disjointed assertions I had made the preceding night, when we lay together. But it is wonderful how they cheered me. I wrung his hand, too deeply moved to speak, and could hardly have felt more triumphant had I been acquitted in full court.

The young parson and I sat together the whole morning and talked of Sussex, of fields, woods, streams, stars, and rain. He also gave me some information about jail life and my fellow-prisoners.

There were nearly fifty men in the ward. Most of them were thieves, pick-pockets, "shorters," and "smashers," the offscouring of the county. Their language was always foul, and they were always fuddled with drink. There was almost as large a percentage of brawlers, scraggers, and stabbers. These brought their crimes with them to jail, and when in liquor made the ward a very Bedlam with their violence. There was a third class, not nearly so numerous, consisting of men who had once been honest and respectable, but who, owing to poverty, drink, or some sudden temptation, had committed a felony.

The wardsman, or chief prisoner, was the fellow who had so minutely catechised me the day of my arrival. No words of my comrade's could describe this wretch's villainy; it was to be brought home to me during the terrible days which followed. Joe Timberlake had been in jail for some years, and it seemed as if his object were to sear away what faint marks of innocency yet remained on the hearts of his comrades. He exercised a horrible tyranny over the ward. The scoundrel had in his possession one of the jailer's whips, and with this I have seen him thrash a fellow till his clothes were in ribbons.

He could do practically what he chose. The jailer never interfered—in fact, he abetted him. Sometimes in the cold evenings Joe would light a fire for the cooking of tripe, herrings, and sausages, and last, but not least, for the heating of a poker, with which, when liquor moved him, he inflicted gruesome tortures on the more helpless of his comrades. If an ordinary prisoner had ventured to do this the jailer would have had him flogged almost to death, but because the tyrant was Timberlake, he never showed himself in the ward, in spite of the shrieks which proceeded from it on such occasions.

Once Joe, more drunk than usual, burnt out a victim's eye. The poor wretch made such an outcry that the governor heard it, and sent the jailer up to investigate. He looked in and saw the fellow rolling over and over on the ground, his hands covering his face; he shook his head at Timberlake, said that he would report him if he did it again, and went away.

Every other day we were turned out into the prison yard, that we might breathe a combination of smoke and smell called "fresh air," and indulge in a few occasional strides called "exercise." In the yard prisoners were allowed to interview their friends, who stood on the further side of an iron grating. Most of my fellow-captives had friends, chiefly of the softer sex, but my heart never beat with the hope of seeing a loved face, and I skulked by myself on the opposite side of the yard, watching enviously the interchange of greeting.

One day as I lounged thus, and had taken my Bible from my pocket for comfort, the young Sussex clergyman came up to me.

"There are some people wishing to see you."

"To see me!" My cheeks flushed and my eyes glowed, but I assured him that he must be mistaken.

"Indeed, I'm not. They were asking for you by name—for Mr. Humphrey Lyte."

"Who are they? Do you know?"

"A man and a girl."

I dashed off across the yard. I expected to see Ruth Shotover. But it was not the beloved face that smiled on me, though the smile was just as sweet. Behind the grating stood Mary Winde and her father. I held out both my hands, while my heart was too full for speech.

"God bless you, lad," said Peter huskily.

"God bless you, sir. This is too great a kindness."

"It was the promptings of our hearts. Directly we had Ruth Shotover's letter telling us of your trouble, Mary and I packed up our traps and came to Maidstone."

"How is it that you are so good to me? So you heard the news from Ruth Shotover. Do do you know where she is now?"

"She is in Maidstone."

My heart leaped and thumped, and my cheeks flushed scarlet with joy.

"How long has she been here?"

"She arrived yesterday with her brother and the Wychellows."

Then Mary leaned forward, and put her hand in mine.

"Humphrey, have you heard that Ruth is no longer engaged to Mr. Enchmarsh?"

"I—I—no one told me."

"Well, it is true, and I'm not surprised—in fact, it is a mystery to me how they ever came to be engaged at all. What should you say, Humphrey, if one day she paid you a visit?"

"Oh, Mary, tell me, did she ever hint that she might?"

"Hint! why, she has been on her knees to Sir Miles Wychellow, begging him to take her; she would have come here to-day if the doctor had allowed it."

"Has she been ill, then?"

"Yes, Humphrey, so ill that she could not leave Ihornden till yesterday, and even then she would not have left if Sir Miles had had his way. He wanted her to remain quietly in the country, but she said: 'I shall go to Maidstone, and I shall stay there till Humphrey Lyte is acquitted!'"

"Then she believes me innocent!" My voice shook with rapture.

"Yes, and so do I," said Mary.

"And so do I," said Peter.

"You are very kind."

"And credulous, some people would say. And let me tell you, lad, that it's only because I know you to be incapable of such a revolting crime that I believe in your innocence. The evidence is dead against you. Sir Miles swears to your guilt, though he thinks it's very likely only a case of manslaughter. By the bye, my lad, as you're a felon in the eye of the law, you won't be allowed the benefit of counsel. Have you considered what defence you shall make?"

I shook my head.

"That's a piece of sinful neglect. Your life is too precious to be thrown away. Hearken, lad—Mary and I had a long talk about you last night, and what do you think was the result of it?"

"Indeed, I cannot say."

"Why, we both vowed that you're keeping something back."

I set my teeth hard, then replied:

"Why should you think that?"

"Because you've behaved so strangely. You deny the murder, but you won't give us a plain tale of what happened, and when questioned you say silly things which you afterwards confess to be untrue. You were with John Palehouse the whole morning of the crime, and you must know who committed it even if you weren't an actual witness."

I was silent, and Peter continued:

123

"You're acting foolishly and wickedly. Your friends can't help you unless you give them the facts."

"I leave that to Curate Kitson."

"Then you're a fool!" exclaimed Peter.

"There is little doubt of that," I cried bitterly; "but, come, let us speak of happier things. Tell me about Shoyswell and all the dear places round it. Mary, are there many moon-daisies at Witherhurst, and many wild fowl on the marshes of Lossenham? Do you remember how we used to gather cowslips at Socknersh? Are they all faded now?"

She answered none of these questions, but once more took my grimy hand in hers, and said:

"Humphrey, Ruth is free, and you too must be free—for her sake."

"The jury, not I, will decide that."

She was about to reply but was cut short by the voice of the jailer ordering us away. So I wrung Peter's hand, and kissed Mary's, and left them, thanking God for two such friends.

I spent the next day in a state of feverish excitement, and when, the morning after, the hour of our "fresh air and exercise" drew near, I could scarcely contain myself. My bright eyes and flushed cheeks made my fellow-prisoners wonder and jeer.

Would Ruth come? Should I see her? I perplexed my heart with useless questions. I could scarcely eat for excitement. Oh, my darling, my darling! When I see you I shall forget all this misery and iron. I shall forget that I am in prison, and think I am in Paradise.

The ward door flew open with a clang, and out we filed. Down the passage we tramped, a regiment of rags and sorrow. A gust of wind blew in upon us as the yard gate was flung back, and we poured into the open space, stumbling and blinking in the unaccustomed light. I pushed my way through the crowd to the grating. I saw a little blue gown.

She stood in a throng of street-walking girls with bold eyes and loud laughter. Vagabonds, loafers, cadgers rubbed their tatters against her dress—the little blue dress in which I had first seen her. She gripped the bars and leaned against them while her eyes roamed from face to face. The next moment she caught sight of me, and her lips parted with a cry:

"Humphrey!"

"Ruth!"

It was all we said. I staggered against the bars, and covered her hands with mine. I did not kiss her—the grating was too close, and round us stood a crowd of leering, ogling, jibing scoundrels and courtesans.

"Dear," I said, after a long silence, "let us pretend that this is the garden-gate."

"The garden-gate——"

"Yes; I want to forget the prison and you are to forget it too. We are to talk of happy things, brightly, merrily, as if only the garden-gate divided us."

"I'll try, Humphrey, but I don't feel merry."

"Nor do I, Ruthie. Still, let's pretend."

"Have you heard?—about my freedom?"

"Yes; Mary told me."

"I can't understand it, I——"

She was interrupted by an exclamation from a figure standing at her side, who might have been made of wood for all the attention I had hitherto paid him, but whom I now saw to be Sir Miles Wychellow.

"Egad, young people! What the devil does all this mean?"

We both flushed crimson, and I realised that my thoughtlessness had placed us in an awkward and shameful position. Sir Miles knew that we had not met since the breaking off of Ruth's engagement, and would naturally infer that we had been carrying on a clandestine love affair while she was still betrothed to Enchmarsh. I made haste to put matters straight.

"You are certainly entitled to an explanation, Sir Miles. I—I have loved Miss Shotover for many months."

"While she was betrothed to another man."

"True, and I confess that I allowed my passion to overmaster me, and spoke words I had no right to utter. But this dear lady put me to shame with her steadfastness and purity, and even if John Palehouse had not been killed and I been arrested, I shouldn't have stayed another hour at Ihornden."

Sir Miles answered nothing, and I realised with a pang that his silence was due to a natural reluctance to tell a poor fellow who would soon be hanged that he was an insolent dog to have aspired to the affections of a lady like Ruth. True, I was of as good blood as she, but I was a tramp, a beggar, a felon, and it was as well that a noose should end my unlucky passion. Ruth must have guessed what was passing through my mind, for her eyes flashed, and she held my hand close in hers.

I broke the embarrassing silence.

"Where is Enchmarsh?"

"At Kitchenhour. Poor fellow! He's in a bad way. He was to have started for the Continent last Tuesday—to see some friends in Holland, I believe—but on his way from Ihornden to Sussex his horse fell on him and broke his leg, so he's now lying at his Manor in a devilish sorry state."

"And how is your brother, Ruthie?"

"He's much better, dear"—then she leaned forward and whispered: "He has been much better ever since my engagement was broken off."

"The Windes told me he was in Maidstone."

"Yes." Then I saw, rather than heard, her murmur: "Poor Guy!" There was on her face that look of motherly tenderness she always wore when speaking of her brother—and my heart burned with strengthened resolution.

"You look very poorly, dear boy," she added softly, stroking my dirty hand.

"I don't feel so," I replied, lying.

"You look a regular ragamuffin!" said Sir Miles bluntly. "Have you no opportunities for washing in jail?"

"Not unless I use my drinking water, which is too precious."

"Do you get enough to eat?"

I did not answer, for I could see the jailer unlocking the yard gates. Our moments of bliss were numbered.

"Oh, Humphrey!" cried Ruth, "it's hard to leave you in this dreadful place."

"Don't fret about me, child. You remember Lovelace's words: 'If I have freedom in my love, and in my soul am free——'"

"'Angels alone that soar above have not such liberty,'" she finished gravely.

"Come in with you, and no loitering!" shouted the jailer.

CHAPTER XVIII

OF THE METHODIST AND MUCH STORM AND TROUBLE

What astonished and touched me most during the days which followed was the kindness of my friends; not only of those who, in spite of appearances, believed me innocent, but of those who thought the worst of me. Sir Miles Wychellow lent me money—I was forced to subdue my pride and borrow, for I was starving—Lady Wychellow knitted me a jersey to wear during the terrible nights when I could not sleep for the cold, and Mary Winde brought me sweet oranges to slake my thirst during the terrible days when I could not rest for the heat. I no longer skulked alone while my fellow-prisoners greeted their friends; there was always a loved face at the grating.

I did not see Ruth as often as I wished, and I realised that it was only because I should almost certainly be hanged I was allowed to see her at all. Sir Miles would have done his best to part us, had he not believed that the hangman would soon perform that office for him.

Once Guy Shotover came to see me. I could not tell by his manner whether he thought me innocent or guilty, and with a tact wanting in many of my visitors, he forebore any direct reference to my plight. Ruth had told me that he had looked better since her engagement was broken off, but in my opinion he looked infinitely worse. His cheeks were redder and his eyes brighter, it is true, but it was the bloom and brilliancy of a decline. As I gazed at him, a voice within me cried: "What is the avail of laying down your life? This man will not live another year." But I silenced the coward in my heart. I did not know for a certainty that Shotover was dying; he might have years and years of life before him for aught I could tell. Besides, let disease slay him, not my tongue!

Poor fellow! I had forgiven him long ago, and my heart was warm with love's brother, compassion, as I looked into his miserable eyes and read their secret the secret—of a sin clamouring to be confessed for its own sake. Soon afterwards he went back to Ewehurst. He hated the town, and felt well enough to resume his clerical duties.

A few days later Peter Winde received a subpoena bidding him give evidence for the prosecution, who had heard that it was he who had given me my pistol, and wished him to identify it in court. There were—and could be—no witnesses for the defence, and though I occasionally considered what I might safely say on my own behalf, I knew that I should be practically in the position of an unarmed man attacked on all sides—and it was cruel to have Peter's hand among those uplifted to strike me down. Mary would not be in Maidstone for my trial. Her servant girl had fallen sick, and she was obliged to go back to Shoyswell. The day before she left she came to bid me good-bye.

"I shall be back as soon as possible, and I pray that when I next see you it will not be through iron bars."

"I pray the same, dear Mary."

"By the by, my lad," said Peter, "I've a piece of news for you—your family are in Maidstone!"

"My family!"

"Yes—your father and mother and Mr. Clonmel Lyte. They must have read of your arrest in the papers. Do you want to send them any message?"

"There would be no use in that."

"Don't you think that their coming to Maidstone is a sign that they've relented towards you?"

I shook my head. My arrest and trial would furnish my father with a good excuse for taking a holiday. "If they wished to have anything to do with me, they would have come to see me, or have sent me word. Where are they staying?"

"At the George. Mayn't I take them a message? They've served you badly, but they're your flesh and blood."

"Perhaps you are right, Mr. Winde. Pray give my father and mother my humble duty."

Peter promised, but no response was made.

My trial was to take place in a week, and many and varied were the speculations in the jail as to what the result would be. The general opinion was that I should be "scragged," and as it was delightful to see a young fellow turn pale and gnaw his lips, in spite of all his efforts to play the game-cock, my comrades regaled me with sickening stories of the gallows, which, owing either to the clumsiness of the machinery or to the hangman's want of skill, was often the scene of frightful agonies.

Sir Miles Wychellow paid me occasional visits, apparently for no other purpose than to wring facts from my unwilling lips. In this he believed he was acting for my good. "If you would only explain matters, instead of scowling and shaking your head," he cried one day when I had been more sullen than usual, "begad! the jury might bring in a verdict of manslaughter."

"Where would be my advantage? The penalty for manslaughter is the same as for murder."

"If you were found guilty of manslaughter, your friends could easily get you a reprieve; but if you're sentenced for murder—gad! it's all up with you! Several murders have been committed round here of late, and the courts are putting down the evil with a strong hand. So, young man, if once you're found guilty of murder, you're hanged!"

I brooded over these words for the rest of the day, and parted with my last hope.

That night I dreamed a horrible dream. I dreamed that I was dead, and that Enchmarsh had renewed his persecution of Ruth. I woke trembling, and gripping my companion's arm. I could not, dared not, sleep again. I sat up and thought, my chin resting on my hand.

It is strange, but till that night I had never considered the possibility of Enchmarsh returning to his blackguardism after my death. I now realised that it was not only a possibility—it was a practical certainty. What could I do? Enchmarsh held his tongue only for fear of mine, and when that tongue was silenced for ever—I shuddered. True, there was his confession safe in my pocket; but if that were found and read at my death, I had died in vain. The secret of Enchmarsh's crime must be kept; I must destroy the fatal paper on the morning of my execution. Then my enemy would no longer have anything to fear, and would once more make Ruth's life a burden and a curse. Whichever way I acted I seemed bound to thwart my own ends, to make my sacrifice of none effect.

I groaned aloud in my perplexity, so that half the ward woke up and swore at me. What was I to do? How was I to tie Enchmarsh's tongue after my own was dust? I prayed for guidance, and the thought came to me, "Confide your secret to a friend; pass it on to one you can trust, who, strengthened with it, will mount guard over Enchmarsh after you have laid down your arms."

But whom should I tell? Peter Winde? Sir Miles Wychellow? I should have no opportunity for telling them. Our meetings were in a crowd, and my secret would run the risk of being heard by half the prison. Besides, even if it were not so, I doubted if either of these men would consider themselves justified in keeping silence after my confession. They would probably insist on the arrest of the real culprit, would drag me from jail and publish abroad my sacrifice—making it useless.

Whom, then, could I confide in? The dawn came shuddering into the room, and showed me the faces of my companions—stern, degraded, peaceless. Then the lad at my side stirred and moaned, for the cruel light fell on his eyes, and roused him out of the sleep into which he had only just fallen after a long night of tossing.

What of him? He seemed attached to me; I had reason to think him faithful; he knew Enchmarsh, and hated him. Nevertheless, I shrank from telling him. But some one must be told, and whom could I tell if not this fellow? Peter Winde and Sir Miles were out of the question; so were all my friends except this poor criminal. Would my secret be safe with him? I thought so. He was in prison for theft, but his crime had been committed under the pressure of starvation; it was not the result of systematic dishonesty and untrustworthiness. Yet he was a drunkard, and though he fought with all the feeble strength of a weak will and a weak constitution against his curse, I had seen him drunk several times during the fortnight I had been in prison. Could I confide the most precious secret of my life to a drunkard, who might any day blab it forth in his cups? Yes, I could rely on him, for he was not as the common toper, who talks and grins and laughs, and opens his heart. Liquor made him sullen and fierce, drove him into some lonely corner, where he would lie with hidden face till at last he fell asleep, to wake ashamed and in his right mind. But would he be in a position to keep watch over Enchmarsh? There was no doubt of that. He had once told me that after his release he was to go to his brother, who lived at Woodchurch in South Kent, and had offered him a fresh start in life at his farm. Woodchurch was only a matter of fourteen miles from Kitchenhour.

I thought, and prayed over my thoughts, till heat and sunshine would no longer suffer my companions to sleep, and they struggled up, groaning, and cursing the light that woke them to fresh misery.

I awaited an opportunity for speaking alone with my friend. It was not long in coming. While the rest of the ward were trying to drown their newly-awakened cares in washy ale, he came to me where I sat in the furthest corner of the room, and offered me a share of some meat he had managed to buy. I declined it, but begged him to stay with me instead of going back to the swilling crowd, some of whom were already drunken.

"Only three weeks more," he said, "then I—but it's cruel of me to rejoice in this way when in three weeks you——"

"Will very likely be hanged. That's exactly what I want to speak to you about. Come close; I do not wish the rest of the ward to hear."

He drew closer, and I whispered:

"I have something to tell you, but first of all you must swear secrecy."

"I swear it," he said simply.

"Thank you. Perhaps you remember that when I first came here you told me you thought me innocent?"

"I did—and I do still."

"Well, I'm going to tell you who the real murderer was."

He started back from me.

"You—you don't mean to say you know?"

"I know."

"Then why in God's name are you here?"

"For reasons I shall soon tell you. Listen. I did not commit the murder, but I witnessed it. The real murderer is a man you know as well as I do."

"Who? Tell me——"

"Harold Enchmarsh."

The fellow's jaw dropped. He seized my arm, and stared at me.

"Yes. Enchmarsh was my friend's cousin, and had cruelly wronged him. High words passed between them, and Enchmarsh in a fit of fury dashed out his kinsman's brains."

"Then you are keeping silence to shield Enchmarsh?"

I laughed aloud.

"The devil, no! I would have dragged him before a magistrate that very hour, had he not threatened a deadly injury to some one I loved."

"What injury?"

"I cannot tell you. I am sworn to keep silence. Let it suffice that it would have ruined a life dearer to me than my own. I promised Enchmarsh his liberty if he would swear to refrain his malice, and to break off an engagement he had contracted with a girl who hated him, but who was going to marry him for reasons I again cannot give you."

"And he swore?"

"Yes, he swore, and I went off happy, in spite of my dear friend's death, for I knew that some one I loved even more passionately would be saved from much sorrow. An hour later I was a prisoner, accused of the crime Enchmarsh had committed."

"Could you not clear yourself?"

"Not without betraying Enchmarsh, which would have meant the anguish of this poor girl I loved. I tried to think of some other way; I soon found out there was no other way."

"So you suffered in silence?"

"I have been silent up to now, and have suffered, if you can call that suffering which is endured for love's sake. But last night the thought came to me or rather I chose to believe that God showed me in a dream—'When I am dead, Enchmarsh will no longer fear betrayal, and he will renew his persecution of this girl I love.' He will either force her once more into an engagement with him, or he will bring on her the sorrow to which I have already referred. Now, it is in this I want you to help me."

"I will do anything in my power."

"It is in your power, I am sure. I merely want you, when I am dead and you are free, to keep watch over Enchmarsh, and if he in any way molests this girl, or her brother, to drag him before a magistrate on a charge of murder."

"My dear fellow, I would willingly oblige you, but I fear that it would be useless for me to bring an accusation of murder against a man, having no proofs, no evidence——"

"But I have both. I have the fellow's full confession in my pocket."

"You have!"

"Yes. I made him write it out five minutes after the crime. So I have a hold on him, and when I am dead I do not wish that hold to be relinquished. I shall give you the paper, and trust that, if need be, you will use it."

"I shall, I swear! But who is this girl, and where does she live, that I may know if he molests her?"

"Her name is Ruth Shotover, and she and her brother live at Ewehurst in Sussex."

"Not far from where I shall be."

"No. But I expect they will leave it soon. It is too near Kitchenhour for their happiness. You must find out where they go, and take care that Enchmarsh does not visit them. If he should renew his engagement with the girl, or molest her or her brother in any way—well, you know what to do."

"And I'll do it."

"I think you have seen Miss Shotover. She has been here to visit me once or twice. She has red hair, and——"

"Ah, I remember her. She came with the magistrate fellow who is always persecuting you for 'facts.' She has a lovely face. I dreamed of her for two nights afterwards. Her brother once came to see you, too, didn't he?"

"Yes; and I'm glad you have seen both the Shotovers, as you will be better able to watch over them. Now I shall show you the confession. But I shall not give it to you till—till we part."

He pressed my hand silently, and I drew the paper out of my pocket.

"Here, read it. You see what power I have."

He read it, knitting his brows.

"How dearly you must love your Ruth to keep silence with this in your possession. If I had loved a girl so dearly I might have been a better man."

"You will leave the old life behind you in this jail," I said, deeply touched; "you will go forward to nobler things."

"I trust so—I pray so. Dick has promised to give me a fresh start. He was always a faithful brother to me. By the by, we must let Enchmarsh know you have told me this. I had better go to him directly I am released."

"Yes but, quick! Give me the paper! The fellows are staring at us."

They did more than stare; they rushed in a body towards us before I had well thrust back the confession into my pocket.

"Hello, Ranter! What've you got there?" cried Timberlake.

"Nothing," I answered, trying to look unconcerned.

"That's a damn lie! I saw you hide a paper somewhere about you. Let's have a look at it."

"I tell you I've nothing!" I cried desperately.

"We'll soon see that. I bet you a hundred to one he's hiding a love-letter. We've left you alone too long, my fine feller. We're going to hear something about that mort o' yours, and see her letters."

"I haven't got a letter."

"Let's see—hold him, lads."

Two fellows seized my arms. The young clergyman interposed. "Here, hands off! Fair play! What if he has got a letter, you've no right to see it."

"Might is right!" shouted Timberlake. "Hold fast, lads!"

He would have thrust his hand into my pocket, while I raged and ground my teeth like an impotent beast; but my friend rushed at him and tore him away. There was a frantic scuffle, and the next minute the poor lad was lying unconscious, his arm broken.

Timberlake sneered.

"Now for our perfect lover," and his hand was in my pocket.

A mist swam before me, and through it I dimly saw the villain draw out the paper and unfold it. I gathered myself together, and the next moment the fellows who held me were rolling on the floor, and I was at Timber-lake's throat.

He staggered, but recovered himself, and we swayed together. I tried to snatch the paper out of his hand, but he was taller than I, and held it aloft, just out of my reach. We struggled frantically, desperation giving me a strength I had never hitherto possessed. I managed to grip his great bare arm, and would have dragged it down, but at that moment we reeled against the window. Timberlake flung himself free.

"If I can't have it, you shan't," and the next moment the precious fragment that I held dearer than my life was whirling in the summer wind, fluttering, dancing, and sinking slowly into the yard.

Then I verily believe that I lost my reason. With a cry of fury and despair I flung myself on Timberlake, and struggled like a beast to kill him. I wanted his life. I was mad.

The rest of the ward, who, though the supporters of the wardsman against his victims, did not love him too dearly to enjoy seeing him paid in his own coin, offered no interference, but stood watching us as we tottered up and down the room. I clutched at his throat, but he tore my fingers away, breaking one of them. I tried to break his back, but he dragged my head down against his shoulder, and pulled out handfuls of my hair. Our clothes were soon in tatters, and our breasts and shoulders uncovered. He was getting the worst of it. I should soon kill him. He shouted, cursed, and screamed. I was silent; I only panted.

I tried to drag him against the wall and dash out his brains, but he bit and tore my encircling arms, and we staggered across the room, mauling one another like two furious dogs. Near the middle of the ward lay my poor friend; we stumbled over his body, and down we crashed. Who would rise first?

For an instant we both lay stunned. Then I sprang to my feet, and the next moment would have murdered him, had not the door burst open and the jailer appeared. I stood petrified, then suddenly came to my senses. Timberlake rolled on the floor in agony. His thigh was broken.

"How now, you beasts!" shrieked the jailer. "What hellish pranks are you up to?"

My fellow-prisoners evidently thought it more to their advantage to take Timberlake's part than mine. "The Methodist's been mauling Joe!" they shouted with one accord.

"Oh, it's you, is it, you fighting devil?" and he gave me a blow in the face that nearly broke my jaw. "I'll teach you to go murdering your wardsman"—another blow, and I measured my length on the ground.

"Here, you fellers, keep him down while I run for help. You young beast! I'll have the skin flayed off your shoulders for this. Keep him down, I say—sit on him, stifle him, throttle him—anything you please, only keep him down."

My companions obeyed, nothing loth, and I was half dead by the time the jailer returned with two subwarders and a surgeon for Timberlake, who had not ceased to roll and scream.

All my fury was gone, and when I was at last pulled to my feet, I stood shamed and mute, while fetters were fastened on my wrists and ankles. Then I was half-dragged, half-carried to the governor's office.

The governor listened to the jailer's indictment, and asked me if I had anything to say for myself.

As I could only shake my head, he ordered me a flogging and three days' imprisonment in a dark cell. No doubt I deserved both.

"Thank God that Ruth cannot see me now!" I thought, as they hurried me down the passage. "Would she recognise this dishevelled, blood-stained, half-naked wretch as her lover?" The thought of Ruth was poignant as death, for once more in front of her stretched the old misery, and I was powerless to save her from it. That scrap of paper which had meant her peace and mine was gone—lost for ever, whirled by the summer wind out of sight or ken. My anguish of mind was too much for my pain-enfeebled body, and I groaned.

The men thought it was horror at my punishment which caused my misery, and one of them, who was a humane fellow, tried to cheer me by saying that the lashing would soon be over, and perhaps not so terrible as I imagined; and as for the dark cell, prisoners that had the cat were only too glad of a little peace and quiet afterwards.

"It's as well 'is mother can't see 'im."

The words seemed to come to me from a great way off, as I was carried back along the passage. I was conscious of little—only that I was being carried, that one man bore my head and another my legs, and that one of my arms was hanging so that my hand dragged along the floor.

We came to a door, and a jailer opened it. Surely that was a black curtain which I saw stretched across the entrance. No, for they pushed me into it. The door shut with a hideous rattle of iron, and the blackness wrapped round me. I tried to push it away, for it pressed upon my eyeballs. Then I sank to the ground, covering my face.

Consciousness slipped away, and I entered a hell of dreams. I was at Brede Parsonage, working in the oast-barn. Clonmel had just been flogging me, and I was thinking how I could kill him. I saw him standing at the corner of the great pasture-field, and stole after him, leaving blood-marks on the grass where my feet had pressed. But when he turned round to grapple me, I saw the face of Harold Enchmarsh, and he shivered like a ghost from my sight.

Then I was in a high, cloudy place, where a great wind was shrieking, and in front of my eyes, dancing, fluttering, whirling in the wind, was a tiny scrap of paper. I struggled to catch it, but it eluded my grasp, and suddenly I fell from the windy place, and consciousness came back with a gasp of agony.

I knew where I was; I remembered what had happened, and in vain I prayed God to kill both knowledge and remembrance. I had been tied up and lashed like a dog because I had behaved like a dog. My shirt was saturated with something that was warm as well as wet. I shuddered. Then suddenly I threw up my arms with a cry of anguish, for I remembered that I was suffering in vain. When I was dead Ruth would be in even a worse plight than if at the beginning I had refused to sacrifice myself, and had sent her brother to the gibbet. I had no hope of living; I could not

134

clear myself without the paper, which had no doubt by this time been trodden an inch deep into the mud. I must die, and Ruth must live on in misery deeper than that from which I had struggled in prayers and anguish to save her.

Oh, that I had allowed Timberlake to read the fatal confession! then at least I should have been free and able to help her—at least, I should not have been in this foul hole, suffocating as a coffin, damp as a grave, and black as hell. How long had I been there? I considered. It seemed an eternity, but I thought that very likely my imprisonment had not lasted more than twelve hours. How should I endure three days of it? I had heard of men leaving the dark cell as shrieking lunatics. The horror of madness made me tremble. I must do something to distract my thoughts—to make me forget the darkness, the airlessness, the damp, the smell, the living things that crawled over my limbs, the pains of my torn body. I tried to repeat a psalm, but my mind was incapable of any sustained effort, and agonising thoughts broke in upon the grand old words of comfort: "The Lord is my shepherd. . . . The Lord is my shepherd. . ." I murmured wildly, staring with strained eyeballs into the dark— "therefore can I lack nothing . . . lack nothing. . . ." I gave up the attempt, for the rest of the psalm had fled from my mind, leaving it a wilderness of terror. I was filled with a vague, horrible fear, which I had often felt at Brede Parsonage, which had often driven me to leave my bed and entreat one of my brothers to take me into his, that the contact of a warm human body might soothe away the nameless horror that gripped me. I was now alone, ill, broken in mind and body. I cowered down in a corner of my prison, my hands clasped against my breast, my eyes staring wildly into the dark. Oh, that dreadful dark! It seemed to enwrap my very soul; it seemed a loathsome material thing; it seemed to crush me. I felt blood trickling down my chin. What had happened? And I remembered. I had bitten my lips to keep down my cries while I was being flogged, and they still bled. I longed to lose consciousness once more, for no phantasmagoria could be worse than the awful reality, and at last I fell into a kind of waking dream. I thought that I was walking with John Palehouse along the Biddenden road. The wind was moaning, the clouds were low. Then suddenly I lifted my eyes to his face, and saw on his temple a little grey bruise. I shrieked and awoke. "John, John!" I cried, till the blackness echoed. "I want you—I want you—come to me—how shall I bear this torture without you?— Come to me.——" Then God sent a merciful blank.

I was roused by a sudden stream of light. I thought it was flames, and covered my face.

"'Ere, take this." The warder kicked me, and thrust a bowl of nauseous-looking gruel into my hands. I tried to speak to him, but my parched lips refused to utter, and it was not till he had all but shut the door that I managed to gasp:

"How long have I been in this place?"

"Maybe three hours," he said, and banged the door.

I fell back with a moan. Three hours! I had thought it twelve, hoped it might be eighteen. I sobbed aloud in anguish. I could not eat my supper. The smell of it alone made me feel sick. I was terribly thirsty. Oh, that they would give me a drink of water! I beat on the door and cried to the jailer, but no one heard.

I resolved to try to sleep, but my shoulders were so lacerated that I could not lie on my back or side, so I stretched myself on my face and prayed God to let me sleep or better still—die.

I did neither.

At last morning came, and when the jailer brought me a fresh relay of gruel, I caught the skirt of his coat—for I could not lift myself from the ground—and prayed him to bring me some water for Christ's sake. He muttered something about "being aginst orders," but the light falling on my face showed him my black, cracked lips, and he had compassion on me. He fetched me a jug of fairly clean water, and left it with me in my cell.

The rest of the day I spent chiefly in dozing, dreaming, or raving. I slept all that night, but an attempt to eat my gruel resulted in a dreadful attack of sickness, which left me so weak that I could hardly move or breathe.

Nevertheless, my mind was more calm and unclouded, and I began to rack my brains for some way of maintaining my hold on Enchmarsh, even though his confession was lost. It did not take me long to realise that this would be impossible. The confession was the only weapon which I could rely on, and without it I was powerless. There seemed no way out of my misery. Ruth's heart and mine must be broken on the same wheel. I ground my teeth and moaned. True, Enchmarsh had no idea that I had lost the paper; he would make no attempt to molest the poor child during my lifetime, but after my death——Oh, it was too horrible to contemplate. I had suffered in vain, sacrificed my good name, offered up my life—in vain. Oh, that I could only live! Let Guy Shotover perish a thousand times rather than that my poor dear should be persecuted, tortured, and shamed by the man from whom I had thought to have saved her for ever. Should I tell my story to the governor, and denounce Enchmarsh, trusting that I should be able without the paper to prove my assertions? Vain thought! I could never do that. Such an action would merely blacken me as a coward, who tried to save himself at the last moment by shifting the burden of his guilt on to another man. If I was to die, at least I should die courageously. Men should say: "He was a blackguard, but he died well."

At last the third day came, and the blessed light streamed in upon me, no more to be shut away till my eyes filmed and closed for ever. I could scarcely stagger up from the floor, and I could not see the jailer's face, so dazzling was the unaccustomed brightness. He dragged me back to the ward, unlocked the door, and pushed me in. I still wore my chains, for I was considered a dangerous prisoner, and no longer allowed to go unfettered.

I expected my former comrades to insult, perhaps to ill-treat me, but they took no notice beyond to nudge one another and leer, as with a jingle of chains I sank down against the wall, too weak to do more than breathe.

I was still unaccustomed to the light—in fact, it was a few days ere I could see as before—and lay with my eyes shut. I did not hear a soft footfall approach me, and started when a hand touched my shoulder.

I looked up, and saw my friend, the young clergyman, his arm in a sling. He sat down beside me, and without a word slipped something into my hand. My fingers closed round it mechanically, and I wondered halfstupidly what it could be.

"It's your paper," said my friend gently, seeing how dazed I was.

"Enchmarsh's confession!" I cried incredulously.

"Yes. I found it in the yard when we were turned out there the other day. It had drifted on to a pile of rubbish."

My joy was so great and my body so weak that I nearly swooned. For a few moments I could not speak, but could only lie clasping the precious paper to my heart.

"You'd better stow it away," said my friend; and as I was too weak and dazed to do anything for myself, he unclasped my hot hand, took the paper, and thrust it into my pocket.

"I am loth to trouble you when you are so ill," he continued, "but I think it right that you should know that the paper is practically illegible."

"What has happened?" I asked faintly, only half understanding him.

"It has been rained upon, and has been sadly torn. It is decipherable now, but a month hence it will be of no use to us whatever."

"What can I do?"

"Ask Enchmarsh to send you another, written fairly in ink. He will not dare refuse you."

"But how can I communicate with him? I thought——"

"It is generally impossible to send secret letters from jail, I confess. But we are unusually fortunate. One of the fellows here is to be released to-morrow, and will smuggle to Kitchenhour whatever you choose to write."

"Can he be trusted?"

"Implicitly. I've employed him before this, and he has never failed me."

"But I have no paper."

"Josh Parkins has some, and will sell you a sheet for half a crown."

"I've no money."

"Yes, you have. I saw the magistrate fellow in the yard yesterday. I told him what trouble you were in, and he gave me a quid for you when you should come out. It was very good of him to trust me."

"Did did you see Ruth?"

"The girl you love, for whose sake you have suffered so terribly?"

"Yes—I love her—did you see her?"

He nodded, and pressed my hand.

"Did you tell her?"

"Yes."

"That I tried to kill Timberlake?"

"I never knew you tried to kill Timberlake."

"I did. I wanted to break his back. Where is he? Is he here?"

"No. He's been removed to the infirmary."

"Thank God! Then—then didn't Ruth know I tried to kill Timberlake?"

"No; I told her what I knew myself, and, of course, not all of that."

"She ought to know—she ought to know the worst of me."

"Don't bother your poor head about that. You'll see her yourself soon."

"Did she cry? Was she unhappy when you told her I'd been flogged?"

"I did not mention the flogging."

"Thank you."

"I told her you had been put in solitary confinement for three days. I thought it best to say nothing about the dark cell. But, come now, poor lad, try and rest a bit. Lean against me."

"Did Ruth send me a message?"

"She sent you her love."

"Did she wear a blue gown?" I continued, hardly knowing what I said.

"Yes—and she was so lovely! But you mustn't speak any more; your poor brain's all confused."

He lifted me, and let my flayed shoulders rest against him instead of the wall. I closed my eyes.

"What about Enchmarsh's letter?" I asked suddenly.

"We needn't trouble about that till the evening. Go to sleep now."

God bless the good fellow! For the rest of that day he held me up against him, soothed me when I was delirious, covered me with his own coat when I was cold, and gave me to drink when I was consumed with fever and thirst. During the afternoon I slept a little, and woke refreshed, both in mind and body. I was still very weak, but felt myself able to grapple with my letter to Enchmarsh, the writing of which must not be delayed any longer.

My friend bought a sheet of Josh Parkins's paper. Parkins had been doing a roaring trade that day, for his fellow-prisoners, discovering that paper was to be had, were consumed with a desire to write love-letters. Seeing his goods in such demand, he became autocratic, and raised his prices. My sheet—a very dirty crumpled specimen—cost me exactly three shillings, and I believe that the last piece went for a crown.

My friend had picked up a piece of stick, which would serve as a pen, but we had no ink. So we used the only available substitute, of which, thanks to the tortures I had lately undergone, there was no lack, and when the ghastly crimson scrawl was finished my friend went in search of our confederate.

He was a tall, wiry, sly-looking man, and did not prepossess me in the least. But my friend insisted on his trustworthiness, and I asked him how much he would charge for taking a letter with all possible speed to Kitchenhour in Sussex.

He scratched his head, leered, and named an exorbitant price, quite impossible for me to pay. I told him that he must ask less, and after a great deal of wrangling he consented to serve me for half the money I possessed, the other half to be made over to him on his return with an answer to my letter. This would mean living on prison diet for a week or more, but my appetite was gone, so I did not fear the ordeal, under which many men had died.

"And 'ow shall oi get to Kitchenhour, mister? Oi've been in Ew'ust village, and can find my way to't well enough from 'ere. But where's Kitchen'am—Kitchenhour—or wotever yer calls it?"

"You leave the high-road just after you come to Mockbeggar," I cried excitedly; "there's a clump of larches on the left-hand side of the way, and a mavis sings there. You go on till you come to a stretch of down all golden with furze, and you can see the Rother in the valley, and the marshes, and the dykes, and—and——"

My voice trailed off in a sob of anguished longing, and I fell back, hiding my face.

My friend tried to comfort me. "There, there! Perhaps you'll see it all for yourself soon. But, come, tell Pearson where he's to go when he leaves the down."

"You can see Kitchenhour from the down," I said brokenly; "it's the stone house on the edge of Wet Level. You can't mistake it—and listen," I added, as he was about to take himself off, "you're to give that letter into the Squire's own hand. No doubt he'll be in bed; he's broken his leg. But never mind, insist on seeing him. And make all the haste you can, and bring the answer to the yard grating, and—and remember, it's a matter of deathly secrecy."

The fellow nodded and slouched away.

The next morning the prison gates opened to him, and he went out into the sun and wind. My heart went with him, and all day long, while my body lay agonised in the stifling heat, my heart was in the fields, among the flowers, and the sobbing notes of stock-doves.

CHAPTER XIX

OF THE METHODIST AND THE STRETCHED-OUT ARM OF THE LORD

The day of my trial was wet and windy. I drove through the streets in a closed hackney, with the blinds down. Fortunately I had a sound constitution, and was almost recovered from my weakness and fever, though I was still far from well. I had never been in a Court of Justice before, and the strangeness of the situation, together with the stare of a thousand eyes, threw me completely out of countenance. I entered the dock pale and trembling, catching my breath, and clutching my throat as if I already felt a rope there.

My trial had evidently created much interest, for the court was thronged. Here and there among the press I saw the severe black garb and stern ascetic face of some minister of Bethel or Salem come to watch the fate of a fellow-Methodist. Women were there, attracted, no doubt, by my romantic story, of which, it appears, several new and enlarged editions were being circulated in Maidstone. I saw many parsons of the Established Church, among them Curate Kitson and the Rector of All Saints', Hastings. Some faces were hostile, some were friendly, some mocking, some curious, all interested.

Not far off were my father, my mother, and Clonmel. It seemed impossible that barely five months had elapsed since I left Brede Parsonage, but I could see how that short time of stress and trouble had altered me by the looks of my family as they stared at my white scarred face.

I saw Peter Winde among the crowd, with Sir Miles and Lady Wychellow. But my eyes did not rest on them; they wandered anxiously, till at last they fell on Ruth. She was pale, but her lips were very red, and her eyes bright as December stars. She did not smile or wave her hand, but her eyes, with her love sitting in them, looked into mine, and our hearts met.

She was so sweet and childlike in her wide hat and muslin gown. I noticed that many girls and women cast envious glances at her as she sat, a dainty bunch of green, beside Lady Wychellow. Surely they would have laughed loud in mockery and disbelief had they been told that she loved and was loved by the felon in the dock, whose coarse blue shirt was so ragged that one saw his skin through the rents, whose hair was all matted over his eyes, and whose fierce black brows were bent in a perpetual frown.

The judge was a massively-built, unctuous-looking fellow, with large white hands, and a multitude of rings. Though slow of speech and movement, he was evidently sound of thought, for his remarks showed penetration and a firm grasp of the case. The prosecuting counsel was a man of refined presence and graceful manner. He had a wonderfully mellow voice, and I liked the straightforward glance of his eyes.

From the first I saw that everything was hopeless. As I listened to counsel's opening speech I realised that had I been an unprejudiced spectator I should have at once set down the prisoner at the bar as guilty; the case was so clearly made out against me. Not one damning circumstance was forgotten—the corpse, the pistol, my flight, my lies, my confession that John Palehouse and I had been alone the whole morning; all these facts were laid calmly, concisely before the court. Counsel dwelt on my guilty looks, on my alternate refuges in lies and silence; he pointed out how I had started, coloured, and nearly swooned at the sight of the pistol, and though continuing to deny my guilt, had been unable to account for my weapon or prove my innocence. In all this he was strictly fair; there was no exaggeration, no misrepresentation. But the calm words were deadly, and when at length he sat down, I saw by the faces round me that my life was not considered worth a farthing's purchase.

The evidence of Curate Kitson and of Pitcher and Green was then heard, and though I had a right to cross-examine the witnesses I did not avail myself of it. Where would be the use? I could prove nothing. After Mr. Green had finished stammering and stirring up the devil in counsel, Peter Winde was called to identify my pistol as his gift. Poor fellow, how his voice trembled! Then the Cranbrook doctor entered the witness-box, and a long discussion followed as to the cause of the bruise on the deceased's forehead. Counsel asked if the prisoner's story of the fall into Plurenden Quarry was possible, considering the nature of the injuries, and the surgeon replied that there were on the body no traces whatever of a fall—the neck was not broken, there were no fractures elsewhere, and no bruises except that on the temple. Again I was asked if I wished to cross-examine the witness, and again I shook my head. Then, as it was nearly five o'clock, the court adjourned, and I was led from the dock. The next day Sir Miles Wychellow was to give evidence; I should make a pitiful effort at my own defence, should see the judge put on the black cap, hear the sentence read. Then—I put up my hands to my throat and shuddered.

The wind was still high, but the rain-clouds had rolled away, and the sky was blue, and bright with the golden glow of afternoon. The people thronged me as I stood waiting for the hackney which was to take me back to jail, and suddenly Clonmel came elbowing his way through the crowd, followed by my father, with my mother on his arm.

"Parson Lyte's coach for the George!" yelled my brother. Then his eyes met mine, and he grinned.

My father stood close by me, but with averted face. My mother's sleeve brushed my arm. She also was looking the other way, but every now and then I saw her neck twitch with the longing she had to turn it. Something snapped in my breast.

"Mother!" I said jerkily and hoarsely.

She turned.

"H—Humphrey—how your face is scarred!"

That was all. Her coach rolled up, and my father helped her into it. Then he and Clonmel jumped in beside her and shut the door. They rattled off over the cobbles, and I was soon on my way back to jail.

During the coal-dark August night, while men slept and shivered round me, I lay awake preparing myself for death. I knew that the time of grace allowed me after the sentence was passed would be all too short, and I should not even have the consolation of being put in a separate cell. The condemned cells were full of the overflowings of the infirmary, of men whom disease, not Mr. Justice, had sentenced. I should have to make what preparation I could among the drunkenness, the lewdness and the violence of the felon's ward.

So I prayed God to help me to forgive the men who had shamed my body and trodden down my soul, and to forgive me, who needed forgiveness more than they all. Then my mind wandered—ever since my punishment in the dark cell I had had delirium at nights—and I thought that I was lying in a great field, bathed in misty starlight, that my suffering and degradation had been a dream. But I woke from this blessed state of semiconsciousness, and realised that I lay with other wretches in a foul hole where most men would not suffer their cattle to sleep.

I thought of the prisoner who had a few days ago gone out into the fresh air and sun and rain. I wondered where he was. He had no doubt delivered my letter, and was hastening back with the reply. Perhaps he was at this very moment walking through the dark mysterious lanes, his nostrils sweet with the smell of the country at night, of sleeping earth and dew-wet grass, his ears thrilling with mysterious night sounds—the flutter of birds suddenly awakened, the howl of a little breeze imprisoned in a cave of bramble and crack-willow, the splash of hidden water falling, the rustle of bracken under a rabbit's feet. Or perhaps he lay asleep in a sheltered field, where the mushrooms spread their tents, and where the thrushes would wake him at the fading of the stars.

Towards morning I slept, and dreamed a dream which I am sure was not born of memory. For I dreamed that I was a little child again, and that I sat on my mother's knee, while she combed my hair in the firelight. I woke as a neighbouring clock struck four, and knew, as I saw the ghastly yellow splash the pale sky outside the grating, that the day of fate had broken.

I could eat no breakfast. I felt sick and faint, and my hands shook. It was strange that I should recoil at the touch of death, I who had so often prayed for it. How I

142

should have rejoiced as a boy at Brede Parsonage if God had said, "This night thy soul shall be required of thee!" All was changed now; life was no longer a drink of deadly wine. Besides, there is a difference between dying quietly in one's bed, when the body is so sick and tired that it would fain be dissolved, and having one's life choked out of one by hemp and a fellow-creature's hands, when the body is sound and warm and full of vigour.

But I forced myself to be calm. I would not meet death like a coward, when the wretched dregs of human kind faced him with a song and a snap of their fingers, joked with the hangman, and laughed in their throes. I walked quietly out of the jail between two warders, and took my seat in the hackney without blanching. The fellows well knew what was passing in my mind; they were familiar with pitiful efforts at self-control, which too often broke down ignominiously.

"There's an infernal jamb in the streets," said one to the other.

"What's up?"

"Can't say. Looks as if it had something to do with———" and he leered at me.

The streets were certainly very crowded; all round me rose and fell the hum of people's voices. Had they come to hear me sentenced? To see whether I blanched or trembled, threw up my arms, or called on God? The nearer we drew to the assize courts the louder swelled the noise, and as we entered the High Street there was a sudden burst of cheering. I stared in amazement from one to the other of my guards. The cheering redoubled, and I made a dash at the blind to pull it aside but was promptly seized and flung back into my seat.

When we came to the court we found a dense crowd assembled, who thronged us as we alighted.

"Three cheers for the Methodee! Good luck to yer, me lad. May the judge rot if you're scragged!"

I was about to question the warders, who hustled me into the building, but before I could speak the door of an ante-room opened, and Sir Miles dashed out.

"Humphrey, was it you who arranged all this?"

"I? Arranged what?"

"Egad! This *coup de théâtre*. Haven't you heard anything about it?"

"No. One doesn't hear news in prison."

"It's all over the town. Wait a moment, warders; I must have a word with the prisoner. Miss Mary Winde has come up from Sussex with the Ewehurst constable, and Parson Taylor of Northiam, and—gad! Humphrey, you don't mean to say you know nothing of this?"

"Nothing—absolutely nothing, I swear it! For God's sake, tell me more!"

"Well, Miss Mary has brought Shotover with her."

"Shotover!"

"Yes. Little Ruthie's brother—with gyves too! The very devil's in it. And hark ye here, young man, a letter has been found, and Enchmarsh of Kitchenhour has been arrested, and—he has killed himself. Here, jailer, quick! Some water!"

I had staggered back against him, and would have fallen had he not caught me in his arms. They made me swallow some water, and I recovered sufficiently to be able to stand and speak.

"Tell me about Enchmarsh—and Shotover—where is he?"

"In the doctor's hands, spitting blood and dying fast."

"Dying! Good God!"

"It's the best thing he can do for himself, poor wretch. He has been arrested for murder on his own confession. Young man"—laying his hand on my arm—"is it true that you have been shielding him?"

I stared at him blankly, hardly realising what he said.

"Is it true?" he repeated almost fiercely.

"Take me into court," I cried, turning to the warders; and much to my relief they led me away.

"Sir Miles wants me to give him facts; it's always 'facts,'" I informed them, not knowing what I said.

On my appearance in dock there was a slight burst of cheering, which was subdued by angry cries of "Silence!" I scarcely noticed it. In fact, I noticed nothing but two faces—Mary Winde's and Ruth's. Mary's cheeks were flushed with tears; Ruth sat with her head against Lady Wychellow's shoulder; her face was tear-stained, but her eyes were dry.

It was all like a dream. I listened with closed eyes and throbbing temples while counsel rose and addressed the court.

"My lord," he said, "I have to address your lordship to-day under most unusual circumstances. Since I opened the case on behalf of the Crown yesterday, I have become acquainted with certain facts which I consider myself bound to examine closely. The reason for my bringing them to your lordship's notice at this stage of the trial is that if your lordship is satisfied, as I must say I am, that they point to the prisoner's innocence, it will be desirable to sift them thoroughly, and possibly to ask the jury to say that Lyte is not guilty."

There was a murmur in the court, but the ushers silenced it, and when quiet was once more established counsel continued rapidly:

"I will hand your lordship a letter which was found in the possession of a man who appears to have been entrusted with it by the prisoner, and I can prove by the evidence of the person who found it that it is in the prisoner's handwriting."

The judge, who had listened attentively, interrupted for the first time.

"What, then?" he said abruptly. "How can the prisoner's letter be evidence in his favour?"

"It is the prosecution which produces it, my lord," said counsel blandly, "and if your lordship will allow me to read it, it will be found to contain references to another document which your lordship will perhaps assist us to obtain in the interest of justice."

Then a filthy scrap of paper, grimy, damp, and scrawled over with blood, was passed up to the judge, who held it between his finger-tips, glanced at it and laid it on the desk before him. There was no need for me to look at it more closely, I knew it only too well. I trembled from head to foot; a mad, desperate, animal joy contended in my heart with a sorrow and a compassion which I thank God were real enough. I was cleared; my name was clean; my body would soon be free. Yet, on the other hand, Shotover was arrested, and Ruth was swallowing the dregs of humiliation and grief. But not through me. There lay the whole point of the matter. It was not I who had spoken; it was God. That I should save my life by sending Ruth's brother to the gallows was horrible, loathsome, too dreadful to think of, but that God should deliver me without any act or word of mine, with His mighty hand and His stretched-out arm, was a matter for awe, bowed head, and thankful heart.

The judge had evidently read some of my note, for he was eyeing me inquisitively and, as I thought, interrogatively. At any rate, I ventured to speak, and said in a low voice:

"I wrote that letter."

"Perhaps, my lord," said counsel quickly, "that admission will suffice for the present, if I may read a copy of the letter which I have here. I can bring forward more formal proof at a later stage."

The judge acquiesced, and counsel read:

To Harold Enchmarsh, Esq., Kitchenhour, Sussex.

"The confession you wrote for me in Plurenden Quarry is by this time very torn and faded. It is still legible, and I can still hang you with it, but I wish you to write me out another, fairly, in ink, for I have revealed our secret to a third party, with a view to protecting the Shotovers from your blackguardism after I am dead. The fellow is to be trusted. You know him. His name is Gerald Frome, and he was once Vicar of Rowfant. If you refuse to do as I wish I shall immediately throw up the whole concern, so send me the confession at once by the bearer of this. I shall give it to Frome, and if you ever renew your engagement with Miss Shotover, or bring about her brother's arrest or death, he will see you hanged for the murder of John Palehouse.

"HUMPHREY LYTE."

There was nothing for me to say. Counsel, judge, and jury seemed to be pursuing their own course without reference to me. The first-named had evidently made careful plans as to the procedure he should follow. He continued his speech, and I soon became aware that if not speaking to me, he was speaking at me, and expected my intervention.

145

"I am not going to say just yet how the letter came into our hands; I shall leave that to my witness, Mary Winde. There is, however, one link in the chain apparently missing, and I think, my lord, that the prisoner alone can supply it. The letter refers to a document alleged to incriminate Enchmarsh directly. If that exists the prisoner can produce it or can give us some clue as to where it is. If necessary we can have him searched again, an operation which has perhaps not been performed as carefully as it might."

I went from red to pale. I had grown so accustomed to the zealous guarding of my secret that I could not even now pluck forth my deliverance.

"Unless the prisoner can show the court this confession," pursued counsel, in the tone of one giving disinterested advice on a comparatively unimportant matter, "the authenticity of the letter may be doubted."

I saw Ruth lift her head, and a quick glance of anxiety flashed into her eyes. I realised that now Shotover was arrested and Enchmarsh dead, an attempt at concealment on my part would do more harm than any revelation I might choose to make. So I thrust my hand into my pocket, and drew out that paper of many vicissitudes.

It was barely legible. It was torn almost in half, smudged, and soiled. Counsel gave a shrug as he took it into his hands.

"I don't wonder the prisoner asked for a new one," he remarked. Then he read it:

"I, Harold Enchmarsh, hereby declare that I murdered my cousin, John Palehouse, by striking him on the temple with a pistol, in Plurenden Quarry, on the fourteenth of July, 1799."

There was sensation in court, and some promptly suppressed cheering. I saw the colour mount and glow on Ruth's cheeks. Then suddenly everything was swallowed up in mist, and I reeled.

"You may sit down, Lyte," said the judge, his voice seeming to come from a long way off; and I sank on the bench behind me, dazed and weak.

Counsel made an observation to the effect that he had persons present who knew Enchmarsh's handwriting, but no one seemed to think that the confession was likely to prove a forgery, so he continued his narrative.

Shortly after the adjournment of the court on the preceding day he had received a message from his attorney telling him that four witnesses for the defence had arrived from Sussex with evidence that might alter the whole course of the trial. Impressed by the short summary of the evidence given in the attorney's note, and considering himself bound by all the traditions of the Bar to see that justice was done in an undefended case, counsel had taken the unusual step of having three of the witnesses—Mary Winde, a farmer's daughter from near Ticehurst; James Apps, constable of Ewehurst; and the Reverend Barnabas Taylor, Rector of Northiam—brought before him at his lodgings. The fourth witness—the Reverend Guy Shotover, curate of Ewehurst was too ill to be interviewed. The accounts given by the three witnesses satisfied counsel that the murderer of John Palehouse was not

146

Lyte, but one Harold Enchmarsh, Squire of Kitchenhour, who took poison shortly after his arrest.

Mary Winde then entered the witness-box, and the court listened, gaping, to her evidence. As for me, I could only sit with closed eyes, and trace the hand of the Lord in all that had taken place.

The prisoner Pearson must have left jail with the seeds of typhus on him, for, smitten with disease, he had wandered from his track, and Mary had found him unconscious in Shoyswell Lane. None of the restoratives that she and her maid applied could unseal his lips, which long before the doctor arrived had stiffened into death. Mary searched his pockets for some clue as to his identity and found the letter! She read it, and at once realised the following facts: I was innocent; I was keeping silence to shield one or both of the Shotovers; Enchmarsh was the real murderer. At first she thought of hastening to the nearest constable and demanding Enchmarsh's arrest, but on reflection decided to go first to Guy Shotover. "Arrest or death!" She realised that Shotover must have committed some crime for which Enchmarsh could hang him, but as to which, in order to save his own skin, he had promised to hold his tongue. So she saddled her horse, rode off to Ewehurst, and found the curate in his study. She told him what had happened, that Humphrey Lyte was going to his death in order to shield him and his sister, showed him the letter, and begged him to explain it.

She described in a few words the interview which followed, but my imagination filled in the blanks. I saw the little lamp-lit room, where Ruth and I had so often sat and played with her black kitten; I saw Guy's face, haggard, terrified; I saw Mary's, resolute, passionate. I heard him lie, vacillate, prevaricate; I heard her insist, command, implore. The coward was brought to bay—by a girl. His mind, once set on the right track, leapt to the right conclusion—Enchmarsh had murdered John Palehouse, but had bargained for his life with the only witness of his crime. What that bargain was the curate also knew. He knew that it was his own worthless life— made a burden even to himself by remorse and fear—that stood between an innocent man and his liberty. How that man had come to know his secret, the ghost which he thought walked only in his own dreams and Ruth's, he could but guess.

Mary had no mercy on him; she wrung his confession from him. Then she did what only a woman would have the tact, the enterprise, the fearlessness to do; she appealed to his courage. She bade that miserable coward be brave, be a hero, counteract by speedy sacrifice the evil he had done, make atonement for his unworthy, craven life by a glorious act of oblation. She pleaded, and his countenance changed; the dead spirit quickened in him; the dumb devil fled; he spoke; he said, "Let me go to the constable and give myself up."

I can only guess the workings of his soul. No doubt it was already weary of the struggle. His remorse had barely been appeased by the breaking off of his sister's engagement. The sin was clamouring to be confessed for its own vileness' sake. And that night, when he realised how a fellow-man was facing that from

147

which he had fled, and was going to death for his sake and Ruth's—when a woman knelt at his feet, and pleaded with shaking voice and tear-blind eyes, the last redoubt of cowardice and selfishness gave way, and the true, noble, selfless man of him ruled in his heart.

Be causes what they may, the effects were these: He and Mary went hand-in-hand to the Ewehurst constable, and he gave himself up.

The constable was then called into the witness-box. He said that he had been routed out of his bed at one o'clock in the morning by Miss Winde and the curate-in-charge of the parish. The latter stepped towards him and cried:

"I have come to give myself up; I have committed a murder." Mr. Shotover looked extremely disturbed and ill, but gave a clear account of his crime and of the motives which had induced him to confess.

Mary then showed the constable her letter, and asked him to arrest Enchmarsh. Apps told her that the evidence was very slight, as the letter might be a forgery, for all they knew. At all events, there must be considerable delay before a warrant could be procured, as the nearest magistrate lived more than six miles off. However, after some thought, he decided to arrest the Squire on the evidence in his possession, and, moreover, admitted that in a case of felony where he had good reason to believe the person accused was guilty, he could proceed without a warrant. So he and Mary set off for Kitchenhour, leaving Guy in custody.

Counsel took the opportunity to say that Apps was to be commended for assuming this responsibility, but I gathered that this was chiefly because the event had justified a piece of independent action somewhat rash in one in his position.

"Miss Winde didn't come inside the house," said Constable Apps, "and it wur an unaccountable long time afore I cud knock anyone up. I wur töald that the master wur too tedious sick to see anybody whatsumever, but I said as how I'd come in the näum o' the law, and the sarvent-lad let me pass. Mus' Enchmarsh wur abed and asleep, but he wakes up when I comes into his room, and when he sees me and hears what I've got to say, he starts cussing and damning at such a räate as I wonders the Old Un didn't fly away wud un then and there. When föalkses asservates their innercence wud too many swears, I'se allus a bit slow at believing um, and I töald the Squire as how he must consider himself under arrest, and tried to put on the darbies. He struggled like a loonatic, but a sick man äun't much of a bruiser, me lord, and I got un fast. Then I showed un Miss Winde's letter, and, sakes! I thought he wur going to have a fit, surelye! 'Where did yer git this, yer son of a harlot?' And when I tells un, he rolls in the bed, and screams and cusses like all Bethlem Hospital. Then, right on a sudden, he lies still, gasping like a fish, and I runs to the door and calls the sarvent-lad to go and fetch another constable from Norjum and a doctor from wheresumever he cud get one. When I turns round I sees Mus' Enchmarsh riz up on his elber, a-putting of a bottle back on the table by his bedside. 'I had to take some doctor's stuff,' sez he; 'I'm feeling that larmentable.'

Then I looks to see what it is he's bin swallering, and I sees on the bottle, 'Pison! Only to be taken externally!' and he'd swallered the whole damn concern!"

"Then I got in a tedious taking, and ran down and called the lad and Miss Winde, and we got some mustid and water, and tried to get the Squire's mouth open to mäake un swaller it; but though we near bröake his jaw, we cudn't get un t'unlock his teeth—and soon he goes all stiff-like and retches, and Miss Winde, she cries, 'Apps, go and fetch Parson Taylor from Norjum!' So I sends off the lad, and good old Parson comes running up in less than no time, and finds Mus' Enchmarsh in the sweat o' death."

Parson Taylor knew the main facts of my arrest and trial, and being convinced as to the authenticity of the letter, at once realised the importance of inducing Enchmarsh to confess his guilt in terms. The Squire was dying fast, writhing on the tumbled bed, tearing the bed-clothes with his teeth; in his anguish he forgot that his admissions would save the hated Lyte, and allowed Taylor to drag from him a half-terrified, half-defiant avowal that he had killed Palehouse—"and I'm sorry I gave him such an easy death." A few minutes later he was seized with violent convulsions, and went to his account.

"Doctor Hewland comes up from Tice'ust," continued the constable, "but he wur a sight too late, and cud only tell us as how the Squire wur dead, which we knewed well enough. Then I and Miss Winde we goes back to Ewe'ust, and, Lord bless us! we finds Mus' Shotover a-lying on the lock-up floor, wud the blood a-streaming from his mouth. So off my lad has to go for Doctor Hewland, and catches the pore gent just getting into his bed at five o'clock in the morning. Doctor Hewland brings the curate round, but sez he'll never live to be tried. Still, Mus' Shotover wur mad and frantic to be up at Maidstone to give evidence, and sez I, 'No doubt as he'll be useful.' So we ships un off in yester morning's coach, and kept un all cockered up at the inn last night. But this morning as soon as he gets to court he begins to spit blood and falls flat. So there he is, lying in one o' the side rooms, and the doctor here döan't think as how he'll ever be in the witness-box—or in the dock or at the gallers, neither!"

The constable's evidence was finished. He had had to be checked once or twice in his garrulity, but had persevered nevertheless in telling what was probably the most sensational story it would ever fall to his lot to repeat. When he had done, there were murmurings, and cries of "Silence!"

The Rector of Northiam—a good old man and a lover of the Word—then entered the witness-box and confirmed all Apps had said. He told the court that he had been roused at about three o'clock in the morning, and summoned to Enchmarsh's death-bed. The constable gave him the facts of the case, and showed him Mary Winde's letter. The effect this scrap of torn paper had produced on Enchmarsh, and the crime

149

to which it had driven him, left in the witness little doubt as to its authenticity. But he at once saw the need for more trustworthy evidence, and conjured the Squire not to enter his Maker's presence with a lie on his lips, but if he were guilty of the murder to confess it and save his soul. Enchmarsh was not the man to care much about his soul, but he was prostrated by horror and agony, and Mr. Taylor managed to wring from him two separate statements, which he wrote down then and there in his pocket-book, and which he now read to the court: "I killed John Palehouse, and I'm sorry I gave him such an easy death," and "I brained that fool of a Ranter, but I shan't live to be hanged for it." He also once cried out in his throes: "This is hellish, but it's not so hellish as hanging!"

The good parson came down from the witness-box, and I have only a dim recollection of what followed. A mist swam before my eyes. Every now and then it parted and showed me a face—the judge's, counsel's, Mary Winde's, or Ruth's. My trial was by no means ended. The judge spoke in low tones to the Sheriff, and counsel had a discussion with his attorney. I was asked by some one who spoke to me over the edge of the dock—I think it was the prosecuting attorney—if I could explain the presence of my pistol in Plurenden Quarry, but I only shook my head. Then after a vague while I realised that Gerald Frome had been brought into court, and called into the witness-box. I heard very little of his evidence, though every now and then a word, a disconnected phrase, drifted on to the ocean where my mind wandered derelict. I was full of strange delusions. I thought it was I who had betrayed Ruth's secret, who had brought about the arrest of her brother. I moaned, twisted, struggled, and would have cried out had not one of the warders put his hand over my mouth.

After Frome had left the court, I recovered my faculties to some extent, and saw that counsel had once more risen.

"My lord," he said, "the evidence we have just heard is of such a nature that I feel compelled to take the responsibility of asking the jury—with your lordship's sanction—to acquit the prisoner. It is true that one important matter has not been cleared up—I refer to the finding of Lyte's pistol in Plurenden Quarry. But apparently there would be opportunities, of which Enchmarsh no doubt availed himself, for abstracting it with a view to casting suspicion on the wrong person. Be that as it may, Lyte's innocence seems beyond question—or, at all events, no jury would convict him now—and I cannot but express my belief that by a timely discovery of the true facts of the case, the prisoner has been saved from death on the gallows, and myself from being a participant in a miscarriage of justice."

He sat down amidst murmurs of applause, and though I was too faint and dazed to fully realise my good fortune, I felt grateful to the man who throughout the trial had acted so generously by me.

There was a brief silence, then the judge said with unction:

"Mr. Lyte, it is with the greatest satisfaction that I have watched the progress of the trial during the last few hours. The law is merciful as well as just, and rejoices to see innocence effectually vindicated. Still, Mr. Lyte, you have yourself to thank for all you have suffered, and I expect you are aware—and if not," he added sharply, "you must be made aware—that in shielding both Shotover and Enchmarsh, you did not act the part of a good citizen, whose duty it is to denounce the criminal and to aid in furthering the ends of justice. You incurred a heavy responsibility, and if not actually accessory after the fact to two murders in such a sense as to render yourself amenable to the law, you were most certainly privy to them, and did nothing to bring the offenders to justice, which they have now apparently escaped. However, I shall say no more on that head. You, gentlemen"—he turned to the jury—"have heard all that has passed, and I feel sure you have done so with satisfaction. It is for you to say that Mr. Lyte is 'Not Guilty.'"

There was subdued applause, then another silence, during which I sat too weary even to thank God. The jury had not, of course, retired, and suddenly I heard the clerk of the court put the question:

"Gentlemen, have you considered your verdict?"

"We find the prisoner not guilty."

"You say that he is not guilty, and that is the verdict of you all."

Then it was as if a black mist rushed on me, wrapped me round and stifled me. I thought I was in the dark cell, and cried, "Water, for the love of God!" then I knew no more.

"There, Lady Wychellow, lift his head a little higher. Now some more brandy that's it!"

I opened my eyes and gazed round me. My head was on Lady Wychellow's lap.

"Ruth," I murmured faintly.

"She is with her brother. There, do not knit your brows so. Close your eyes, and don't fret."

I shut my eyes obediently, but I fretted hard. Where was I? What had happened? Ah, I remembered I had betrayed Ruth. I had saved myself by revealing her secret after having been faithful almost unto death. I writhed my head on Lady Wychellow's knee and moaned.

"What's troubling you, dear lad?" asked a voice I knew to be Peter Winde's.

"Ruth," I murmured, "I have betrayed Ruth—she told me a secret—I revealed it to save my life!"

"No, no, lad. You're raving. You kept it to the end. Your poor mind's been brooding so fiercely over this confidence that you've come to think you've betrayed it. Nothing of the sort! Don't you remember how Mary found your letter, how Shotover confessed, how Enchmarsh——"

I passed my hand over my forehead. Then I started up.

"Yes, I remember. Oh, Mr. Winde, am I free? Shan't I have to go back to jail?"

I gripped his hands, and a shudder passed over me.

"No, poor fellow, your prison days are over, thank the Lord!"

"Where am I now?"

A voice from behind me answered:

"In one of the ante-rooms of the court, egad! You were carried here after you fainted in the dock."

I turned round and saw Sir Miles Wychellow. I held out my hand to him; he had been a good friend to me.

"Well, Don Quixote," he said huskily, "your campaign is over."

"Why do you call me Don Quixote?"

"Begad! Because Cervantes said, 'Don Quixote is a madman!'"

"You think I was mad to shield Shotover?"

"I don't think it was a particularly sensible thing to do."

"But I did it for Ruth's sake."

Peter Winde pressed my hand.

"I understand you, dear lad," he said kindly; "and God will accept your sacrifice."

"Where's Mary?"

"She—she fell faint and ill, and went to rest at our inn. You shall go there soon, but first you must speak a word of comfort to a poor soul that's passing into God's presence sorely sin-stained."

"Shotover?"

"Yes. He's in the next room."

"Dying?"

"I'm afraid so. The doctor gives him no hope. He has been in a decline since winter, and all the horror and excitement of the last two days have brought on a terrible bleeding from the lungs. He's so weak that the doctor won't allow him even to be moved to an inn. He'll die before the stars come out."

"I will go to him—if you really think I can give him any comfort."

"I am sure you can. He has been asking for you. Poor fellow! He wants your forgiveness."

I rose with difficulty to my feet.

"Gad! hadn't you better rest a while before seeing him?" said Sir Miles.

"I would rather go to him now."

Peter Winde made me lean on his arm, and led me into the next room.

Shotover lay on the floor, for the place was bare of furniture, but his head was softly pillowed on his sister's lap, and her red hair fell and touched his face, while in his own hair I saw her fingers twisted. She lifted her eyes as I came in, and said:

"He's here."

"Come to my side and take my hand. . . . I'm dying, and I can't see. . . . Are we alone?"

"Yes," for Peter Winde had stolen away.

"That's well. . . . I'm not going to thank you—I could never do it. . . . It would take a lifetime, and I shall be dead in an hour. All I want to do is—this!"

He took Ruth's hand, and laid it in mine.

My fingers closed round hers hungrily. Neither of us spoke. We were united after long parting, and after much tossing had reached the haven where we would be. Silently she laid her face against mine, and I kissed her cheek and the tears upon it.

Guy turned his head on Ruth's knee, and sobbed.

"God forgive me for keeping you two apart! What a wreck I have made of my life! What a wreck I have all but made of your love! . . . What shall I answer God when He reckoneth with me? . . .' Love without sacrifice is dead.' . . . Then I have never loved . . . and how shall I, having never loved, enter the presence of God Who is Love?"

He groaned aloud, and I sought for words to comfort him. But I could think of nothing save a sentence from the Communion service he used to read so reverently. I laid my hand on his forehead, and whispered:

"'Not weighing our merits, but pardoning our offences, through Jesus Christ our Lord.'"

After that he lay quieter, while a little breeze, sweet enough to have been born in Sussex, blew in upon us.

"Ruth," said the dying man at last, and his voice was only a whisper, "I want to hear you say that you forgive me."

"Why will you speak this way? What have I to forgive? Have I not thanked God for you, and loved you most when you sinned most?"

"'Loved most when sinning most.' Such is the love of women. 'Not weighing our merits, but pardoning our offences.' Such is the love of God."

And with that he died.

We could not mourn for him who had escaped the gallows by dying in the arms of those he loved. We closed his eyes and smoothed the hair upon his forehead, and Ruth kissed his lips. The sunshine crept up to the wall, and the little wind began to blow chilly. Still we sat hand in hand, our tears falling like a benediction on the face of the dead man upon our knees.

CHAPTER XX

OF THE METHODIST AND THE RETURN WITH JOY

Before the evening was very far advanced I again became light-headed, and as there was no room for me at the Black Ship, where the Wychellows were staying, I was put to bed in a little chamber in the New Inn, where Peter and Mary lodged. Peter sat with me through the whole night, during which I tossed in almost ceaseless delirium. I was possessed once more with the idea that I had betrayed Ruth's secret, and Peter afterwards told me that he had often to hold me down in bed, so frantically did I struggle to rise and fling myself at Ruth's feet, beseeching her forgiveness. It is strange, but to this day this phantom haunts me, and I constantly awake trembling, with the belief that I have been faithless to the most solemn trust ever confided to me.

During my few clear intervals I lay quiet and contented, fingering the sheets which were so clean and soft, or turning myself lazily on the feather mattress. I felt that all this cleanliness, comfort, and peace must be a dream, and that I should soon wake to find myself in jail, amidst stench, dirt, airlessness, and crowded unwashed humanity.

About eleven o'clock I was conscious. Peter had just made me swallow some milk, and had laid me back on the pillow as tenderly as my mother might have done if she had cared for me. There was a knock at the door, and I heard Mary's voice.

"Father, go downstairs and have some supper. I'll watch by Humphrey while you are away."

Peter glanced at me as I lay with my cheek on my hand, breathing softly.

"He's quiet enough now, poor lad. Thank you, dearie, I'll go down if you will stay here, and remember to call me if he gets excited."

She promised, and soon the door closed after him.

Mary pulled a chair up to the lamp, and drew a little book out of her pocket. I lay watching her with drowsy half-closed eyes.

"Mary," I said suddenly.

"What is it, Humphrey? I thought you were asleep."

"I've never said 'Thank you' for all you've done for me."

"I did nothing—except what anyone else would have done in such a case. It was God Who showed strength with His arm."

"I have thanked Him, but I have not thanked you. Come to the bedside, and let me thank you as I ought."

Mary rose, and came mechanically to the foot of the bed.

"I tell you that you've nothing to thank me for," she exclaimed with some abruptness. "Please do not say any more about it."

She drew aside the window curtain and looked out. The moon and stars were shining. I sighed rapturously.

"Oh, Mary, how sweet it is to see the moon without any bars between. I saw her last night in jail, and there was a great black bar across her face."

"I'll leave the curtain drawn back if you like it."

"Thank you. What a glorious sky! Mary, don't you remember—the moon was lying on her back just like that when you and I met for the first time, when we ate our supper in the hayloft?"

"I am not likely to forget," she answered sharply. I had never seen Mary in this strange abrupt mood before.

She evidently realised that she had spoken hastily, for she turned round from the window with a smile.

"Let me arrange your pillows for you," she said in a voice that trembled; "they are almost on the floor."

She shook and smoothed them. Her hand happened to touch my hair, and she drew it hurriedly away.

"Now try to go to sleep. Are you comfortable?"

"Yes, thank you, Mary."

She went and sat once more in the lamplight, and opened her book. Suddenly I saw a tear fall on the page. I shut my eyes, and drew the bedclothes high over my head.

A few minutes later I fell asleep, and dreamed that I was at Shoyswell, and that Mary and I sat in the gable barn among the hay, as on the night of our first meeting. We watched the moonlight in the fold and on the fleeces of the sheep, while the little moon lay on her back between the oasts, and Mary sang, "Glory to Thee, my God, this night."

The song died away in a sudden scream of wind outside the casement, and I awoke. Mary had left the room; Peter sat in her place. The window was still uncurtained, but the moon was gone, and there were raindrops on the pane.

The next morning Peter urged me to stay in bed. But I was far too restless, and I thirsted to see Ruth. So, after a little persuasion, he gave in, and lent me some clothes to wear instead of my own rags and tatters.

My heart was full of fears as I walked, leaning on a stick, up the High Street to the sign of the Black Ship. It was true that Shotover had put Ruth's hand in mine; he was free from all pride, and demanded of Ruth's husband but one qualification—that he should love her even as she loved him. Yet Sir Miles was different, and now Shotover was dead, he had the direction of Ruth's affairs. I remembered how coldly he had looked on our love when I was in prison, and my heart failed me.

155

I soon reached the inn, and asking for Miss Shotover, was shown into a private sitting-room. A few minutes later the door opened, and I sprang forward eagerly to meet—not Ruth—but Sir Miles! To my surprise, he grasped my hand, and clapped me heartily on the shoulder.

"Begad, young man, you look better after a decent night's rest. Ruth slept ill, and is only just risen, but she will be with us in a moment."

I gazed at him bewildered.

"Sir Miles, do you know what Guy Shotover said? what he did?"

The baronet looked graver.

"I know it, my lad. I was with the poor fellow a few minutes yesterday morning, and, though every time he spoke he nigh suffocated, he begged me not to keep you and Ruthie apart."

He was silent a moment, then continued:

"I don't deny, young man, that I had looked higher for the child. You're gently born, I know, but I wanted her to lead an easy life, and have a house of her own, and servants, and silk gowns, and such things as a maid loves. But after what happened yesterday I have come to think differently. A man who could suffer so much for her sake, even though he be poor and friendless, is worthy of her—yes, lad, you've proved yourself worthy;" and he clasped my hand once more.

I was too much moved to reply.

"And now," he continued, "I've some questions to ask you. When is the marriage to be?"

I gnawed my lip angrily.

"It's all very well to speak of marriage when I haven't a penny in the world."

"But, my dear fellow, now poor Shotover's dead, Ruthie has enough——"

"Sir Miles, if you think——"

"There, there—don't devour me quite. I didn't mean that you should live on her money. What I wanted to say was this—that what she has and what you can earn ought to be enough for you both."

"But I don't earn anything—at least, except as a farm-hand. Do you refer to that?"

"I do. Gad! if you take Ruth on the roads with you, you will have to sleep under a roof. You must lie at inns instead of in the fields, and have rafters, not clouds, over your heads in time of rain."

"But I never thought of taking her on the roads. I can't imagine her tramping the highways, and being hungry and tired. She has not been bred for such a life."

"You mean to wait till you have a chapel somewhere—which may never be at all. Egad! as you young people insist on being married, and as I'm weak enough to allow it, there had better be no waiting; that would be dreary enough for the girl as well as for you. Besides, she is less unfit for the roads than you for Little Bethel. My lad, you're a vagrant born, and I'd rather see Ruthie wearing out her soles on the highway than you eating out your heart among streets, chimneys, and conventionality. And she need not be hungry or tired, you can take care of that."

"Then you mean," I cried, trembling, "that we can be married at once?"

"As soon as the banns are up—certainly."

I bowed my head. The room swayed and seemed full of fire.

"And Ruth?" I asked faintly. "What does she think of this?"

"What I think, lad, and what you think—and here she is to tell you the same."

The door opened, and Ruth came in. Sir Miles slipped out, but before he was well away I had caught her to my breast. She was all in white except for a black ribbon twisted in her hair, in token of her love and sorrow for the dear, unworthy Guy. She felt a thin, frail thing as I clasped her to me, but the shadow was quite flown from her eyes.

It was some time before I recovered my health and strength, and I spent the days of convalescence happily enough. Every one was good to me; it was sweet to lie alone in the little room in the gable, and the hours when I sat with Ruth's hand in mine and her cheek against mine were unutterably blessed.

About a week after my release I was visited by my friend in adversity, Gerald Frome. I had not forgotten him when God opened to me the prison gates, but had written to him, and had sent him what little comforts I could afford. As soon as he was set free he came to thank me, and to ask me for my prayers. It was he, not I, who deserved thanks, for without his care and tenderness, and the support of his arm in a terrible time, I verily believe I should have died. I earnestly prayed our Lord to have mercy on him, to save him from the old curse, and lead him to better things. Three months later he died. Perhaps that was the only possible answer to my prayer.

Peter and Mary Winde were unable to stay in Kent for my marriage. Peter was obliged to be back at Shoyswell for the hop-picking, and he and his daughter left Maidstone about a week after my release. It struck me that Mary was eager to go.

On the evening of their departure I was sitting alone in the inn parlour, when they came to see me.

"We start for Sussex in an hour," said Peter, "and before we go, we both want to give a wedding present to the lad who has been a son and brother to us."

"You have indeed been a father and a sister to me."

"We had some difficulty in choosing our gifts, for how can we give you house-linen, china, damask or such things as are usually given at a marriage, when the sky is to be your roof, the soil your floor, the tree-stump your table, and when the landlady of the White Hart or the Blue Boar will provide the sheets for your bed? So you must forgive me if I make this my present."

He handed me a small tin box, which I found to contain a cheque for five pounds, and while I was seeking in vain for words to thank him, Mary gave me a Bible bound in black leather, and told me she had given one like it to Ruth.

"So you can think of me when you read God's word."

"I shall always think of you, Mary," I cried, my tongue loosed at last; "I shall always think of you, Mr. Winde. You are my truest, dearest friends, of whom I am not worthy."

Tears choked my voice, and Peter shook my hand and laid the other hand on my breast, and if I had not known him for a staunch Methodist, I should have thought he had made the sign of the cross there.

Then I turned to Mary, and was seized with the old impulse. I did not resist it this time, but caught her in my arms and gave her my first and only kiss. I felt how hot her cheek was under my lips, and her hand in mine was trembling and burning. When I drew back and looked into her eyes, I could have sacrificed all I possessed not to have given that kiss.

"The coach leaves the Star Inn at half-past eight," said Peter, breaking the awkward silence. "Mary, you and I must be starting. You will come with us, lad?"

"Certainly. Have you said good-bye to Ruth?"

"We've just been to the Black Ship. Come, Mary, run upstairs and put on your hat and cloak, my dearie."

A few minutes later Peter, Mary, and I were on our way to the Star. The sun had set, and the sky was iron grey, flushed in the west. We had not long to wait till the coach was ready to start. Then a hasty pressure of hands, and good wishes called on the night air, while the Maidstone Rocket rattled over the courtyard stones.

I walked back to my inn with a slow, grave step, and sat for some time brooding alone; but at ten o'clock I went to see Ruth, and forgot all my depression.

After that the days flew quickly, till our wedding morning, the twentieth of September, broke at last. We were to be married very early, for we wished to leave Maidstone by the nine o'clock coach. This would reach the cross-roads of Three Chimneys at noon. Then my wife and I would walk to Ewehurst to superintend the selling of the Parsonage furniture and livestock, and that tramp through the Kentish and Sussex lanes should be our honeymoon.

I rose at five and dressed all trembling. My heart was full of a joy as pure and an awe as sweet as that with which it had throbbed on the morning of my confirmation or of my first sacrament. The streets were dim with morning fog, which did not reach as far as the housetops, so that from my window in the gable I looked down on a creamy, opaque sea. Once out of doors, the thick yellowness was all round me, and I groped my way with difficulty to All Saints' Church.

Inside the church everything was very dark, and I had to call up a sleepy old verger to draw up the blinds and light a few lamps that parson might see to read the service.

I was early, and knelt for some time alone in one of the worm-eaten pews. A robin was twittering outside, and I thanked God for that little song of hope. Ruth arrived at last with Sir Miles and Lady Wychellow. My bride wore no jewels or brocades, lace or veiling, only a simple muslin gown, with roses at her breast, and a chip hat tied with broad ribbons under her chin. She was, and looked, a child, but sorrow had crowned her with an early tender womanhood. I kissed her silently, and we knelt in the old pew side by side.

On the stroke of seven, parson bustled in, his surplice crackling with starch. He was a brisk, excitable little man, and evidently enjoyed the romance of a wedding 6 at such an early hour. The service was soon over, and Ruth and I came hand-in-hand from the communion rails, wedded husband and wife, "for better for worse, for richer for poorer, in sickness and in health, till death us do part."

The fog still lay thick upon the streets, but the rays of the risen sun made crimson smears on its yellowness. We went to the Black Ship Inn, where a simple wedding-breakfast was prepared, and I do not think that Ruth and I spoke a word the whole of our way. After breakfast we said good-bye to the Wychellows, for we were to walk to the coach alone. The good baronet and his wife knew that we needed no company in our happiness.

On reaching the Star we found we had nearly half an hour to wait before the coach started, but it is strange how quickly the time passed, though we did little more than stand hand-in-hand and watch the clouds in their lazy drift. Then "Take your seats, ladies and gentlemen!" cried the guard, and all was bustle and confusion. The next moment the horses had plunged forward as the ostlers let go their heads, and we were lurching and rolling out of the yard and down the street.

Maidstone was soon behind us; the jail, with all its hideousness of sin and sorrow, was like a dream from which we wake shuddering and thanking God that it is day. My past life seemed to me then as a baptism of tears, from which I had come strengthened, healed, and purified.

Through hopfields and orchards, heavy with their September riches, through cornfields where reapers bent whistling over their toil, where scythes swished and hones sang. Through Shepway, Wormlake, Stallance, and Motynden, and thus to Headcorn, where we stopped to water the horses. Then on past Great Love, Hungerden, and merry little Shepherdswell, till suddenly the coach drew up at the cross-roads of Three Chimneys, and the next moment Ruth and I were left standing beside the bundle that held our chattels, watching a cloud of dust spin away towards Cranbrook.

We were at the same cross-roads where the constable and I had stopped the Maidstone coach barely two months ago. Then I wore gyves on my wrists, now my only shackles were Ruth's soft hands, clasped over mine as she put her lips to my face.

"Humphrey—husband!"

I could not answer for gladness, but kissed her mouth and took her hand, and led her down the lane.

We had a long tramp in front of us, but heat and weariness seemed to have taken fright at our love, and to flee before our face. We walked gaily hand-in-hand, singing like children. At Dockenden we halted, and went into a field through which ran a little stream. By the side of this stream we ate our mid-day meal of bread and cheese, and drank of the delicious water, Ruth drinking from my hands. Then suddenly my heart reproached me.

"Little girl, you have been gently bred, and here am I taking you to tramp the roads with me!"

"Faith! That's just what I love, Humphrey."

"But you are too sweet and delicate to be a common mumper's wife."

"What nonsense you talk! As if you were a common mumper!"

"You will often be tired."

"I shall not mind with you beside me."

"You will have a frugal board and a hard bed."

"I shall not mind with you to share them."

"Ruth, how can you sacrifice so much for a fellow like me?"

"Lud! I'd sacrifice the world for a fellow like you. But come, Humphrey, why should you and I reason together in this way? When I promised to share your life, I didn't mean only the sweetness and the sunshine of it, but also the bitterness and the rain. Now, let's hurry on, or we shall never reach Ewehurst to-night."

As it happened, we did not reach Ewehurst that night, for in spite of Ruth's words we loitered on our way, and night fell as we reached Crit Hall. We did not care. Love prefers starlight to sunlight. Our tongues were loosed, and we talked of many things—of our first meeting, of Shoyswell, the Windes, and of John Palehouse. Then we talked of Guy, and our voices fell to whispers.

On and on, past Beretilt and Four Wents, across the Furnace Stream, through the uncanny shades of Mopesden Wood. We had left the road, for the grass was softer than the marl to our feet.

"Ruth," I said, "we must be nearing Sussex."

The night was very wonderful. The great flat fields lay round us in a stillness broken by the sough of the wind through the grass and spurge. Evening moths, fat and white, fluttered heavily in and out of the fennel and chervil, waving like fragile spooks in the light of the first stars. It was a perfect ghost time. We found it hard to believe that those tall, pale forms which appeared and disappeared in the dark were only the giant hemlock as the wind waved them in and out of the moonlight. An owl raised his note of sadness, the whirr of bats' wings troubled the brooding air. Far away at Soul's Green a bell was tinkling, now clear, now soft, as the wind swept it, and every now and then an unusually strong puff brought the bleating of some outcast from the fold.

"Ruth," I cried, "how sweet the country is to a man who has been in prison!"

We tramped on, and passed a group of cottages known as Delmonden. Their little windows shed oblongs of light upon our path, and by that light I saw the tears hanging in Ruth's eyes like stars.

"Wife," I said, "directly we are in Sussex I shall kiss you."

"But how will you know when we are in Sussex? We are nowhere near the Rother."

"But the Kent Ditch, dear. We shall cross the Kent Ditch—and then I shall kiss you."

Only a few yards further on we came to a reedy channel, where the wind swept the osiers with a moaning sound.

"There is no bridge," said Ruth.

"I'm glad there is no bridge," said I. And I caught her up in my arms, and waded with her across the Kent Ditch, and clambered on to the shore of my goodly heritage.

We were in a hop-garden, and the wind gently bowed the overweighted vines, while their steamy scent crept into my nostrils, soothing and sweet. The night was very clear, or rather let me say the morning, for it was past one, and the autumn lay an hour old on the breast of the sky, swaddled in stars.

"Wife!" I cried, and clasped her to me, and kissed her again and again. It seemed as if I should never have my fill of kisses.

When at last I drew back my head, she stole her arms round me, and looked up into my face. Two tears crept down her cheeks; one fell on her lip, and I kissed it away. The wind lifted a sob, and swept upon us from the huddling fields of Kent, and blew a strand of Ruth's hair across my mouth. I held it there while the blast sobbed again—blustered—and was still. Far, far away, a shooting star crossed the sky above Shoyswell, and I saw it sink among the woods like a burning eye.

Printed in the USA
CPSIA information can be obtained
at www.ICGtesting.com
LVHW011052050224
770980LV00020B/560

9 781502 502193